SHOULD YOU KEEP A SECRET?

LISA DARCY

www.bloodhoundbooks.com

Print ISBN 978-1-914614-83-5

ALSO BY LISA DARCY

Lily's Little Flower Shop

My Big Greek Holiday

To my readers all over the world, thanks! I write because of you.

CHAPTER ONE

STELLA

When I said 'I do', I never thought I'd end up saying 'I don't anymore'. Divorce? Not me. Ever.

And I'm not divorced ... yet. But my husband and I are separated. Garth has a girlfriend. Actually, he's living with her. I'm not feeling sorry for myself though, I'm in a good place. Happy with my life, friends.

Garth and I met in the early noughties at an inner-city bar in Sydney. He came out with the ridiculous pick-up line, 'Do you believe in love at first sight, or should I walk past you again?' Yes, it was dumb and cheesy, but obviously I was in the mood for dumb and cheesy, because I laughed. He was cute. It helped that he was unsure of himself and nervous as hell. And at least he didn't say, 'What time do you have to be back in heaven?' I have standards.

Within a week, we were in love. Three months later, we moved in together. The following year, Harry was born. I often wonder whether we'd have stayed together if Harry hadn't been conceived. We were running on a treadmill of relentless forward motion. Then I fell pregnant with Hannah. Two kids! Marriage would complete the circle. So Garth and I did what was expected. Three months before Hannah was born, we united as Mr and Mrs. I even forwent my maiden name – Templeton. I know that's not politically correct, but I liked Garth's surname, Sparks.

Stella Sparks. It had a glamorous ring to it. Besides, the name Stella Templeton had never done me any favours. I hoped Stella Sparks would.

Our marriage was good, really good ... until it ran out of steam.

The bartender coughed and handed over my change.

It was my shout. Place? Local pub, a rooftop bar in an oasis of luxurious greenery. Three girlfriends hanging out on a Thursday night, catching up for drinks. Date? January thirtieth, two days after the start of the school year. It felt more like two months. Teenagers!

Loud conversations and laughter bounced off walls. I picked up the bottle of wine and headed back to the girls.

'So,' Carly said as I sank into a comfy wicker cane chair, 'what's everyone's mantra for the year?'

She'd asked the same question the last three years, and I couldn't for the life of me remember what I'd said twelve months ago. I poured the wine instead of answering.

Jesse groaned. 'I'm not playing this game.'

'Why not?' Carly snapped. 'What else are you doing?'

We clinked glasses, and she took a large gulp before continuing. 'Anyway, I've got mine – fuck buddy.'

'Carly!' Jesse shrieked.

I shook my head. Carly could be a loose cannon, especially after a few drinks. She liked to shock people, and Jesse always fell for it. I wasn't sure if Carly was serious or not. Her marriage had been through its ups and downs over the years, but she hadn't complained about Brett recently.

'That's not a mantra,' I told her.

She smiled and flicked her long blonde hair behind her shoulders. 'My game, my rules.'

With a slow, deliberate movement, Jesse picked up her glass. 'I know what I want.'

'What does that mean?' I asked.

'It means I know what I want from life, and this is my year to go for it. That and maintenance. I'm finding wrinkles on my ears. I can't wing it these days. I need to look after myself, otherwise...'

We all had issues. Jesse thought her husband, Steve, was having a mid-life crisis because he was arrogant, rude and hated her friends. He wasn't having a crisis, he was just a prick, full stop. But Jesse seemed devoted to him and did everything she could to keep him happy, including Botox, beauty care and endless sexual favours. She hoped that if she kept herself looking gorgeous and him feeling manly, one day he might tell her he loves her like he used to. And she does look great – flawless olive complexion, intense green eyes, wavy sandy-coloured hair. Jesse's a real catch, unlike Steve, who's rather ordinary.

'What about you?' Carly asked me, snapping her fingers to bring me back from my mental drifting. 'We need your mantra.'

'I can only commit to a month. Anything beyond that's a bonus.'

She sighed. 'Get on with it.'

I took a sip of wine. 'Fun.'

'Too short,' Carly said.

'How about "I take control of my life"?'

Jesse and Carly looked at each other. Carly swigged her wine before answering. 'You can do better.'

'What? It's not like maintenance and fuck buddy are so great.'

Carly shrugged and cast her eyes around the room.

'What about "I choose to be happy"?' Jesse said, looking anything but.

Jesse had great highs, where she was on top of the world, all smiles, hugs and good times, tempered by times when she felt low, sad and uninteresting. She'd been in a depressed phase since before Christmas and was finding it hard to pull herself together. Her little quirks had returned too – foot tapping, repetitive counting.

'Finding a suitable fuck buddy would definitely make me happy!' Carly cut in.

'What's got into you tonight?' I asked.

'Nothing. Just being honest.' She nodded towards a group of men at a nearby table. 'Maybe one of them is up for the job.'

I rolled my eyes, then turned a deep shade of pink when I followed her gaze and realised who she was talking about.

I'd met Mike seven weeks earlier at Harry's end-of-year school speech night. We were both seated towards the back of the hall, and I'd noticed him immediately. He was tall and tanned, had collar-length salt-and-pepper hair with a bit of a fringe thing happening and an easy smile. Even more interesting was the absence of a wedding ring...

After the speeches were over, I'd made a point of bumping into him in the canteen line-up for weak tea and heavily sugared chocolate slice.

'Come here often?' I'd asked. A pathetic opening, but it was all I had.

'Only when I'm certain there'll be attractive women here.' He smiled broadly.

I extended my hand. 'Stella Sparks.'

He took it. 'Mike Thompson. Divorced?'

'Presumptuous.' I grinned. 'Separated.'

'Me too.' His tone was light. 'Sorry. People talk. You're in fine company though.'

'I dread to think what else you've heard.'

'All good, I promise.'

Instant rapport? I wouldn't go that far, but he was laidback and handsome. Bonus points: he didn't appear up himself or sleazy. Another thought struck me: if he knew about my marital status, he must have noticed me before.

We got talking, and the following week, we met for coffee ... And that was as far as it had gone.

'Can I interest you in a library card?' was one of the lamer sentences I'd uttered. Yes, I'm a librarian, so it wasn't completely random. Still.

'Is it hot here or is it just me?' was another one. Idiot. We were sitting outside under pine trees in the summer sunshine. Pink crepe myrtle and white gardenias were in full fragrant bloom. Cows roamed a neighbouring paddock. Idyllic.

The meeting was a disaster. I spilt coffee down my white linen shirt and struggled to make conversation even though our speech night encounter had been easy.

Mike reached out and placed his hand over mine to stop the trembling. 'Everything okay?' He had a wide generous smile, and a relaxed confident manner.

'Yes, no. I'm nervous. Worried people will see us and talk.'

'Stella, we're drinking coffee, not groping each other in the middle of the street. At peak hour' – he laughed – 'with our kids, ex-partners and ex-in-laws looking on.'

'Or kissing in the library.'

'Do tell.'

'You'd be surprised.'

Mike raised his eyebrows. 'I've been missing out.'

I hardly remember the rest of our conversation ... Mike acted light and flirty, and I guessed I came across as some moronic twit. But I'd put it behind me, determined to focus on my children and newly found freedom.

Then, horror of horrors, I'd run into him at the supermarket two days ago in the fruit and veggie section. I'd stammered something about how nice it was to see him again, that I was meeting friends that night and wouldn't it be great if he could come along. Lo and behold, there he was, barely three metres away and smiling at me.

I smiled back. Jesus! I felt sixteen again, although I had absolutely no intention of revisiting that annus horribilis.

'See,' Carly said. 'You're eyeing them off too.'

'You're all talk,' I said, dismissing several erotic thoughts from my head. I wasn't looking for a romantic interlude. I liked Mike, but I was terrified of falling in lust only to have it fall apart. Yes, I was getting ahead of myself, but that's me.

'I'm not and I'll prove it to you.' Carly stood and walked towards their table.

Several men turned to look at her. Carly's a stunner – athletic, tall, a bit like a greyhound. A good-looking greyhound with long blonde hair. Lately though, when we're out together, I feel as though I'm minding an eighteen-year-old. It gets tiring, especially when I have to go home and deal with my own teenagers.

Maybe if I'd stopped Carly – grabbed her arm and pulled her back – events wouldn't have escalated the way they had.

CHAPTER TWO

'Everything okay with you?' Jesse asked, refilling my glass.

'Sure,' I said.

'Kids doing okay?'

'They're teenagers. Their lives revolve around themselves and their friends. They're not happy with the separation and Garth's new girlfriend, but they're handling it.'

'It can't be easy.'

'No, but there's no alternative.'

Jesse glanced at Carly, who was flirting up a storm with her new friends. 'Should we do something about her?'

'She's a big girl. Give her ten minutes.'

Jesse nodded. 'Sometimes I envy you. You're free. Have no one to answer to.'

'Except my kids.'

'That's different. They won't always be living with you. You can have your own headspace. You can please yourself, not always be worrying about what your husband thinks.'

'How's it going with Steve?'

'Same old, same old. He can't get enough sex, but he doesn't care about me enough to introduce me to his new colleagues. I had to beg him to take me to the company Christmas party. A couple of times when I joined in the conversation, he frowned, as if I was about to say something wildly inappropriate.' She sighed and looked up from her glass. 'And you know what, Stella? I never do. I keep it all hidden.'

I wanted to tell her to wake up to herself and dump her dickhead husband. But I'd told her that a few times already. I wasn't going to spoil this conversation by suggesting it again.

'I'm just being dramatic.'

I wasn't so sure. And what did she mean about keeping things hidden? From what Jesse had told me, Steve spent a lot of time working late and hardly noticed her when he was around, except when he was after a blow job. He hadn't always been so dismissive of her. When I'd met him several years earlier, he'd been open, accommodating and much kinder to Jesse. These days, I hardly ever saw him. Before Garth and I split, we'd occasionally had them over for a barbeque, but Steve usually ended up drifting away from the conversation towards whatever the kids were watching on television, or else he'd sit there raising an eyebrow if he didn't agree with what was being said, leaving the impression he thought he was superior to us, that we should be honoured he'd deigned to be in our company.

'And,' Jesse said, 'I really want another baby.'

I took her hand. 'You any closer?'

She sipped her wine, then shook her head. 'I don't blame Steve. I know he's busy, tired and fed up. He doesn't want to add to the pressure by having another mouth to feed.'

'You can afford it.'

'Emotionally, Stella. Steve says he doesn't have the energy or time to devote to raising another child. Although he's also said it would be "fiscally irresponsible to bring another child into this unpredictable world".'

'You're talking about a baby, not a new car.'

She shrugged, and we both looked at the empty bottle on the table.

'Should I buy another one?' she asked, just as Carly bounced back.

'I've met the most amazing guys,' she told us. 'Mike's a dad from school, and the others work with him. We're all heading to a party later. Want to come?'

I glanced at Mike who was looking sheepish.

'I don't think it's a good idea,' I said, recalling the disastrous coffee date.

'But they're doctors.' She noted the empty bottle. 'Who's for more wine?'

'I'm in,' I said distractedly. 'They don't look like axe murderers, but you never know.'

Jesse nodded. 'Looks can be deceptive.'

'Please!' Carly snorted, and headed towards the bar.

'Stella, has Liz mentioned anything more about the full-time position coming up? I wanted to talk to her today, but she was sighing and shaking her head a lot so thought it best to avoid her.'

Wise.

Jesse is a librarian as well. That's how we met ten years ago, working together at the library, cataloguing nonfiction. Liz is our newish boss (six months) and has a few issues with Jesse.

'Not really.' I let the words hang.

Thankfully, Jesse's mobile rang. She took it from her bag and walked outside.

When I told people my profession, they immediately gave me a sly – or in many cases, not-so-sly – once-over, then said, 'You don't look like a librarian.' As if it were a compliment.

'Really,' I'd say. 'And what are we supposed to look like?'

They'd throw me a few stereotypes from the 1950s and my eyes would glaze over. No, I didn't wear thick horn-rimmed glasses. I'd never worn my hair in a bun, nor was I mean or a spinster. I did wear cardigans though.

Carly returned with a new bottle of wine and poured a couple of glasses. 'Want to join them?' she asked, looking over at Mike and his friends.

I shook my head, scratching imaginary itches on my arms. 'You go. I'll wait for Jesse.'

'Whatever.' And Carly was off, back to flirting with Mike's friend.

He had messy dark curly hair that sat just below his collar, a three-day growth, and was tanned and tall, just like her. Mike was probably a bit older than we were, but the other two looked young, well under thirty. I felt a bit rude not going over to say hello – I had asked Mike here, after all. But I was still scratching myself. It was better to say nothing than to start a conversation and say something stupid.

'Hey,' Jesse said, returning to our table, 'Steve's just rung. He's been held up at work. I told the babysitter someone would be home by ten, so it looks like I'm done for the night.'

'But this is *our* night, Jess,' I said, wounded. 'We've been planning this for months. Can't you ring the babysitter?'

'Truthfully, it's not worth it. Besides, I'm tired.'

A squeal drew our attention to Carly, who was standing with Mike and his friends.

'Sorry to dump her on you,' Jesse said.

'Don't worry. I'll see she gets home in one piece.'

Jesse pushed her way through the crowd towards the exit. Carly was sitting on the doctor's lap.

Mike smiled at me, stood, beer in hand, and came over. 'This seat taken?'

I stammered something unintelligible. Where was my brain?

'It's clear you weren't going to join me.' He sat down. 'So, do you want to talk about the coffee date?'

I blushed. 'It wasn't a date, and no, not really.'

'Pity. I thought it went well, until you stopped returning my text messages.'

'I sent you messages.'

'*Thanks* and *Nice to see you again* weren't the kind of messages I had in mind.'

'Look, I'm no good at this. I'm...' My cheeks were on fire.

'You're what? Gorgeous? Interesting? Have a great smile?'

'Stop. I'm too old for games. Besides, you're only saying those things to get me into bed.' Shit! Did I just say that out loud?

Mike smiled. 'I'm not.'

Great! Not only had I said something wildly inappropriate, but he didn't even fancy me.

'Not that the thought of kissing you hasn't crossed my mind, but I'm not trying to rush you.' He drained the last of his beer. 'Not right now, anyway.'

I beamed, pretty sure I was a bright shade of beetroot.

'Stella, Stella, the night is young. Toby's taking me to a party.' Carly was swaying about ten centimetres from my head.

Standing to steady her, I said, 'You don't even know the guy. Let's go home.'

'Yes, I do. He's Toby and he's a doctor. He feeds monkeys at the zoo in his spare time.'

I looked at Mike, who was conveniently preoccupied reading a crumpled docket from inside his wallet.

'Right,' I said to Carly. 'Toby sounds like fun, and if you feel the same way about him tomorrow, you two should meet up. But,' I whispered, 'you have a husband and child waiting for you at home.'

She slumped into a chair. 'Piffle. You're such a party pooper.'

At that moment, Toby appeared. 'No pressure, but we're taking off.'

'Hold your horses,' Carly squealed, standing again. She looked at Mike and me. 'You coming?'

I couldn't let her go to the party by herself, so I tailed her outside. Mike followed.

'There's really no need,' I said to him.

'It's cool. Besides, you could probably use an extra hand.'

He was right. I needed to stay with Carly, but I hadn't driven, and I couldn't fit into the car she was about to climb into, a black Lexus hybrid.

Mike leaned over to Toby. 'We'll follow you.'

Toby nodded and told him an address. Carly got in beside him, which completely foiled my plan, because I'd been hoping to get her into Mike's car and then ask him to drive us straight home. Then I'd planned on ditching Mike too – I needed some distance from him.

'Carly,' I hissed. 'You don't know these people.'

'Sure I do,' she slurred. 'They're from some hospital.'

She closed the door and Toby pulled away from the kerb. Bloody hell! This wasn't the scenario I'd imagined.

Within seconds, I was in the passenger seat of Mike's SUV, following Toby up the Pacific Highway. At least we were heading in the direction of home.

CHAPTER THREE

Mike and I made small talk as he concentrated on keeping up with the zippy Lexus. Mike's dashboard clock read 10.04. Where I really wanted to be was tucked up in bed, not chasing Carly to who knows where.

As I listened to Mike, my thoughts drifted back to what he'd said earlier about wanting to kiss me. Did he actually *say* he wanted to kiss me or just that the idea had crossed his mind? Maybe my fantasies were getting in the way of reality. Either way, surely kissing couldn't be a bad thing. Or maybe it could.

'Tell me,' Mike said, 'what do you do when you're not trying to keep up with your party-loving friend?'

'Besides trying to keep up with my kids and my job at the library?'

He glanced across. 'I still can't picture you as a librarian. You're too...'

'What?'

'I was going to say sexy but thought you might slap me.'

'Good call.'

'Okay, alluring ... feisty? Can I get away with feisty?'

We pulled up behind Carly and her new mates in an ordinary suburban street barely a kilometre from my mother-in-law's retirement village and around three kilometres from my home. No loud music filtered from any of the houses, which all looked the same – low-set, blond-brick homes with well-kept, green front gardens. There was nothing in sight to suggest a party was going off inside one of them.

Carly was leaning against Toby's car. She wasn't making a hell of a lot of sense, but at least she was upright.

'Now what?' I asked her.

She looked at me, then at Toby, then at Toby's friend, Pete, who had been in the car with them.

Pete winked and started off along the pavement towards a white gate attached to a white picket fence. 'This is it.'

'Doesn't look like much of a party,' Mike said next to me.

I nodded. 'Feels like we're popping in to visit Grandma.'

Pete led us down a side path. Halfway along, he stopped at a red wooden door. Okay, this is where we find out there's been a severe case of mistaken identity; we've arrived at the wrong address in the wrong suburb and we're about to invade an elderly couple's home. They've probably been asleep for hours.

I expected Pete to knock, only to be confronted by angry pensioners. What I didn't expect was for him to extract a key from his jeans pocket.

'Voila,' he said, unlocking the door and pushing it open. He stepped inside, urging us to follow.

Common sense told me to step away and head back to the road, but before I could grab Carly, she'd tottered inside. I followed, straining to make out anything in the dark. The dim lights gave off a soft red glow. As my eyes adjusted, I saw we were in a big room – a living room? There were several oversized sofas, and lamps of various shapes and sizes draped in fine chiffon scarves; there even seemed to be a smoke machine–

'Pete!' The voice belonged to a woman.

I squinted. What the hell? She was practically naked. All she wore was a sheer black baby-doll top, fluffy black high heels and barely-there knickers. She also had huge breasts. Playboy Bunny came to mind.

Around the room, couples and throuples cuddled on the oversized sofas. What had we walked into?

'You've brought new playmates,' the Bunny said, hugging Pete.

Mike nudged me.

'This is a bit different,' I said, leaning against a wall for support. We'd stumbled into Hugh Hefner's suburban counterpart.

Pete wasted no time. In an instant, he was naked and had joined several others on a nearby couch.

To be fair, Toby seemed as shocked as we were. 'Don't look at me. I had no idea Pete was into this ... whatever this is.'

Carly put her head on my shoulder. 'This isn't quite what I had in mind when I said I wanted a fuck buddy.'

'Be careful what you wish for.'

'I went to an orgy once or twice,' she went on, 'but I was nineteen. Way overwhelming, so I had a few lines of coke. But this ... wow!'

'Coke?' I blinked. 'You're kidding me!'

'Look, Stella! These people aren't drinking Red Bull and vodka.'

I scrutinised the trays of drinks being passed around. Carly was right. They also held small dishes that probably contained other substances. I glanced at Mike and Toby. I couldn't hear what they were saying, but they looked uncomfortable.

'I could go for it,' Carly continued. 'Anonymous sex.'

'Carly!'

'What? I could be persuaded. Look at Pete – he's just dropped his pants and gotten into it.'

Pete was receiving a massage and more.

'Yeah, but I'd need the coke, or at least an amphetamine-based synthetic drug like Ecstasy,' Carly mused. 'And it'd have to be with someone attractive. I couldn't do it with anyone who had bad breath or belly fluff.'

'This is turning you on, isn't it,' Toby said, leaning into her.

She smirked. 'Of course not. I'm shocked. Don't know where to look.'

Pete and a woman holding a pulsating strobe-lit vibrator started doing things to another woman that were possibly illegal. She seemed to be enjoying herself though, given her shrieks.

When a naked man with a gold fringed tassel attached to his flaccid penis bounced up to us with a tray of drinks, I was too shocked to refuse.

'We like to make the newbies feel welcome,' he said, looking each of us up and down. 'I'm Quentin. After a drink, you'll feel more comfortable. When you're ready, I'll introduce you around.' He smiled and bounded down the corridor.

Drink spiking? I caught Mike's eye, and he shrugged. Suddenly I wasn't thirsty. I didn't want to lose control, not here. I put my untasted drink on a nearby table. Mike did the same. Carly and Toby looked at us, peered at their drinks and downed them in one go.

'I needed that,' Carly said with a giggle. 'Wait till the school mums hear about this. It'll rock their world.'

Understatement.

What was a party like this doing in the suburbs? Wasn't it better suited to the inner city? Was I being judgemental? Yes. As I looked around at the entwined bodies, it occurred to me that maybe these people lived in the neighbourhood. I couldn't see Mrs Farns (Year Eight support) or Mr Daniels (Computer Studies) getting into this kind of thing. The school's headmaster, on the other hand, was a dark horse – actually, a dark, quiet and all-too-ready-to-dress-up horse. And maybe there were a few divorcees in the area who'd get a kick out of this? Then again, maybe swingers, or whatever these people called themselves, did this kind of thing as far away from their own environs as possible.

As for divorcees, what was I thinking? I was soon to be a divorcee. Was this what I expected people to think of me: that I'd turn to orgies to get my kicks as soon as Garth was out the door?

I nudged Mike. 'Ever been to one of these before?'

He shook his head. 'Not sure it's my scene.'

I eyed a dominatrix who was teetering on twelve-centimetre stilettos. She gave a man dressed as a slave a few lashes of her whip, then picked up a paddle and spanked him with it.

'Electric paddle – won't leave marks,' said Quentin, the tasselled-penis man, back beside us. 'Most people like to be hurt, but no one wants to have to explain welt marks when they get home.'

'Hmm,' I said.

A sign hung on the wall nearby: *Welcome to Master Mitch's and Mistress Sherri's Haven. Go hard or go home.*

Every day, I drove past hundreds of homes, no doubt where tuckshop mothers and cricket coaching fathers lived – what did they get up to after hours? How would you know? Everyone was so busy with their own lives, tending to their gardens and weekly agendas. How did anyone have time to go to these parties, let alone source sparkly costumes and dazzling accessories? Maybe it was all done online.

One couple seemed heavily into the domination/submission

routine. He looked absurd, crawling around like a baby, sucking a dummy, wearing a nappy, a thick spiked dog collar around his neck. A few more people joined them – grown men on their hands and knees being dragged along by their red-lipsticked, black-corseted mistresses.

I nudged Carly. 'You don't see that every day on the North Shore, do you?'

What kind of people subjected themselves to this treatment? How could they enjoy it? Was the butcher from my local supermarket crawling around in a nappy? Or perhaps the guy who owned the pizzeria? The local bank manager?

'Anything goes,' I overheard Quentin say to Mike. 'As long as it's consensual. We're all adults. But remember your safe words.'

Safe words?

Quentin explained. 'Red means stop, yellow means this is getting intense and green means keep it up, buddy.' He slapped Mike on the back and disappeared into the throng.

'You wanna get out of here?' Mike asked.

I was about to say 'yes', when Carly whacked me on the arm.

'What is it?' I said when she hit me a second time.

'Look,' she said, pointing.

I was staring at a dominatrix who looked slightly familiar – Tami from the news agency? – when one of the nappy men looked up. At first, I thought I was mistaken.

Shit! I wasn't. It was Steve. Jesse's husband.

Everything around me seemed to freeze. Steve? Was I hallucinating? How long had this been going on? Was it legal? Did Jesse know?

I had to make a split-second decision. Stay still and hopefully remain invisible? Or make a run for the door? If we moved too quickly, we'd be spotted for sure, but if we stayed where we were, the group, including Steve, would walk – crawl – straight into us.

'The door,' I whispered to Carly.

She turned to follow me but tripped on a rug and fell into my back. She cried out. I turned and pulled her arm to keep her moving, but it was too late. Steve had seen us.

I could tell he was trying to place us, to figure out how he knew us. Seconds later, it clicked. It probably didn't help that Carly was staring at him, open-mouthed.

Steve was one cool customer. Only for the briefest moment did he look horrified. Then he winked. Did he really think we were players?

'Let's keep this to ourselves, ladies,' he said, standing up. 'We wouldn't want anyone else finding out about your nocturnal activities, would we?'

'Our nocturnal activities?' Carly hit back. 'You mean yours?'

It was hard to take Steve seriously considering he was wearing a red studded collar teamed with a white nappy. Thank goodness for the nappy. I had no desire to see my friend's husband's tackle.

His mistress tugged on his collar. He dropped to his hands and knees, and she dragged him away. Poor Jesse. Imagine being married to that.

Toby, Mike, Carly and I made a hasty exit onto the street.

'What do we tell Jesse?' Carly asked, sounding exhausted.

I had no idea. How could we bring it up? Invite her for drinks and say, 'By the way, do you know your husband frequents sadomasochistic sex parties?' Or maybe, 'When your kids were babies, did you notice Steve getting unusually excited by the sight of their dummies and nappies?' I thought not. And would Jesse believe us? I could hardly believe it after I'd seen it for myself.

'We let it be,' I told Carly.

'I can't believe you're saying that.'

I couldn't believe I was saying it either, but would Jesse thank us for telling her? 'Let's sit on it a few days before we do anything.'

CHAPTER FOUR

JESSE

Jesse drove like a maniac the two kilometres to her house, palms sweating, head aching. She'd only consumed two glasses of wine over three hours. Small glasses at that. But imagine if she got pulled up for drink driving and lost her licence. She'd never live it down.

She drove into her tidy two-car garage, then took three deep breaths before getting out of the car and trudging inside the house. As she neared the family room, she heard Anna, the babysitter, talking on her mobile. Jesse stopped, exhaled deeply, clenched her hands and entered the room.

Anna looked up and smiled. 'Gotta go,' she said into her phone, before putting it in her handbag and standing. 'Good night?'

Jesse nodded. 'Sorry about the mix-up. I thought Steve would be home by now.'

Anna shrugged. 'No drama.'

Jesse walked her to the front door, paid her sixty dollars and said goodnight. Then she started her nightly routine. First, Jesse checked on her nine-year-old twins, Ollie and Emily. She kissed them both lightly on their foreheads and whispered, 'I love you.'

In the darkness, she picked up discarded clothes and scattered toys, then roamed the house checking all the doors and windows were locked.

Satisfied her home was in order, Jesse texted Steve and got ready for bed, pulling several mushroom-coloured cushions off the grey duvet. But she couldn't settle, annoyed that, once again, Steve had ruined her night. She flipped the light switch on and off three times before climbing into bed.

Light on again, she reached across to her bedside cabinet, pulled a leaflet from the top drawer and scanned its headline. *Take charge of your life TODAY! Join the Secret Women's Business society. Let US help YOU make a difference!* Jesse nodded. Yes! She desperately wanted to take charge of her life. *Don't put your life on hold. Start living TODAY, in the NOW!* The words spoke directly to her, compelling her to act.

She slumped back against the headboard. Who was she kidding? Jesse couldn't imagine going to a meeting or getting along with the types of women who'd frequent such gatherings. Deflated, she shoved the leaflet back in the drawer.

She checked to see if Steve had returned her text. Nothing. No doubt he was angry with her. She shook her head. That was the wrong way round: Jesse should be angry with him. It wasn't as if her going out should have posed a problem. Anna was more than willing to babysit, and Jesse was the one who'd organised her, as well as cooked dinner for the twins. The house was tidy – as it always was. No, the real problem was that Steve was a control freak. He didn't like her going out, and he hated her friends. The last time Jesse had been out with the girls was close to three months earlier.

Her most recent social outing with Steve had been his work Christmas party, but that had been a fizzer. Jesse would have liked to have had more fun; she was certainly open to it. It was a Hawaiian theme, so she'd worn a hula skirt, a coconut bra, the whole bit. Everyone had made an effort to dress up. But Steve was on edge the whole night. Every time she opened her mouth, he'd stared at her, silently urging her to keep quiet. So she'd sipped soda and lime (she was the designated driver, as always), made superficial chat and spent the rest of the time on the outskirts of conversations.

At one point, she'd overheard some of Steve's colleagues complaining about the hours he kept. 'His lack of commitment rivals Max's in accounts,' said one sales guy, who Jesse recognised but didn't know by name. She'd put it down to jealousy. Steve worked ridiculous hours, and he knew how to network – he'd spent most of that night doing just that, talking 'global economies' with various people.

After ignoring her nearly all evening, when they'd arrived home, a pissed Steve had demanded a head job in the kitchen, fluorescent lights and all. Yes, they still had regular sex, but sometimes it felt to Jesse that they were just two bodies going at it. Steve didn't like to kiss, so they hadn't for the last few years. It was all about getting on with the job and getting his rocks off. She thought it would be nice if he occasionally returned the favour, but he wasn't interested. That's what her marriage seemed like to Jesse most of the time – a job. And not a very fulfilling one at that.

Still, she lived in a lovely home, though probably a bit bland and beige for her liking. The only fun room was Emily's, all pinks and bright greens, with fittings and flamingo wallpaper that screamed joy.

But at least she wasn't Stella, who was about to go through a divorce. Jesse had been truly shocked when Stella and Garth split. They were best friends. Stella laughed at Garth's jokes; he listened attentively when she told stories. Their kids were well-adjusted, normal. If it had been Carly and Brett who were divorcing, Jesse wouldn't have blinked. But Stella and Garth? They'd seemed solid.

The way Stella had explained it, these days they were more friends than lovers. 'Garth's like a pair of old slippers. And they're not comfortable anymore. They're tired, thin and worn. I still love him, but I'm not in love with him.' But wasn't that what marriage was supposed to be? Best friends who have sex? Stella seemed quite fine with their separation, but who wanted to live with the stigma of divorce?

Jesse shook her head. Despite her reluctance to acknowledge it, sometimes she thought her marriage might be heading there too. She and Steve hadn't been happy for months. His moods were getting worse, and she was losing patience trying to figure out why. He seemed to have lost interest in her – they never talked properly nowadays – but at the same time, he'd become completely paranoid about what she was doing, where she was going, and who she was seeing.

The combination of neglect, increasing absences and his obsessive need to know what she was doing twenty-four hours a day had brought back Jesse's quirks. But Jesse believed marriage was for life. Her own parents had stuck it out, so why couldn't she? She had children, after all. Besides, Steve had no other family in Australia. His parents were long dead, and his brother lived in Johannesburg.

Jesse checked the bedside clock: 1am! She considered phoning Louisa in San Francisco but thought better of it. Her sister would be rushing out the door to the gym before work. Instead, she ran through the day's to-do list: an open morning for Ollie's class, shop for dinner, buy a gift for Steve for Valentine's Day.

She must have dozed off because she woke with a start when Steve climbed into bed.

'Hey,' she said, reaching over to cuddle him.

'Shattered,' he grunted and turned his back on her, falling asleep almost instantly.

Jesse sighed, relieved that he didn't want sex. She was still annoyed with him for ruining her night out though. She rolled over, thinking back to the leaflet and the phrase *Start living TODAY, in the NOW!* How impossible that seemed.

CHAPTER FIVE

CARLY

Carly woke with a killer hangover. Brett wasn't beside her, but there was a full glass of water on the bedside table. She gulped it down before checking her Fitbit. Eight. Shit! Brett would have left for work over an hour earlier.

She struggled out of bed and wrapped herself in a light dressing gown. A quick survey of the house revealed that Will had also departed for school. She walked back into the bedroom and was about to flop down on the bed when she saw her phone flashing – a text message from Toby. Instantly, she was transported back to her drunken flirting the night before, when she'd been not-so-secretly rebelling against her mundane suburban life. It had seemed like a good idea at the time...

'We're heading to a party,' cute Toby had told her. 'You keen?'

Was she keen? He could have told her he was off to wrestle crocodiles, and she'd have joined him.

But now? In the harsh light of day, it was a different story.

Hands shaking, she read his message. *What a night, hey? Not what I expected. Dinner next week?*

She shook her head, deleted the text and called Stella.

'Please tell me we didn't end up at a suburban sex party last night where we sprang Steve dressed as a baby.'

'Okay.'

'Good. I was hoping it was all a bad dream.' Carly paused. 'I've driven along that street so many times.'

'Same.'

Carly took a breath. 'Toby was cute.'

'Yeah. Not so sure about his friend Pete.'

'He sent me a text.'

'Who, Pete?'

'No. Toby.'

'I'm not surprised. You were all over him.'

Carly winced. 'Don't remind me. I'm an idiot. What are we going to do about Jesse?'

'Like I said last night, let's leave it for the moment.'

'Stella, Jesse has a right to know. We can't keep this a secret. What if the situation was reversed and Jesse and I had seen Garth there – back when you were together – wouldn't you want to know?'

'It's too bizarre. I can't get my head around it. The last thing we need is for Jesse to shoot the messengers. Let's leave it twenty-four hours so we can at least come up with a plan.'

'Isn't it better to rip the plaster off quickly? Jesse's going to be hurt either way.'

'I'll think about it.' Stella paused. 'How are you?'

'Hungover. Ashamed. Embarrassed.' Carly rubbed her right shoulder, forcing the imaginary pain away.

'Okay, you've painted a pretty clear picture. Take two Nurofen Plus and go back to bed.'

After hanging up, Carly curled up on the bed, wrapped a soft cotton blanket around her, and pieced together the events of the night. After an awkward run-in with Steve, the four of them had hightailed it out of the house, leaving Pete behind. Last

Carly had seen, he'd been enjoying the attentions of three women dressed up as headmistresses. Where did people find the energy? All she'd wanted to do was cut loose – drink wine, maybe dance. Then she met Toby, and now he'd texted her.

What the hell had she been thinking, flirting with him? Things weren't great with Brett, but that was no reason to behave the way she had. The shame was overwhelming. Carly felt physically ill – shaking, stomach cramps – and not just from the alcohol she'd consumed.

Earlier in the night, Stella had annoyed her by calling out Carly's inappropriate behaviour. Carly should have listened, but she'd been having a good time and wanted to forget everything that was going on in her life for a couple of hours. Forget that her elder son, Nicholas, had gone to Cornwall, England, on a gap year, and that her other son, William, had less than two years left of school before he'd be taking off as well. Then what? She'd float around alone in a big empty house while Brett continued to work twenty hours a day, seven days a week.

She missed Nicky intensely. He'd said numerous times that he hated her using his pet name, but when she did (if he was in a receptive mood), his face lit up like he was seven years old again. It made Carly feel like she was dancing on clouds. Her heart broke that she wouldn't get to see that adorable smile for another eleven months, especially being thousands of miles away.

Carly got up and walked into the kitchen, searching for something to make her feel better. She glanced at the fruit bowl on the table. Mango? Passionfruit? Apple? She ate half a banana and instantly wanted to throw up.

Had she really told Stella and Jesse she wanted a fuck buddy? She'd only been joking ... sort of. Bloody hell, she wasn't a bad person. It was just that Brett spent more time at work than he did at home. And when he was here, he was preoccupied and tense. He had two iPhones and it wasn't uncommon for both to be glued to his ears at all hours – when he wasn't chained to his iPad. The closest sexual companion Carly had these days was her vibrator, the Rockin' Rooster. Brett was too busy keeping track of the money market, concerned about 'hostile takeovers' and 'significant mergers', to trifle with her.

It hadn't always been this way. At the beginning of their relationship, everything was shiny and thrilling. The first few times had been awkward: they were both inexperienced and had to work out how to kiss so their teeth didn't collide, how to make their bodies fit together. But six weeks into their relationship, it clicked. That was one day she'd never forget.

They'd met up during Carly's lunch break. As soon as she saw him, the palpitations started: nerves, excitement, desire. When they kissed hello, she felt the frisson between them.

'Hungry?' Brett asked, staring at the menu.

Carly was hungry, but not for food. Underneath the table her foot nudged his. Boldly, she placed her trembling hand on his thigh under his board shorts, desperate to touch his skin.

He reached over and kissed her. 'I'm already hard,' he whispered. 'Let's get out of here.'

She smiled, allowing him to take her by the hand and lead her back to his car. They leaned against the bonnet, and he kissed her deep and slow, his hands cupping her butt, their legs entwined.

'Get in,' he said softly.

Irresistible desire ... she couldn't even think about refusing.

Less than ten minutes later, they arrived at one of the few National Parks in the area. He stopped on a secluded track surrounded by sky-scraping eucalypt canopies, moss-covered logs, and dense fern carpets. Greens of every hue filtered through the sunlight. It was damp, humid, and hot. Kookaburras cackled above.

'What about rangers?' Carly managed half-heartedly as he tilted the front passenger seat back as far as it would go and angled himself above her.

'I don't know. Do you want more than two of us in the car?' He was already pushing up her skirt. 'Live dangerously, Carls.'

She grinned, grabbing at his shorts, pulling them down. It felt so naughty, fucking in broad daylight where anyone could walk by and catch them. But Carly didn't care. Neither did he. They were young, possibly falling in love, so what the hell did it matter? Brett was right. *Live dangerously.*

Carly wriggled down the seat till her bum was practically on the floor.

'What are you ... oh,' Brett said, as she took his penis in her mouth.

What must it have looked like from the outside? Brett gripping the headrest, rocking back and forwards, Carly thankfully hidden from view.

He'd been almost delirious as he reached down and pulled at her hair. 'Come up, I want you now. I can't wait any longer.'

They manoeuvred themselves into position and he thrust inside her, his grip slipping to her waist. Carly pulled her mouth away from his and tilted her hips into him, allowing maximum penetration. They rocked together, Brett sucking her breasts, bringing her to orgasm before letting himself come. That was when Carly had known Brett was her soulmate. They'd be together forever. Carly savoured the memory.

She looked down at her erect nipples. They hadn't had car sex, or any other kind of sex, in a long time.

In the early days, even though they had two boisterous toddlers and lived in a tiny two-bedroom inner-city terrace with a mortgage that made them gag, they were in love, horny and happy. When they went out with other parents from preschool, they'd listen to them complaining about the lack of sleep and sex. Brett and Carly couldn't understand it. They couldn't get enough of each other. She was the luckiest woman on the planet: two adorable sons, and a husband who loved her and loved being a dad as well. She'd hit the jackpot. And when he was away on business – phone sex.

Finances improved and a few years later, the family moved, and Carly contented herself decorating their perfect 1880s Federation home, nestled in an half acre of manicured lawns. A taste of Carly's style – brightly painted turquoise walls, local artwork, antique furniture, boldly patterned sofas, and a vibrant yellow ottoman. A mix of old and new. Quirky. Fun.

Life changed around six years ago when Nicholas started high school. Brett was increasingly busy with work – lots of travel, late-night conference calls. To alleviate the boredom and loneliness, Carly threw herself into volunteering on several school committees. Then, they kind of stopped talking. Brett hadn't seemed overly concerned. Whenever Carly mentioned that they had nothing in common except the boys, he'd look at her quizzically and say, 'That's a major common interest, don't you think?' Carly would agree and they'd limp along for another few months.

These days, they were lucky to make love once or twice a month ... and she'd been dead unlucky since New Year's Eve.

Sometimes Carly wondered if Brett was having an affair. That would certainly answer a lot of questions. Last week, during one of their discussions, she'd asked him if he was seeing someone else. He hadn't been shocked because she asked this every four months or so. He said no. When she suggested they might like to sleep in separate rooms, he just shrugged and mumbled something unintelligible. The next morning, she apologised as did he, Brett even suggesting a night together in the city, just the two of them. Brett had good intentions, but they hardly ever came to fruition.

Carly walked into the bathroom, contemplated having a shower and thought better of it. She didn't have the physical energy. Still, her mind wouldn't rest.

She thought again about Toby and the fuck buddy business. She didn't want to fall in love. She just wanted a playmate. A handsome playmate. Then again, she was married. In all their nineteen years of marriage, she'd never been unfaithful, and she doubted she'd ever have the courage to. It was all bluff, a fantasy. Yes, she'd fondled Toby's hair the previous night, but that was as far as it had gone. It wasn't as if she'd tried to take his clothes off and have sex with him in a public toilet. Still, she felt like a tool.

In the distance, the phone rang. As she reached it, the answering machine kicked in. Just as well. It was Brett, and she was way too ashamed to talk to him.

CHAPTER SIX

STELLA

After the phone call from Carly, I drove to the library. I couldn't stop thinking about last night. We all knew Steve was odd. Okay, odd's probably not the right word. Smarmy. The Steve I knew was always in control and immaculately dressed: Armani suits, Ralph Lauren polos. The Australian marketing director of a huge international pharmaceutical company, he prided himself on his appearance, so clean and neat. But seeing him the previous night (wearing a nappy for goodness' sake) changed everything.

Carly had a point. Sooner or later Jesse would find out, but I didn't want to be the one to tell her. At least, not yet. Not until we had more information. But then what more did I need to know? I guess I didn't want to get involved in that part of Jesse's life. It was a nightmare and instinct told me to stay clear.

Jesse called an hour later when I was neck deep in cataloguing a swag of new titles. 'Did you end up going to the party?'

'Jesse, hi. Yeah–'

'Sorry I ditched you. It's just with Steve working late, I didn't think it was fair to keep the babysitter waiting.'

I stifled a cough. Steve! How exhausting leading a secret life. 'Sure. What time did he get home?'

'Late. Two-ish maybe. He was up at the crack of dawn this morning, bleary-eyed but ready to face another day.'

Sure.

I said I'd fill her in on the details later and tried to end the call. Not only was I uncomfortable talking to her, but the cataloguing wasn't progressing as smoothly as I'd hoped.

'About the books I stacked yesterday...'

'It's okay, Jess. I've fixed them. No need to worry.'

'Maybe I'm becoming a bit preoccupied again.'

'You're fine.' This wasn't a conversation I could have with Jesse over the phone. 'Let's talk about it when you come in next week? Okay?' Silence. 'Jesse?'

'There's one more thing, I'm serious about applying for the full-time position when it comes up.'

I looked skyward, trying to formulate my words. 'I know, but what about Steve?' I could barely say his name out loud. 'He doesn't even like you at the library part time.'

'I'll work on him.'

In truth, Jesse was becoming a problem at the library. Although she was thorough and dedicated, once she became fixated on something, like tidying the magazine racks, it took her the best part of a morning. A few times recently, she hadn't been able to stop clenching her hands. I'd take her into the bathroom and help calm her down, but it usually took a good half-hour. The situation couldn't continue indefinitely, but I was hoping to find a solution to satisfy Liz, the manager, so Jesse's job remained secure. As for a full-time position? There would be no way Liz would agree.

Then there was Steve. What a fuckwit! Maybe I needed a man's perspective – I could ask Garth. Maybe he already knew. But nah, Garth couldn't keep a scandal that big to himself.

I had no time to deliberate further. Business at the library was brisk. At eleven, I was running toddler hour, but some parents didn't seem to understand that it wasn't a babysitting service. You couldn't dump your kids in front of the reader (twenty-one-year-old Gracie, studying English literature at university) and dash off to the shops. Which meant I was on parent patrol.

'Can't you just watch them for a minute?' one hassled mother asked after I caught her trying to bolt out the automatic doors.

'No,' I replied, polite but firm. I really wanted to say, 'Does this look like a day-care centre to you?' The nerve of some people.

She slunk back over to toddler hour and her two-year-old twins, no doubt wishing I was dead.

On my lunch break, I found two text messages and a couple of missed calls on my mobile. The first text was from Carly apologising again for her behaviour the night before and suggesting a movie afternoon tomorrow – Saturday. The second message was also from her: *OMG! Ring me ASAP.* It had been sent an hour ago.

I checked my voice messages. The first was from Steve. That was a worry. When I heard his voice message, I had to play it again.

'Stay the hell away from my wife, hear me? Jesse doesn't need the likes of you putting silly ideas in her head about working full-time at the library. And on that other matter, I'd advise you to keep your mouth shut if you know what's good for you. I repeat, stay away from her.'

My hands trembled, and my throat was dry. I was furious. The nerve of him ringing and leaving threats!

The second message was from Carly; she sounded frantic. *'Did Steve call you? I'm still shaking. Ring me!'*

I replayed Steve's message. Under the circumstances, he was in no position to tell us what to do. And regardless of whether we saw Jesse or not, we could still tell her what we'd seen the previous night. Steve couldn't stop us ringing her or texting her. She was our friend. I spoke to her practically every day.

I phoned Carly.

'Did he threaten you too?' she asked.

'Yeah.'

'Stella, I'm rattled. What are we going to do? Did you talk to him?'

'No, he left a message.'

'Same here. The guy's a nutter.'

'Look, I'm shaken too, but I don't think he'll do anything silly. He's scared we're going to tell Jesse, that's all. I think he's bluffing.'

'He didn't sound scared. I'm worried.' Carly took a breath. 'Maybe we should steer clear of Jesse for a while? We don't want to make matters worse.'

I forced my voice to remain calm. 'We haven't done anything wrong.'

'Shit! I sent her a text message about the movies tomorrow, the three of us.'

'Carly, did you hear me? We've done nothing wrong. If we suddenly stop talking to her, she's going to think it's strange.'

'Yeah, but maybe we should keep a low profile just for the next week.'

I sighed. 'What is this? *Lupin?*'

'Worse.'

'So now you don't want to tell Jesse?'

'Yes, I want to tell Jesse. I also want to call the police. Steve's threatening us. Who knows what he's capable of?'

'Okay, but like I said this morning, let's give it twenty-four hours – enough time for Steve to calm down and for us to come up with a plan–'

'Like what?'

'Like whether we tell Jesse or not. But, Carly, we've got to be united.'

'I say rip the plaster off and let the police deal with Steve.'

'It's not that simple.' I raked my fingers through my hair. 'Did you tell Brett?'

'No way. Then I'll have to explain how we ended up at that party.' She paused. 'I just keep wondering how long Steve's been doing this stuff.'

I shook my head. 'Who knows? But seriously, it's best if we say nothing for the moment. If it all blows up, you'll have to tell Brett. Try to ignore Steve.'

'And Jesse?'

'Let's take a step back, keep things as simple as we can for now.'

I heard Carly sigh. 'Okay.'

After I'd hung up, I sat for a time thinking about Jesse. Despite my bravado with Carly, I didn't know what Steve might do. Normal people would be extra nice if they got caught out like that, but that wasn't Steve's style. He wasn't normal. He was always right, no matter what. He could be caught with the crown jewels in his pocket, and he'd still deny it.

I couldn't begin to imagine Jesse's reaction if she found out. She'd be devastated, her life in tatters.

I deleted Steve's message and then wondered if I'd done the right thing.

CHAPTER SEVEN

The rest of my shift flew by in a blur. Before I'd had time to blink, it was three, and I was heading out the door to pick up Garth's mum and take her shopping. I did this most Friday afternoons. Just because Garth and I were divorcing didn't mean I had to divorce June. She'd been good to me over the years, especially when Hannah and Harry were younger, picking them up from day care, babysitting. She'd been a saviour.

And after Garth's dad, Vince, died, looking after the children gave her increased purpose and meaning. Running around after little kids doesn't allow much time to wallow in your own grief and misery. So, no, I didn't see why the kids and I had to give up June.

Besides, she wasn't any closer to accepting the situation. She'd been forgetful lately and Garth had needed to tell her a couple of times about our parting. 'What about your father?' she'd said to Garth at a family dinner post-separation. 'He's not well; his heart will give out when he hears.'

It had taken us all a few moments to process what June had said. Vince had been dead eight years.

'Silly me,' she'd stammered when she realised. 'You've got me completely worked up. I still think of your father as being with us. It's hard to believe he's been gone all these years.' She recovered enough to add, 'You and Stella had such a beautiful wedding! The croquembouche was a culinary masterpiece. I've never tasted anything so delicious.'

That was true but, as we explained, a sublime wedding dessert was no reason to stay together indefinitely.

Our separation had been a shock for most of our friends. Perhaps it would have been easier for others to understand if we'd had a huge blow-up or showed warning signs of discontent, and it probably didn't help that I didn't feel the need to tell anyone but family and our closest friends that Garth had hooked up with a colleague.

Truthfully, my romantic life with Garth had been kaput for several years. Occasionally, we'd tried to reignite the flame by having weekends away from the domesticity that had engulfed our lives, but the passion never lasted. Seven months ago, we'd gone to Fiji, just the two of us. Without Hannah and Harry, we'd quickly realised what we'd known deep down for years. The kids were the glue holding us together, and when they weren't with us? Well, we wished they were.

Garth and I had never been the sort to hold hands while walking along the beach, cuddle at the movies or kiss spontaneously. There were rarely any public displays of affection. That wasn't us. At least, it wasn't me. But it seemed these were the exact intimacies Garth had been missing. Soon after Fiji, his idle lunchroom chat with a colleague turned into coffee at a nearby café ... which turned into lunch, and the lunches quickly progressed to dinners. Thankfully, the affair wasn't drawn out. Garth had the decency to tell me he had feelings for Amanda. I didn't blame him. In fact, I felt relieved. I wouldn't say I was happy our marriage was over, but I understood where he was coming from.

In early January, he moved into Amanda's apartment. I couldn't think of anything worse than shacking up with a new partner minutes after leaving a long-term relationship, but there you go. It was what Garth wanted, so good luck to him. The kids weren't as accepting of his new life. It was incredibly stressful for me having to coax them into ringing their dad or having a meal with him. As for staying the weekend with him and Amanda, forget it. That meant that when the kids weren't at school or with their friends, they were my responsibility. It was wearing me down.

Aside from the issue with June – she had no idea Garth had hooked up with Amanda and was now living with her – things weren't too awkward. Garth had come to Hannah and Harry's end-of-year speech nights, though, because he'd been running late, we didn't sit together. Hence why I'd noticed Mike. We'd chatted amicably after Hannah's dance concert, and watched Harry play his end-of-year cricket match. We'd even ended up having Christmas lunch together – although not with Amanda. I wasn't ready to play happy families with her and neither were the kids.

Garth's new apartment (or, rather, Amanda's) wasn't particularly close, but it was on the train line, so if the kids wanted to go there after school or on weekends, they could. I knew Garth would have preferred to see and speak to Hannah and Harry more often, but right now, they weren't keen on their dad living with somebody who wasn't their mother. I appreciated that. I keep telling Garth it wouldn't matter who she was: the kids weren't comfortable with their father having a girlfriend, period.

Harry had commented that he already had one mother and 'two would be torture. A stepmother, ugh!'

I thought that was jumping the gun: Garth hadn't said anything about marrying Amanda. Then again, I was as surprised as they were when Garth had announced he was moving in with her.

'It's just wrong,' Harry had said.

'Totally gross,' Hannah agreed. 'See, Mum! You're not in the loop. You don't even know what's going on with Dad.'

She was probably right – not about it being gross, but about me not being in the loop. I didn't feel bitter or angry. I was sad for the kids that they didn't have two parents living together and raising them, but this was the way it had turned out. It could have been a lot worse. Imagine if Garth and I hated each other and fought over custody, visitation rights and the house. Ugh, indeed!

The person who seemed to find it most difficult was Garth himself. When I'd seen him last weekend, he'd looked as if he were carrying the weight of the world on his shoulders.

'You should be happy. New girlfriend, new life,' I'd said.

'Yeah, but the kids hate me.'

'They don't hate you. They just don't like seeing their dad slobbering over his younger girlfriend, especially in public.'

'I don't slobber, and she's not that young.'

'You know teenagers. They can't stand to think their parents might be having sex, especially with other people. They'll come around. A few of their friends' parents are divorced. A couple have even remarried. It's a sign of the times.'

'How about you, Stella? How are you doing?'

'If that's your subtle way of asking if I'm getting any, the answer is no. And I have no intention of meeting anyone either. I just got rid of you.'

Inside my head, a voice said, 'Liar! What about Mike?'

'Don't you get lonely?'

41

I shook my head. 'Why the sudden interest? I'm doing just fine.'

Maybe Garth had wanted me to ask him about his new life, but I didn't go there. It wasn't my job to stroke his ego and tell him what a fabulous catch he was anymore. He was doing okay ... and if he wasn't? Well, it wasn't my problem.

Rather like Jesse and Steve weren't my problem. Yes, I'd prefer not to have seen Steve trussed up like a baby. Maybe our chance encounter last night would persuade him to come clean to Jesse. *Guess what, honey? I love dressing up as a baby, sucking on a dummy and being spanked.*

But after the voice message, I doubted it. Steve wasn't a nice person. It was possible that something like this could tip him over the edge. It might not be Jesse's or my problem, but we'd become embroiled in it. While my head didn't agree, my heart wanted to check in with Jesse more, not leave her at Steve's mercy.

CHAPTER EIGHT

When I pulled into June's carport, she was all dressed up and sitting in a cane chair (her back perfectly straight), waiting for me on her veranda.

'June, hello. What are you doing outside? It's far too hot.'

'Nonsense,' she replied, kissing me briefly on my cheek.

On the road again, I asked about her shopping list.

'The usual,' she said, 'but with Garth's birthday coming up, I want to buy him something special. Golf balls, maybe.'

'He hasn't played in a while,' I ventured.

'He played last weekend when David was visiting.'

I took a deep breath. David was Garth's brother and, to the best of my knowledge, the last time he and Garth had played golf together was a good five years ago.

'Are you sure, June? I think it might have been a bit longer.'

'No, we went to the clubhouse afterwards for a barbeque, remember?' She paused a moment, then added, 'You might be right. Golf balls would be wasted on Garth. They all seem to end up in the pond.'

I wasn't sure if she'd remembered how long ago that barbeque had been, or if she'd just changed her mind. I didn't want to push it, so I simply nodded and drove on. Maybe she was just absent-minded, but it had crossed my mind that she could be showing early signs of dementia. I batted the thought away.

June had always been eccentric, more so since Vince died. Example: she had plenty of hair but liked wearing headscarves and turbans. Today she was sporting a lime green and orange turban, a flamboyant look without being completely over the top. When Vince was alive, she'd only worn them on special occasions, because he wasn't overly fond of them, but as soon as he passed, she said, 'Bugger it. I'll be dead a long time. I'm going to wear my drapings every day.' And that was it. June was famous in the neighbourhood for her fabulous turbans and scarves. I suspected she liked the attention.

The rest of the afternoon passed uneventfully. We shopped at the supermarket, then went to a department store where June bought Garth a navy shirt. I dropped June home and helped unpack the groceries, then left her with her latest Harlan Coben and knitting. I should spend more time with her, but there were only so many hours in the day, and often I found myself running out of time and energy.

As I got back into the car, my mobile rang. The screen flashed 'unknown number'.

'Hello,' I said tentatively, worried that it might be Steve.

'Stella?' It was Mike. 'I'm ringing to apologise.'

Lightning bolt! My hands were instantly clammy.

'I'm mortified Pete took us to that ... um ... place,' he went on. 'Maybe we could meet up again?'

'At another swingers' party?'

'Preferably not.'

'Pity, I kind of enjoyed it.' What was I saying? I wasn't skilled at impromptu flirting. My face flushed hot.

There was silence on the other end of the phone.

'Mike?'

'Yeah?'

'I'm joking. I have to admit though, some of those scenes keep popping into my head.'

'Have you spoken to your friend, the one whose husband–'

'No! Well, I have but not about that.'

'Yeah, not easy. You really don't think she knows anything? What about the cocaine?'

'What do you mean?'

'He was probably high. You saw the coke on those trays. We're getting a lot more middle-aged men suffering cocaine overdoses in emergency these days. Your friend's husband fits the profile.'

What a mess.

'So should we try meeting up again for coffee?' Mike asked. 'Or, better still, dinner?'

My heart pounded and the phone shook in my hand. I had to be sensible. I liked Mike, but I didn't need any complications. So, as much as my body hated me, I gave him a vague response, thanked him for dropping me home the previous night and wished him a good weekend.

'You can't avoid me forever,' he said as I went to hang up.

'I can try.'

Mike laughed. 'That's not going to work. You're already hooked.'

'So am not.'

'So are.'

I hung up smiling. I was so hooked it was ridiculous.

Garth phoned later that evening. The kids were happily tapping on their computers – Instagram, Snapchat, downloading music and no doubt participating in other activities I'd banned them from doing – and I'd just poured myself a glass of cold Sauvignon Blanc and was settling in to watch *Pride and Prejudice*, my favourite version with Colin Firth as a buff Mr Darcy.

'We need to talk,' Garth said.

Sounded ominous. Why, oh why, had I answered the phone? It was Friday night. I'd been enjoying myself.

'What about?'

'Mum.'

I sat up. 'June? What's the matter? I saw her this afternoon. She's fine.'

'She seems to have a problem with Mandy.'

So, it was Mandy now, not Amanda? 'Back up. You've introduced them?'

'Tonight. I turned up with Mandy to take Mum to dinner. It was a disaster.'

I looked at my watch. It was only just after eight. 'Jeez, it must have been if you're home already.'

'Mum kept asking for you. Wouldn't let up. I tried explaining, but she wouldn't listen. Just kept saying it wasn't the right way to treat my wife, and that Dad would be very disappointed. I think it's going beyond her normal forgetfulness, Stella. I'm worried about her. I knew something was up when I arrived. She wasn't dressed for dinner and kept rabbiting on about the garden hedge, saying it needed trimming. I don't know what to do.'

'Trim the hedge for starters.'

Garth sighed.

'How did Amanda react?' I asked.

'She was shocked, obviously, especially as Mum kept calling her a homewrecker and telling her I was old enough to be her father.'

'That's harsh. Her much older brother, sure, but father?'

'It's not funny. Mum was rude, Mandy's in tears, and all of a sudden, I'm very tired.'

'Okay, well, I'm sorry for you but–'

'Could you check in on her tomorrow?'

I could have said no, but given my feelings for June, I didn't. 'Sure, but Garth, I think you should take June to her doctor. Get the clinic to run some tests.'

'You think it could be' – he struggled to say the word – 'dementia?'

'Could be.'

He sighed. 'Yeah. How are the kids?'

'Good. Busy. You know what they're like.'

'I miss them.'

'Want to talk to them?'

'Maybe tomorrow.'

We hung up and I went back to watching Mr Darcy. Specifically, that scene with Colin Firth carrying on in the lake with the wet shirt. It got me thinking about Mike. Well, fantasising.

What would I do with him if he was in front of me ... naked? I'd be terrified ... almost.

I figure I'd tie him up and have my way with him, after I'd teased, kissed and probed my way about his body.

Bondage? Where had those thoughts sprung from? It wasn't like me at all. I was normally so sensible. The sex party antics had affected me more than I wanted to admit.

I shook my head. I had children ... responsibilities. But the thought of Mike's hands and lips caressing–

Stop it, Stella!

Still, it made me wonder ... why didn't I just say yes to his invitation to meet up again?

CHAPTER NINE

JESSE

Jesse was in the kitchen on Friday evening preparing a prawn laksa and waiting for Steve to come home. Wine was chilling in the fridge, and Emmy and Ollie were occupied playing games on their iPads. (A Friday after-school treat.)

She was looking forward to a family evening with the four of them enjoying dinner together and then watching a movie like *Peter Rabbit* or *Coco*. But whether that would happen or not largely depended on Steve's mood. These days, any exchange between them had a nasty habit of spiralling into an argument. She'd say something he misinterpreted, or he'd say something she took the wrong way. Something was always upsetting him – the kids were too loud, the toothpaste wasn't the right brand. She was walking on eggshells and didn't understand why.

Her mind jumped to her job at the library. She wanted that full-time position, but Stella was right. Steve didn't like her working. He was much happier when she was at home all day. She'd done that when the twins were little, but she'd missed the library, being surrounded by books and interesting customers – her tiny slice of independence. After the twins had started school, she went back to working part-time.

Stella had organised Jesse's current position at the library: two days a week, ten until three, always a Thursday and alternating Mondays and Fridays. Easy. Jesse loved working with Stella and Gracie, not that their rosters always coincided. And they were good to her, helping her out on bad days when she got stressed. And she did get stressed, especially when it was her turn at the customer enquiries desk. Why couldn't people wait in line to be served? Instead, they clustered around the desk and coughed or said 'ahem' to get her attention. She knew they were there; she wasn't blind. Couldn't they see she was already serving someone? The polite thing to do was to stand back, give the person in front of them space and wait their turn. It wasn't brain surgery. Then there were the patrons who asked unnecessarily protracted questions and wouldn't stop talking long enough for her to answer them. They just kept going on and on.

Jesse stirred the laksa. Yes, her job was sometimes stressful, but she was confident her issues could be ironed out, especially if she worked full-time. For starters, she'd have more time to complete all her duties.

She jumped when Steve walked into the kitchen. 'Hello.' She beamed. 'I didn't hear you drive in. Good day?'

'Long.' He kissed her on the cheek and peered over her shoulder into the pot on the stove. 'Smells good.'

'Prawn laksa. Drink?' She walked to the fridge and pulled out a bottle of wine. 'Petaluma, one of your favourites.'

Steve walked into the next room to greet the kids, while Jesse poured two glasses. She took a small sip from her own, knowing she'd tip most of it down the sink later. She needed to stay in control.

Steve came back in, picked up his glass and took a mouthful. 'What's new?'

He seemed relaxed and responsive, so Jesse jumped in. 'Darling, about the position coming up at the library.'

She waited for a response ... Nothing.

'I'm thinking about applying.'

He took a longer sip and let her statement hang in the air before replying. 'You still banging on about that? We've been through this before, Jess. Our family comes first. You can barely manage a part-time job. If anything, you should cut back your hours. The kids are your priority, or at least they should be. I have my doubts after last night.'

'Emily and Ollie *are* my priority, always! You know that.'

'So you say, but what about those afternoons when you've been held up at work?'

'One afternoon, Steve. One! And Mum picked them up. The kids were none the wiser.'

'But I was.'

Jesse started to twitch. She needed to turn some switches on and off, but Steve was watching, monitoring her behaviour as always. Her hand sneaked out, searching for a button to press. 'It would be nice to have some extra cash coming in.'

She meant it, though she could never hope to match what Steve earned. Her job probably brought in a twentieth of his, reducing her to little more than a financial footnote. Money equalled power. Steve earned all the money, therefore he had all the power. It played on her mind. Whenever she asked him for extra money, say for new cushions, he questioned it. It wasn't that she didn't have access to his money, she did, but it was assumed she would stick to a monthly budget. But at certain times of the year – like November and December, the Christmas shopping months – it was tough. In January too, when she had to buy new school shoes, uniforms and so on. Steve had no idea how much everything cost. Jesse put as much as she could on lay-by, but she couldn't lay-by shoes. The kids' feet grew too quickly.

'We have enough money,' Steve said. 'Is this about the new plates you bought last week?'

The kitchen plates – she'd forgotten about those. She'd been shopping at the supermarket and there'd been a homewares promotion on mid-priced crockery. Jesse had spent sixty dollars on the plates, which were discounted from a hundred and ten, but Steve hadn't been impressed.

'It's not about the plates, Steve, though if I were working more, I wouldn't have felt so guilty about buying them.'

'You're not making a sound argument. You bought them, regardless.' He stared at her, waiting for her to say something, to challenge him.

There was little point in continuing. He was a much better debater than Jesse. She usually felt like an illiterate imbecile after one of their discussions.

Steve put an arm around her. 'I know you like being at the library, it's your escape. But with the long hours I work, it's not fair on the kids. Is it?'

At that moment, Emily bounded in yelling, 'I beat him. I beat him again at *Stand-Up Rafting*. I can ride the rapids better than anyone in this house!'

'Oh yeah?' Ollie shouted, running in after her. 'I'm better at *Rallyball* than you.'

Just as quickly, they raced out again, Emily screaming, 'Are not!'

Jesse sighed. 'You have a point.'

'I know I do,' Steve said triumphantly. 'You barely have enough time for all of us as it is. I run a distant third here.'

'That's not true. It's just that there's always something going on with the kids – homework, excursions, sport, music.' She felt overwhelmed just listing their activities.

'Exactly, so how could you manage a full-time job on top of everything else?'

Jesse gave up and turned back to the laksa. Sometimes she wondered if Steve was jealous of the time she spent with Emily and Oliver. She needed to work harder at getting the balance right so all three of them were happy ninety per cent of the time. But then where did that leave her? Where did her personal satisfaction and happiness rate on the scale? Perhaps if she could work up the courage to attend one of those Secret Women's Business meetings, she'd learn the mystery to keeping everyone happy and satisfied, including herself.

'At least you're over that silly idea of having another baby,' Steve said, draining his glass.

That took her by surprise. 'Why do you say that?'

He shook his head. 'You're talking about a full-time job at the library.'

'Oh, but I do want another baby. That hasn't changed.'

'Really? I'm sorry I brought it up. Make your mind up, Jesse. Do you want a full-time job, or do you want another baby? You can't do both! Besides, you know we can't afford another kid – not even with your minimal financial contribution. When's dinner?'

Jesse stared at the pot, blinking back tears. She hadn't added the prawns yet. 'Ten minutes.'

Steve put his empty glass down on the bench. 'Right. I'll have a quick shower.'

Jesse stared as he walked out of the room. She felt a great sadness at the thought she might never be pregnant again or get to hold another newborn – *her* newborn – in her arms. She loved the twins to death and was serious about her library career, but that didn't mean she didn't want another child.

'You need to get your nervous habits under control before we can discuss having another child,' he'd said on several occasions, when he wasn't telling her they couldn't afford it or that it was fiscally irresponsible.

Jesse knew she was only nervous because she didn't know what was up with him. She wouldn't feel so anxious if he treated her better.

CHAPTER TEN

Jesse had had such high hopes for that night, and now they'd had two disagreements in the space of twenty minutes. The weekend stretched ahead. She couldn't bear the thought of more arguments; the tension and stress were too much. Steve was a footy fanatic but unfortunately football season hadn't started yet. The Australian Open had finished, so there was no tennis to distract him. There would be motor racing and wrestling on Cable, but that wouldn't interest him for long. She could always offer the usual sexual services to get him into a positive mood, but she resented performing these favours and getting nothing in return, not even a thank you.

Blinking away more tears, she told herself to get a grip. Steve had a busy schedule. She needed to back off. Be grateful for what she had, who she was, and what they had together as a couple and a family. She was just being greedy. Once Steve was out of the shower, everything would be fine. She just needed to relax.

Giving in to her urge, she opened and closed the fridge door three times. Immediately, the tension eased from her neck and shoulders as she counted down. Ten, nine, eight ... She knew she shouldn't do it, but she always felt more in control afterwards.

'What are you doing?' Steve asked.

She jumped. 'Nothing,' she answered, caught out and wishing she could snatch back the last two minutes.

'Bloody hell! I saw Ollie doing the same thing the other night. Are you taking him back to that psychiatrist?'

'Shush, keep your voice down. Ollie's doing fine. And he was seeing a psychologist!'

Jesse shook her head. Sometimes she almost hated Steve. She stared out the window to her car in the driveway. Sometimes she felt like getting in it and driving away. People like Carly fantasised about fuck buddies, but, when Jesse fantasised, it was about escaping, grabbing her two kids from school one afternoon, leaving town and never looking back. They'd head north-west into the country, where they'd find a pretty cottage in a friendly town – somewhere with a white picket fence and a few acres. It would be sunny every day, they'd grow fruit trees and be happy. Just the three of them, away from the stress and hassle of city life. Jesse would make jam and bake cakes and biscuits for the local weekend market. Their lives would be idyllic.

'So,' Steve said, 'care to tell me about last night?'

'Last night? With Carly and Stella?'

He reached for the wine bottle. 'You seem to spend a lot of time with those two.'

'Before last night, I hadn't been out with them in months. They're good fun.'

'Isn't Stella getting a divorce? Do you really think she's a good influence, especially given the way things are with you?'

Jesse bit her tongue. Good influence? How old was she? Twelve? 'Are you saying Stella's a bad influence because she's separated? That's ridiculous.'

'Ridiculous? I'm ridiculous because I think you spend too much time with vacuous women who are out on the prowl? What did you get up to last night?'

Jesse counted backwards before speaking. 'I was home by ten. And you know exactly where I was for the three hours before. At the pub.'

'So you say.' He stalked out of the room.

She took a deep breath, needing to keep it together for the children's sake. To buy herself a few minutes, Jesse fussed about the kitchen, tidying up, washing dirty dishes, wiping down benches. Finally, she could procrastinate no longer.

As she went to get the bowls for dinner, she noticed a new message on her phone from Carly, sent much earlier in the day: *Either of you keen on the movies tomorrow pm?* The message had been sent to Stella as well.

Had Carly forgotten what it was like having nine-year-olds in the house? As if Jesse could take off to the movies at a moment's notice! Still, it would be a nice escape.

She peeked into the lounge room where Steve was playing with the twins. He was still handsome. Most men his age were losing their hair and gaining a paunch. Carly's husband, Brett, was getting rounder by the day. Garth was a bit like that too, but Stella had said that since he'd moved out, he'd joined the gym.

'Dinner's ready,' Jesse called.

She dished up the laksa, determined to stay optimistic and bright. As she sat down to eat, she kept telling herself she could do it. She had to do it. It was her job to ensure harmony. Marriage was a compromise. Sometimes you had to do things you didn't want to, to keep the peace. It was called managing the situation.

Thankfully, the kids had so much news to share, their enthusiasm was contagious. They chattered about school, swimming classes and sport. Then Ollie mentioned a movie he wanted to see on the weekend because 'all the other guys have seen it'.

'Not me?' Emily said.

Ollie shook his head. 'Of course not you. You're a girl!'

'I'll take you,' Steve said, looking up from his laksa.

Wow, that was a surprise, Jesse thought. Progress.

Ollie beamed and punched his fist into the air. 'Yes! Boys' afternoon.'

Jesse smiled. 'Excellent. Carly's invited me to the movies tomorrow too. I'm sure we can see something that you'd like, Em, so all three of us can go.'

'Yay,' Emily said, bursting with excitement.

'You see too much of that woman,' Steve cut in. 'She's a bad influence – I don't want her around Emily.'

On and on he went. Jesse couldn't understand it, especially in front of the children. It was only an invitation to the movies, not an invite away on a girls-only weekend to Melbourne. In the end she cleared the bowls away and said, 'Forget I ever mentioned it. I won't go.'

She put the kids to bed, read them each a story and then took herself off to bed. If Steve was in a foul mood and didn't have the decency to explain why, so be it.

But by the time he came to bed, she'd calmed down.

She rubbed his back. 'What's up? Have I done something wrong?'

He shook his head. 'Just tired, that's all.'

'Maybe you need to get away from us for a weekend. Why don't you and your mates go to the Gold Coast for a golfing weekend?'

Steve loved the Gold Coast, but Jesse found Surfers

Paradise seedy and depressing. Too many cracks in the pavements. She reasoned that Steve heading away for a weekend with his mates every few months might mean they could avoid a family holiday there later in the year.

'So now you're trying to get rid of me, is that it?'

She couldn't win.

Steve nodded off while Jesse lay in bed, wide awake.

She glanced at her phone. Two WhatsApp group messages. The first was from Carly. *Sorry, something's come up, and I can't do movies tomorrow. Rain check? xxx* The second, from Stella. *Sure, there's not much good on anyway. Xx*

Jesse took a deep breath, relieved she didn't have to come up with her own excuse. She needed a good night's sleep, but given that Steve was snoring, she snuck out of bed and into the kitchen to ring her sister, Louisa, in San Francisco.

'When am I going to meet him?' Jesse wanted to know about Louisa's new boyfriend, Philippe.

As usual, Louisa was her non-committal self. 'Maybe during our summer break. It really depends on what courses I'm teaching.'

'Can you at least text a photo?'

'I guess I could do that.' Louisa laughed. 'How are things with you? Ollie and Em?'

'Busy, good.' Jesse wasn't in a chatty mood, so why had she rung her?

'And the library?' Louisa asked.

'There's a full-time position coming up I'd love to get.'

'But?'

'Steve doesn't want me to apply for it.'

Louisa sighed. 'Jesse, go for it if that's what you want.'

Jesse wanted to wrap up the conversation. 'I guess.'

'How can you stand it? Day after day? Don't you want to scream?'

'This is my life,' Jesse said, irritated. 'I have to get on with it. My home, my kids, my life. No one else is going to live it for me.'

'But some part of you must yearn for freedom and adventure?'

'Maybe. But it's not my time yet. One day it will be, but not today.'

The call ended and Jesse sat in the kitchen. Another conversation that hadn't gone according to plan. But Louisa was Louisa. 'Get outta there, Jess. Run away. Come over to San Francisco and stay with me.' As if.

If only Louisa would come home, they could have a meaningful relationship like sisters were supposed to.

CHAPTER ELEVEN

STELLA

Usually I was up by seven, even on weekends, but today I slept in until eight. Something of a miracle for me. Must have been all those dreams about Colin Firth, or maybe Mike. At least I'd been able to forget about Steve and his threats. Almost. Still, I'd texted Jesse and Carly last night responding to Carly's cancellation of the movie date. Good! We didn't need that complication.

At breakfast, I asked the kids if they'd noticed anything odd when they'd spoken to their nanna recently. They looked at me as if I had two heads and went back to what they were doing. Harry and Hannah weren't really in speaking mode these days. They were teenagers, the world revolved around them, and if it didn't? Well, they weren't interested. I got it, but I'd appreciate more than the occasional grunt from time to time. Harry was the worst – attached to his iPhone or computer twenty-four seven. Hannah was a bit more communicative: she'd chat about friends, music or the latest movie she'd seen – if she was in the mood. If she wasn't up for a talk, forget it. Monosyllabic answers all the way. So I hadn't really expected much of a response when I quizzed them about June.

Then I'd moved on to their dad. 'He'd really like it if you both stayed overnight some weekends.'

'Yeah,' Hannah said.

'Yeah, you will?' I replied.

'Yeah, no. Can't this weekend. Lucy's party.'

I shook my head. 'Harry?'

He was wolfing down an overflowing bowl of Weet-Bix. 'Nup. Exams.'

'Come on, guys. You need to see your dad, and I need a break.'

'Thanks a lot,' Hannah said. 'I'm sorry we're such a burden, ruining your perfect life!'

Perfect life? What the...? 'You're not a burden, darling, but Dad misses both of you. He wants to see you, take you out to dinner, the movies–'

'I'm good,' Harry said. 'Anyway, if he wants to see us, why can't he come here?'

'Because he wants to show you his new apartment.'

They rolled their eyes.

'I don't think so,' Hannah said. 'I don't want to stay overnight with Dad's lover.'

Well, when she put it like that. 'Can you at least call him? Go to the movies or something with him tomorrow?'

They shrugged and scarpered, leaving me to clean up the breakfast mess. As well as that, I had the daunting prospect of baking scones to take to June's. She loved scones, so as much as baking didn't appeal to me, I gave it my best shot.

'Hi, June,' I said when she opened her front door two hours later. 'How are you this morning? Thought you might like some scones. They're still warm.'

Nothing seemed amiss. June was dressed in an orange jumpsuit, yes, the mind boggles, and sported a purple and cream turban. When I think of colour, June always springs to mind.

Clearly, she'd eaten cereal for breakfast – the porridge container was sitting on the bench. She seemed in high spirits as she put the kettle on.

'Go for your walk this morning?' I asked.

June was one of those people who got up before daybreak and walked every morning without fail, cyclones and blizzards the exceptions, but both as unlikely as snow falling in the Sahara.

'Of course. Best part of my day,' she said briskly.

I'd never been up before sunrise, except once, to catch a 6am flight to Darwin. Of course, when Hannah and Harry were babies, I was often awake at that time, but I'd worked hard to erase those memories. Sleep deprivation and I did not sit well together.

June pulled out two teacups from the cupboard. 'Beautiful morning, bet it's going to be a scorcher.'

'Garth tells me dinner last night wasn't so good?'

June turned to me and raised her eyebrows.

'What?' I asked.

'I don't know why he had to bring that woman.'

'And which woman would that be?'

'Why? Has he got a few?'

'Good one, June. Not to my knowledge. But seriously, he said you wouldn't talk to Amanda.'

'Did he? Well, what does he expect? Taking up with a woman who wears plunging necklines. They should both be ashamed of themselves. What about you and the children?'

'I'm fine. You know Garth and I have separated, right?'

She looked at me as if I had two heads. I knew which side of the family my kids had inherited that from! 'Of course I know, but that doesn't mean I'm happy about it. In my day, you stayed married until you died. There was no other choice. Marriage or death. End of story.'

'Thankfully, times have changed.'

I covered several scones with strawberry jam and whipped cream while she poured boiling water into the teapot. 'Come and sit down.'

She inspected the spread. 'Lovely. Where did these come from?'

'June! I baked them this morning.'

'Yes. Silly me.'

Over the tea and scones, we talked about June's plans for the following week. I listened carefully to her every word. She certainly seemed to know what was going on with Garth and dismissed the previous night's events as him being 'overly sensitive'.

June adjusted her turban. 'Garth's never liked confrontation. One bark and he's off like a dog with his tail between his legs. In some ways, he's still a child.'

I couldn't argue with that.

After an hour and a half, I'd decided that June had her wits about her, but was pissed off with Garth for not staying married and miserable like half the population.

On my way home, I drove down swinger street. In daylight, it looked even more suburban: immaculately maintained sidewalks, neat kerbing and guttering, row after row of nondescript brick homes. I parked two houses down from the house in question and walked to the gate. There wasn't a red light by the letterbox, or empty beer bottles on the front lawn – in fact, there was a red and purple welcome gnome standing to the side of the entrance. The curtains were open. There was nothing to suggest this home was anything but ordinary.

Across the road, a man, maybe my age, was mowing the grass. Had he been at the party on Thursday night? Were all the neighbours involved? I returned to my car and started the ignition. Maybe I'd come back another day and check out the letterbox to determine if Mitch and Sherri really lived there. Of course, I could have rung Pete – he had a key, after all – but I didn't have his number. Maybe he knew Steve from the parties?

I wondered how Jesse was getting on. I thought about stopping in at her house but decided against it. I was wary of Steve and didn't want to add to Jesse's troubles by showing up unannounced.

When I arrived home, the house was empty except for the Cavoodle and the Burmese, who were engaged in their familiar Mexican standoff routine, this time over a rogue slice of ham. I don't know why Barney (dog) bothered pretending to be brave, Shirley (cat) always won. Without the kids around, it was almost too quiet. Not that I was complaining. It was nice to have time to just *be*.

Coffee in hand, I tucked my legs up and settled on the sofa, staring at stacks of books on the coffee table. Whichever room I was in, they pleaded 'read me'. Books ruled my tables, be they bed, office, side, kitchen. They also cluttered two ottomans in the sunroom. I couldn't imagine a life without books. No wonder I became a librarian.

Could I be friends with a non-reader? Hmm. Probably not.

Light flooded in through a shuttered front window and I looked down at my oak wood floor, laid down in a herringbone pattern, practical for pets and children, but also stunning to look at. Skimming the books in front of me, I picked up an advanced copy of Jane Fallon's latest, *Just. Got. Real.* and began reading.

My tranquillity was shattered minutes later when my mobile rang.

'Stella? Did you see Mum? Is she okay?'

I'd forgotten to report back to Garth.

'June's fine. She was probably tired when you saw her, having an off night.'

'I'm so relieved. I mean, it's not good she was rude to Mandy, but I was worried it might be something more.'

'As I said last night, you should take June to see her doctor.'

'Really?'

'Yes, really, Garth. As much for your peace of mind as hers. Don't worry, I'll organise it.'

He sighed. 'Thanks. I appreciate it.'

'No worries. Enjoy the rest of your weekend.'

'What are the kids up to?'

'The usual: hanging out with friends, refusing to clean their rooms. Why don't you call them?'

'Because they don't want to talk to me. Are they home?'

'Not right now.'

'See. I'll catch them later.'

Poor Garth. In my kinder moments, I felt sorry for him. The kids didn't want to spend time with either of us, but at least they were living with me. I could nose my way into their bedrooms occasionally and force them to talk. They weren't about to friend me on Facebook, but they weren't entirely locking me out of their lives either. I needed to get stricter with them about spending time with their dad.

CHAPTER TWELVE

CARLY

It was Sunday morning, and Carly had spent another sleepless night ruminating over her behaviour with Toby, seeing Steve at the party, and what Jesse would do when she found out. Steve's message had rattled her. Rattled and intimidated her.

Regardless of what Stella said, Jesse would learn Steve's secret, whether they told her, or she discovered it another way. Carly could leave an anonymous note in her letter box, but how awful would it be to stumble on it like that? Alone, with no support? Much better for Carly and Stella to tell her in person and provide the support she would need.

But that left Steve. Carly had no doubt he was a tyrant at home and would prove to be even worse once exposed. Cornered animals lashed out.

Over breakfast, Brett looked at her expectantly, as if he knew exactly what was going on in her head. She tried to keep a poker face.

'What are you up to today?' he asked, not unpleasantly.

Carly forced a smile. It was on the tip of her tongue to tell him about Steve, but she thought better of it. She'd have to explain about the party, why she was there and who she was with. She closed her eyes, imagining the scene.

'You went to a party with three strangers?' he'd say. 'You allowed three men you didn't know to take you to some party in a private house? You got into their car? Whatever possessed you to do such a thing? How much had you had to drink? How did you meet them?'

She could always blame Stella, say that she'd dragged Carly along, but Brett would never believe her. He'd quickly realise it was Carly who'd made Stella go. No, she really wasn't up for that discussion. It was better Brett didn't get involved. She and Stella would handle this alone. They should go to the police. Steve had threatened them.

'The usual,' Carly replied in the offhanded tone she'd perfected when she didn't feel like talking.

He shrugged. 'Okay, well, I'll see you after Will's basketball game.' He kissed her lightly on the cheek and was gone.

Brett! The distance between them was widening into a chasm. She knew she was as much to blame for it as he was, but really, what did they share these days?

Sometimes, like now, Carly found herself staring into nothingness. Waiting the day out, so she could go to sleep and not have to think anymore. Wishing her life away.

She wandered back into the kitchen. The house felt so empty without Nicholas. She kept telling herself the gap year in the UK was good for him: he needed to spread his wings; experience life; find out what it was like not having an automatic dishwasher, cleaner and maid at his beck and call.

Nicholas had left on 2 January. He hadn't wanted his parents to drive him to the airport; Carly would cry and cause a scene. 'That's so not cool, Mum,' he'd told her, even though Carly had promised him she wouldn't.

On New Year's Day, Nicky had let Carly help pack his suitcase, mainly because he was hungover from the night before. She'd washed and ironed and packed. Held it together. Nicky's flight the next day was at four thirty in the afternoon, so they mooched about in the morning. She made him his favourite breakfast – pancakes, bacon, hot chocolate, the whole bit – but all too quickly it was one o'clock and time to leave.

'Don't touch anything in my room,' he'd said on the drive to the airport. 'I might come back in a year.'

'What do you mean, "might"?' Carly asked.

Brett looked at her. 'What the boy's saying is that after living away from home for a year, he may get a taste for it. There's no guarantee Nick's ever going to live at home again.'

Carly's eyes brimmed with tears. 'If I thought that, Nicholas, I'd never have let you leave.'

'Mum, you promised,' he warned.

Inside the terminal, swarms of teenagers from Nicholas's school milled about, far too excited about their upcoming gap year adventures to consider their heartbroken parents. Carly recognised most of the parents kissing their children goodbye, not all by name but by sight. She didn't want to socialise. Her entire focus was on her eldest son, who was deserting her, flying the coop ... You couldn't tell Carly there weren't favourites in families. In Carly's house, it was Nick and her, Brett and Will. How did it work when parents had more than two children? It didn't mean she loved Will any less; it was just that she and Nicholas were simpatico. They got each other.

Right from the very start, Nicky had been hers; he'd always gone to her first when he was upset, happy, hungry. She used to have to encourage him to talk to his father, so attached was he to her. But Will ... well, with Will, Carly had found out what it was like being the second wheel. William sought his father out in every situation. William was Brett's and Carly hadn't minded so much ... until now. Until Nicholas had left her.

Several years back when Nicholas and William were at primary school, Carly thought about having another child. Seriously. But Brett was blasé. 'What more could we want?' he'd asked as his boys darted around the soccer field, freezing and covered in mud, but happy.

A baby girl, Carly's mind had responded, but she'd pushed those feelings aside. She had her son, Nicky – the one who'd inherited her blue eyes and her habit of rubbing his right shoulder when he was stressed, the one who wanted to explore life outside his own neighbourhood and take risks. Brett had his son, Will. Will who, with his father's build and temperament, was always ready to defend his dad.

Thinking back, another child would surely have caused disequilibrium. She was glad they had just the two boys.

Carly went to the computer, switched it on and logged into Facebook, then Instagram and Snapchat. She checked Nick's status update at least once a day, sometimes more. Apparently, it was bitterly cold and snowing in Cornwall, but Nicholas was having the time of his life coaching the senior rugby team, or assisting, at least. *Pub night, Friday! Schoolies sneaking out to join us*, he'd reported recently in one of his updates. He certainly sounded busy and happy, as if he'd found his purpose.

There was no update today.

Carly had been banned from writing on his wall – in the early days, she'd written *I love you, Nicky* and he'd heatedly told her never to do that again. How was she to know her post would be read by his 2,358 friends? Now she sent him an email: *Missing you, Nicky. Hope the weather isn't getting you down. Love Mum xx*

Carly missed him. Norman, their ginger tabby cat, missed

him too, and she was sure Brett did as well, although he hadn't said much beyond the fact that it was Nicholas's rite of passage and Carly should stop bombarding him with emails and social media messages.

Probably the only one who was happy with the situation was Will, who'd just started Year Eleven. There had always been healthy competition between the boys. They'd always bickered and fought. The two couldn't play tennis or eat a meal together without it ending in a brawl. Carly imagined William was quite chuffed about Nick's departure. No more having to share the remote, the computer, or the car once Will got his licence.

Last night, Will had slept over at a friend's house. He'd started going to gatherings nearly every Friday and Saturday night. She wasn't so naive as to think he was all pure and innocent. He'd had a girlfriend for five months last year. That had ended in October, and he'd been heartbroken. 'Mum, I was in love.'

In love! All of sixteen and he was in love. She'd tried giving him the big sex talk, but he hadn't wanted a bar of it, just yelled, 'Muuum!' whenever she broached the subject.

Nicholas had had a couple of short-term girlfriends but nothing serious. He'd always had groups of friends. And when he'd found out he was going to Cornwall for twelve months, he'd told Carly, 'No point finding true love now and having to break their heart when I leave the country.'

Carly glanced at the clock: 11am. Long, tedious hours of loneliness stretched ahead. That evening, a Sunday night, Brett was attending a business dinner. She wondered if it was anything like the business dinner Steve had supposedly been at. Brett had invited Carly along, but she wasn't up to it. She felt too insecure, too lost. In fact, the only time she felt good about herself these days was after a few drinks.

Maybe she needed a hobby. She used to be busy all the time: teaching Nick to drive, volunteering for committees, hosting school functions. This year, she hadn't wanted to do any of that. She'd had enough of committees and morning teas. But she was thinking seriously about what she was going to do for the next forty years. She didn't want to be sitting at home feeling sorry for herself for the rest of her days.

Carly had worked in retail merchandising after she'd left college. That was how she'd met Brett. She was setting up a display of the latest Dior fragrances in a city department store, and he'd walked up to her seeking advice on what perfume to buy for his mum's birthday. She'd found out later his mother's birthday had been the previous week.

Before Carly knew it, they were married with toddlers. She hadn't given her career a second thought. Then, when they moved to the big house, her days were filled frequenting vintage and op shops in search of the perfect lamp or vase for their home. That is, when she wasn't volunteering at school.

When Will started high school four years ago, she'd returned to paid work, taking a job merchandising for a clothing company. She'd jumped in headfirst: the hours were long but rewarding. It had been exhilarating. But a few months after she started, she'd come home one night when Brett was away to find Nick and a couple of his mates drinking and behaving like drunk fourteen-year-olds.

Carly had quit immediately; she'd become complacent about parenting, and this was the result. Brett had fully supported her. In fact, he'd cut back his travelling for a few months too. Since then, Carly hadn't worked. As for Nick, it had appeared to be a one-off incident. She hadn't seen him drunk again until he was of legal age.

She considered doing a university course as a mature-age student. Wouldn't that be great? Nick was starting a commerce degree the next year, not that she wanted to study commerce. But surely, she could find an interesting course to keep herself occupied. The university was big enough for them both.

Leaving the computer switched on, Carly walked into Nick's bedroom. She'd asked him to do a big clean-out before he'd flown to the United Kingdom, but after his final school exams, he'd partied with friends. Then it was Christmas, and suddenly, he was gone.

She opened a cupboard. There were toys shoved at the back from when he was seven. Carly stared around the crowded room, at clothes Nick had outgrown, the paperbacks he had no intention of reading, his past exam papers, assignments and school texts. She hadn't thrown anything away because she'd thought Will might use the past exam papers and the books. But Will didn't read. As for exams, he crammed the night before – when he wasn't on his iPhone or computer.

She retrieved a ladder from the garage and several garbage bags. This was going to take some time, but if she approached it methodically...

Most items on the top cupboard shelves were from Nick's middle school years – cap, tie, sports carnival ribbons, and lots of photos stuffed into school diaries. She put them to one side and kept going. What she'd thought were keepers years ago (Year Eight maths books, exercise books crammed with French notes, English and history essays), they could firmly live without. When on earth was Nick ever going to look at those notes again? She threw book after book on to his bed, pleased to be making space in the cupboard.

Maths! The rows they'd had over that subject. Years Nine and Ten had been a struggle, with the distractions of hormones, first girlfriends and friendship dramas. Study had been well down Nick's list of priorities. But he'd ended up taking the subject right through to his final year and done well, torment and heartache quickly forgotten.

Carly was easier on Will, not that she'd admit it. She and Brett had gone through the hideousness of Year Ten with Will, and she was hoping he'd follow in his brother's footsteps and settle down this year.

Stuffed away at the back of the cupboard were Nicholas's two favourite cuddly toys: Rupert the Bear and a huge yellow Pikachu. Carly took them out, smelled them, her eyes watering. She looked inside the cupboard again. The top shelf had been cleared, but she was only a third of the way through the total job. She checked her watch. She'd been going for close to two hours.

Climbing down from the ladder, she stared at the mess on Nick's bed and groaned. She'd created more chaos than she'd thought possible. Papers and books were strewn everywhere.

'Hey.' It was Will.

She jumped and turned. 'How'd you go?'

'Smashed 'em. Sixty-four to twelve.'

'Ouch.'

'What are you doing?'

'Cleaning out Nick's room.'

'He'll be pissed.'

'Will.'

'What? He will be. Don't try doing this to my room.'

Carly shook her head. 'Where's Dad?'

'In the kitchen. We bought meat for a barbeque.'

Will wandered off and Carly looked again at the pile of junk on Nick's bed. She couldn't do any more right now; she'd lost her enthusiasm.

'Mum,' Will shouted from his room. 'Is it okay if Harry comes over?'

Stella's son, Harry, and Will had been best mates for years.

'Sure,' Carly called back. 'But clean up your room first.' She paused. 'And then let me know when pigs are flying overhead.'

'Ha. Good one, Mum.'

CHAPTER THIRTEEN

An hour later, Carly was back in Nick's room. She had to practise what she preached: when you start something, see it through till the end.

She gathered the books and bits of paper off the bed. If she threw it all in the recycling, Nick would never notice, so that was her plan – all those old maths books and notebooks, gone. No point getting sentimental over geography and algebra. But she'd keep his school diaries. Carly flipped through the one from Year Eight. He'd crammed it with ticket stubs, photos, notes. So cute. Those from Years Nine and Ten were similar, bursting at the seams with paraphernalia.

His Year Eleven diary wasn't as thick; obviously he'd got past the phase of pasting in every photo and note. And his Year Twelve diary, even thinner. When she opened it, a couple of pieces of paper fell out of a card. She picked them up and put them back inside, but curiosity got the better of her and she started reading.

You're great, the card said. *When I see you smiling, wow! Please tell me we'll be friends forever*. It was written in large curly writing and signed '*B*'. Who on earth was B? Brenda,

Bridget...? Carly couldn't think of many names starting with B. There was no date but given she'd found it in his Year Twelve diary, she assumed it was little more than a year old.

The next was sad and pleading: *Don't tell me what we have isn't special. This friendship means everything to me. I've seen into your soul. Please talk to me. B*

Carly sat on the bed. On all the notes, the girl had drawn a bumble bee just above the B. Cute. But who was this poor girl, and why hadn't Carly heard of her before? Nick had dated a Lauren and an Ella. He'd taken Lucy to the semi-formal in Year Eleven and Maddie to the formal in Year Twelve. But a B? Bernadette? Becky? Carly couldn't come up with a name she remotely recognised. Why hadn't Nicholas told her about B?

She scanned the diary again. It was full of scribbled notes, assessment dates, and telephone numbers. It was like looking for a needle in a haystack. She shook the diary to see if anything fell out. Success! Several notes – none of them relevant, except the last one. *Nick, maybe when you finally grow up, you'll realise what you've thrown away. B*

Poor broken-hearted B. Was there anything more devastating than the angst of teenage love? Especially unrequited love. Heartbreak didn't get any easier, but at least when you were older you were more capable of putting things into perspective. B ... B ... Brooke? Bree? Bailey?

Carly couldn't stop thinking about B on Sunday afternoon. She kept going over names in her head, trying to remember events, parties, gatherings, meetings of significance. Nicholas was a rugby head and sport took up most of his waking hours. He'd studied only when he had to and spent most Saturday nights at the movies with his mates. He wasn't into the party scene, going out every other night to get drunk and crack on to girls. But maybe that was all a facade. He could have been seeing lots of different girls and just not bringing them home.

The only B Carly could come up with was Bella Anderson, who lived a few streets away. She was around Nicholas's age, and they'd gone to the same primary school, but she'd attended a girls' school in the city. It was time to ask a few casual questions...

Carly wandered into the kitchen where Will and Harry were scoffing chocolate cake and ice cream.

'So, I've been clearing out Nick's room.'

Will turned to Harry. 'Mum's in a cleaning frenzy.'

'Yes, and I'm starting on yours next.'

Will went to object, but Carly got in first. 'Joking. Look, do either of you know a girl whose name begins with B?'

'Totally random, but okay,' Will said.

'We've got a hot chick in our tech class called Bridie,' Harry said, smiling.

'And there's Billie in my English class,' Will said. 'Why do you want to know?'

'Just curious.' She probed further. 'Anyone from Nick's year?'

Will laughed. 'How would we know?'

'I just thought there might have been someone he was close to, whose name started with B.'

'Nup,' Will said, stuffing his face with ice cream.

Carly busied herself cutting more cake for them and dishing up the rest of the ice cream. 'Or a girl whose nickname had something to do with a bumble bee?'

The boys started laughing so much that they spat ice cream and cake over the bench.

'Buzzy bee.' Harry giggled.

'Buzzing around the locker room...'

'And the showers...'

'Okay, let me in on the joke, boys,' Carly said, pointing her very sharp Global knife at them.

'It's nothing,' Will said. He and Harry glanced at each other and giggled some more.

'Waiting...' she persisted.

Long beat.

'Buzzy Bee was one of the assistant sports coaches at school last year,' Will said.

Carly's mind raced. Nick had been going out with an older woman? It made sense that she was into sports, but a teacher? That couldn't be good. And she'd been pursuing him? No wonder he hadn't told her about it. Had they done anything illegal? Nick had turned eighteen last June, but if she was ... Oh. My. God. A teacher!

'Yeah, always hanging around the senior boys' locker room, checking them out,' Harry added.

'That's not very professional,' Carly said, raising her eyebrows, keeping her voice calm.

'No, Mum. Not professional at all.'

Both boys laughed some more.

'We all knew he was gay,' Will said.

'Pardon?'

'Mr Busby – he was always trying to crack onto the senior guys,' Will explained.

Carly put the knife down. 'What?'

'Relax. He only lasted a term before they shipped him off to Tasmania or Siberia ... somewhere.'

She took a deep breath. 'You shouldn't say things like that about the teachers. I'm sure he was just being friendly.'

'Yeah,' Will agreed. 'With guys he wanted to pork.'

Carly reeled. 'What? What are you suggesting?'

Will rolled his eyes. 'Nothing.'

Carly glared at him.

'Seriously, Mum, forget about it.'

Harry licked his fingers. 'Thanks for the cake. It was great.'

Will finished his last mouthful. 'Yeah, really good. Harry, you playing COD?'

Carly silently groaned. When would he grow out of these computer war games?

'Nah,' Harry replied. 'Better get home.'

'Say hi to your mum,' Carly said as Harry scooted out the back door.

'Sure.' He gave her the thumbs up before disappearing into the garden.

In a daze, Carly cleaned up their mess. B was male? Nicholas's B was a sports coach called Mr Busby? That made no sense at all. She couldn't believe Nicholas would get involved in something like this. Who was this Mr Busby? Where had he come from? What did he look like? Had he coached Nick? She'd take action. Make a formal complaint to the school. Nicholas had obviously been harassed, stalked by a lunatic. A teacher.

She raced back up to Nick's room and read the letters again. Why hadn't Nick told her? Or Brett? They could have helped him. Maybe he had tried to talk, but she and Brett had been so caught up with their own problems they hadn't listened to him. They'd shut him out because they were too busy arguing.

No wonder the kid had been excited about going to the UK – he was escaping B and leaving his parents, who'd done nothing whatsoever to protect him. While Carly had been conjuring up imaginary fuck buddies, her son had been pursued by a lunatic and scared out of his mind. It would have been too much for him to handle: a young kid being sexually harassed by a man. Why hadn't he spoken to her about it? Carly had let him down. She'd failed him.

Unless Nick had encouraged the attention, at least initially.

Maybe Nick was gay.

He could be gay. Carly wouldn't have an issue with it. But a teacher? No. It was wrong.

The question was: what to do now? Tell Brett? Talk to Stella?

Perhaps the best course of action was to send Nicholas an email.

In the study, Carly turned on her computer and stared at the screen a very long time before typing: *Hi Nicky, how are things in Cornwall? We miss you. The house is empty and quiet without you. Hope you are doing fine and the weather's not getting you down. Please write soon. Love you, Mum xx* (She added one of those ridiculous smiley faces.)

It was impossible to ask the question she desperately wanted to ask. What was she supposed to say?

Hi Nick, I found letters from your admirer, Mr Busby. Was this guy harassing you? Or did you have a friendship together? Just wondering if there was anything going on, because when I put two and two together, I keep coming up with four. I'm totally fine if you're gay...

If she started down that road, she'd never stop. Besides, it really wasn't a conversation they could have via email. The most sensible thing was to let the matter drop, at least until she could talk to Nick. Still, something niggled at the back of her mind about the time when he was fourteen and drunk with mates.

CHAPTER FOURTEEN

JESSE

The weekend was a disaster thanks to Steve being a complete misery. Jesse was trying to be supportive – she understood he had a demanding job; he told her often enough – but it was the weekend. Time to let up. Regardless, nothing Jesse said or did was right. He even seemed suspicious when Jesse said she wasn't going to the movies with Stella and Carly. Instead, she spent a mother/daughter Saturday afternoon at the local shops, drinking milkshakes and buying Emily inexpensive costume jewellery.

'Did you see anyone?' Steve had questioned when Jesse and Emily arrived home half an hour later than expected.

'Of course we saw people.'

'Who?'

'A couple of mums from school. Why?'

Steve wanted to know what Jesse was doing, where she was going and who she was seeing, even Sunday morning when she'd popped to the bakery to buy croissants. It was weird. And he was jumpy, chewing his lips, sniffing, rubbing his nose and his eyes. Normally it was Jesse who was anxious.

That afternoon, Emily was helping Jesse in the garden,

planting petunias into clay pots, when Steve walked outside just as Emily accidentally spilled potting mix.

'Emily! Be careful!' he shouted. 'You're making a mess.'

'Settle down,' Jesse said, seeing that Emily was about to burst into tears. 'It's a driveway.'

'She has no respect for other people's property,' he yelled. 'It's a filthy mess.'

'It's okay, Steve. We'll wash it down.'

A bizarre outburst. He calmed down eventually, but his foul mood lingered.

When Jesse prepared the kids' favourite dinner, spaghetti bolognaise, he barked, 'Why can't you cook a decent meal?'

Straight after eating, the kids scurried to their room to play Monopoly by themselves, clearly not wanting to deal with bickering parents. Jesse was exhausted. Fed up.

After yet another outburst – about his business shirts not being ironed correctly – she lost it. 'Our marriage is hanging by a thread,' she shouted, itching for a scene.

'What?' Steve fumed. 'One minute you want another baby, the next minute you're telling me our marriage is crumbling. You're all over the place, Jesse.'

She shook her head. Maybe she was. She couldn't control herself, clenching her fists so she wouldn't start switching lights on and off. Or closing doors. Checking the oven.

She stormed out the front door and got in her car.

'You're not leaving me,' Steve shouted as she revved the engine. 'I'll never allow it.'

How could she have let things get out of hand like that? she asked herself as she drove to her mum and dad's. She was the one who needed to keep things running smoothly. Her role was to support Steve and look after the kids, not to storm out of the house. This was definitely not managing the situation.

Arriving at her parents' home, she composed herself to face a barrage of questions.

'Where are Steve and the twins?' her mother, Dot, asked when Jesse walked in. 'Why aren't they with you? What's the matter?'

'Nothing, Mum,' Jesse said wearily. She nodded to her dad, who was watching *MasterChef Unplugged*.

'Have you heard from your sister?' Dot continued, barely stopping for air.

Jesse had needed to go somewhere quiet. Big mistake coming here. She should have gone to the movies, alone.

Thankfully, her grandma, Milly, walked into the room with a pot of tea. 'Jesse, I thought I heard you come in. Cuppa?'

Jesse smiled and took the cup Milly handed her.

'That husband of yours looking after you?'

'Of course,' Jesse replied shakily.

'Hmm. Drink up. We've got apple crumble too.'

'Thanks.' Apple crumble was the last thing Jesse felt like eating. Sickly sweet. 'How's church, Grandma?'

'Please don't indulge her, Jesse,' Dot said. 'Milly and her happy-clappy new friends!'

'It *is* a church,' Milly replied indignantly.

'Do you even pray there?'

'What are you talking about, Dot? I pray.'

'I'm not talking about your fancy New Age church prayers. I'm talking old-fashioned, word in the Lord's ear type praying. The kind of praying that gets answered,' Dot said, putting her teacup down on the coffee table.

'Mum,' Jesse said. 'Don't be mean.'

'Mean? You don't have to live with her.' Dot shook her head. 'Now drink your tea, Mother. Be quiet.'

'See how she bosses me,' Milly said to Jesse. 'I don't know how Bernard's put up with her for thirty-six years.'

'Thirty-nine actually,' Bernard said, looking up from the television.

Milly walked out of the room whistling an unfamiliar tune. No doubt about it, she was shrinking by the week.

———

The house was dark when Jesse arrived home. The kids were asleep and so was Steve, though he rolled over when she lay down beside him. A few moments later, he wrapped her in his arms and pressed his naked body against hers.

'I'm sorry,' he whispered. 'This is the third month in a row the team haven't made target, and I'm taking it out on you and the kids. I can be a moody arsehole.'

Jesse tugged off her T-shirt and underwear and turned to face him. 'It's okay,' she said, stroking his hair.

'Mmm,' he groaned as his hand reached up to take hers and guide it towards his erection.

Moments later, his full weight was upon her, and he was grinding. She wanted him to kiss her, but he turned his face away and continued pumping. Jesse needed to believe that everything would be all right between them, but the hurt and rejection was too much. She silently wept as he built to his climax.

CHAPTER FIFTEEN

STELLA

Sunday afternoon Mona, June's neighbour called. 'June's had a fall. She's okay but she's been admitted to St John's hospital. I can't reach Garth–'

'I'll be right there.'

I arrived twenty minutes later as June was receiving her X-ray results. My eyes bulged. One of the attending doctors was Toby, Carly's friend from the other night.

'Small world,' he said.

'Are you looking after her?' I asked in what I hoped was a pleasant manner. Yes, he was old enough to be a doctor, and his name badge read *Dr Toby Mitchell*, but all the same, I was nervous.

'Relax, Stella. Yes, your mother-in-law's had a fall, but I've mended many broken arms, mostly belonging to seven-year-old boys and seventy-year-old women. You'll be all right, won't you, June?'

'You scared me,' I said, bending down to kiss her.

'As it turns out,' Toby told June, 'there are no broken bones, but you've got extensive bruising and swelling. I'm going to wrap you up and keep you under observation for the next couple of hours.'

'That won't be necessary, young man.' June winced in pain.

'June,' I said quietly, 'we should let the doctor get on with making you better.'

'I'm not ailing.'

Toby gestured to the nurse to wheel June into a nearby examination room, then said to me, 'The other night was weird, hey?'

I nodded and looked around at the other doctors, nurses and orderlies. 'I don't know what I'd say to Pete if I ran into him again.'

'No fear of that. He's not on today. Neither's Mike for that matter.'

'Mike?' It took me a moment to register. 'The three of you work at this hospital? Together?'

Toby nodded.

Small world indeed.

I left him to get on with wrapping June's arm and sat in the waiting room with a watery cup of tea and a copy of *Woman's Day* circa 2016. I tried Garth's mobile again, updating his voicemail that June had no broken bones but was being kept under observation for the next couple of hours.

I glanced up at the wall mirror. I was a mess: no make-up and my hair was in need of a good wash. I'd left home so quickly, I hadn't changed out of my scruffy house clothes – cut-off denim shorts and a faded blue T-shirt. I guessed now wasn't the time to be worrying about my appearance, but I was relieved Mike wasn't at work.

By the time June had been given the all-clear – she'd probably badgered Toby into submission – Garth and Amanda had joined me. Amanda looked stunning. Her lipstick had been carefully applied, her short black hair was shiny and neat. Her plunging neckline, perhaps inappropriate for the hospital, showed off her generous cleavage.

'Mum,' Garth said, after a nurse wheeled June into the waiting room, 'what were you doing standing on a ladder in the garden?'

'Trimming hedges. I told you they were growing out of control. Who's this?' She pointed to Amanda.

'June,' I interrupted. 'You know Amanda, Garth's friend.'

Amanda smiled but said nothing.

Toby introduced himself to Garth and asked him to sign several sheets of paper before handing over a bottle of painkillers.

'Mrs Sparks is free to go,' Toby told Garth. 'But she won't be able to do much for herself the next few days.' He turned to June. 'Don't worry, you'll get used to the bandage and sling soon enough.'

Garth nodded and the penny dropped. 'Doctor Mitchell,' he said, 'Mum lives by herself.'

Toby regarded the four of us. 'Mrs Sparks should be fine to go home in four or five days, when the swelling and bruising have subsided, but in the meantime, it's best if she stays with family.'

He smiled at me. 'Nice seeing you again, Stella. And, Mrs Sparks, I'll see you in two days, okay?'

June nodded, and Toby left the room.

Garth did a double-take. 'You know him?'

I didn't answer. 'So, June, what are we going to do with you?'

'I guess you can come home with Mandy and me,' Garth said.

'But I don't have a spare bedroom,' Amanda said, looking anxious.

'That won't be necessary,' June said. 'I don't want to be a burden. Nor do I want to be in the same house as that woman.'

'Mum,' Garth said firmly, 'you're coming with me.'

'I'm not a bloody invalid,' June barked. 'My arm's bruised, that's all. I'm sorry I'm such a bother. Anyway, I want to go to *my* home. I'll manage quite well on my own, thank you very much.'

Garth sighed. 'You can't do that. The doctor said you need to stay with family.'

'That's ridiculous. I don't need a babysitter.'

'Maybe not,' I soothed. 'But we'd all feel a lot happier if you stayed with Garth.'

Amanda shot me a warning look.

'Or perhaps,' I said, thinking aloud. 'You could stay at your mum's, Garth.'

'That wouldn't work,' he replied, his face contorted, fingers scratching his head.

I was about to ask why not, when June said quietly, 'Okay, I'll stay at your house.' She nodded to Garth. 'Yours and Stella's.'

'But Mum, you know I don't live with Stella. It's hardly fair–'

'If June wants to go home with Stella,' Amanda said, placing her hand firmly on his arm, 'that's what she should do.'

'I said I want to stay with you, Garth,' June said, her voice rising. 'You and Stella.'

'But–' Garth started.

'But nothing. You can't expect Stella to look after me while you go off with one of your dalliances.'

Amanda flinched. 'I'd hardly call me a dalliance.'

'Really?' June said, looking her up and down. 'I would.'

'June!' I took her hand in mine. 'It isn't like you to be so rude. Is it the drugs?'

Amanda snorted.

'No, it's not the drugs,' June replied. 'I just don't like her.'

'Mum!' Garth was almost hyperventilating. He looked at Amanda. 'I'm sure it's the medication, sweetie.'

The nurse coughed. 'Shall we go?'

She was waiting to wheel June to the lobby, where she could relieve the hospital of any further duty of care. We followed her and June down the long corridor to the hospital's front doors.

'What are we going to do?' Garth whispered in my ear.

'Clearly she's not going to Amanda's, which will be a huge relief to–'

'I'm right here. I can hear you,' Amanda said.

I turned to her. 'And are you relieved?'

'Yes, of course, but–'

'If June's not going with you, and you're not prepared to stay at her house for a couple of days, then obviously she'll have to come home with me. It's not as if I don't have the room.'

I patted June's good shoulder. 'The kids will be thrilled to have you stay, darling.'

She rolled her eyes. 'My own son doesn't want me. Is this the way I brought you up, Garth?'

I loved the way she spoke to him as if he was still twelve.

We thanked the nurse, and Garth carefully helped June out of the wheelchair. 'Where's your car?' he asked me. Evidently, he'd decided he wasn't up to arguing any more – with his mother or with Amanda.

'Good question. I was so flustered when I arrived...' I looked around. 'It might be ... yes, this way.' I set off down the hill towards the underground car park.

Garth helped June into the car. 'I'll come over tomorrow to see how you're doing, Mum. Okay?'

'Don't do me any favours,' she said.

He attempted to kiss her cheek, but she turned away and he ended up kissing her very grey hair.

'Right, I'll see you tomorrow,' he called to me as I got into the driver's seat.

'Sure,' I said. 'Bye, Amanda.'

Garth grimaced again, and the two of them walked back in the direction we'd come, Amanda clinging on to Garth as if he might suddenly float away.

'You okay?' I asked June as I drove out of the car park and turned left onto the Pacific Highway.

'I feel silly.'

'About Amanda? Don't worry–'

'Amanda? Certainly not! I'm talking about falling off my ladder and into the compost. I don't care what she thinks. She's a woman who looks like a thin Liza Minnelli with a ridiculously large bosom.'

I smirked. She did a bit.

CHAPTER SIXTEEN

When we arrived home, the kids were waiting for us. Well, waiting was a bit of a stretch. Harry was on the PS5 playing some war game and shouting, and Hannah was playing Wordle and watching TikTok videos.

'How about you guys stop what you're doing for a moment and say hi to Nanna,' I said when June and I walked into the rumpus room.

'Hey, Nanna, how's your arm?' Hannah asked. At least she had the decency to look up momentarily.

Harry grunted. 'Hey.' He didn't pause to stop gunning down enemy soldiers.

I made June a cup of tea and settled her on the deck with the day's newspapers while I walked down the hall to make up the sofa bed in the study. I hadn't stopped to consider how her being here would impact us. Not that there'd be a problem, but the kids had their routine, and I had mine. Everyone was going to have to make some adjustments.

I had to laugh when I thought about Garth. He'd been so hassled at the hospital – his mother, wife and girlfriend in the same room and him trying to keep everyone happy. Amanda looked as if she'd swallowed nails. And Garth's reaction to Toby as it dawned on him that we knew each other ... I'd almost seen his brain working as he tried to figure out the connection.

Toby! I rang Carly to fill her in. Sure, I could have walked the fifty metres to her house, but I was feeling lazy. Lazy and tired.

'That's so embarrassing,' Carly said. 'What did he say? What did you say? I can't believe the one night I go out and get smashed, I meet toy-boy Toby.'

'The one night?'

'Whatever. What I mean is, I was never supposed to see him again.'

'Even though he's rung you?'

'Twice, actually. I was so out of it, I forgot I'd given him my number.'

'I believe you scribbled it on his arm, several times.'

'I'm married, for Christ's sake.'

'And how's that going?'

'Fine. Good. Not that great. The usual. So, June's staying with you?'

'Looks like it.'

'Nothing more from Steve?'

'Nope.'

'And you'll see Jesse at work on Thursday and Friday. What then?'

'Let's see how the next few days pan out.'

I hung up and noticed a text message from Mike.

Stella, is your MIL okay? Toby said she had a fall.

Yes, fine. Staying with me and the kids for a bit.

Sounds like you need an escape. Dinner?

LOL. I rather like June. I don't need an escape.

Sounds like you do. How about tomorrow night? It's the one evening I have off this week.

I looked skyward and smiled. What the hell? *Sure, I'd love to.* I glanced at the message and retyped, *Sure. That would be nice. X.*

We'll work on nice. Will confirm details tomorrow. xx

I smiled and set about cooking a chicken stir-fry. A dinner date with Mike! I really needed to up my flirty conversational skills.

June was outside resting in the late afternoon sun, the kids were still on their computers, and I had time to think as I chopped broccoli and shelled peas.

It was odd seeing Garth with Amanda. It wasn't like I was jealous. And I didn't dislike Amanda, but I'd felt ... nothing. She was just another person. I was sure she was perfectly nice, but I had no compulsion to get to know her, to find out whether she preferred green tea, Earl Grey or a latte first thing in the morning. As for Garth, I got the impression he was swimming out of his depth. I loved him. I always would. I wasn't quite sad, but I wasn't in high spirits either.

At six o'clock, the phone rang. Speak of the devil.

'How's Mum?' Garth asked.

'Fine. No problem at all.'

'Good, good.'

'And you?'

'Mandy's not happy. We fought the whole way back to her apartment.'

'That's no good.' I really didn't want to have a conversation about his domestic bickering.

'Anyway, we've decided it would be better if Mum stayed with us,' he went on. 'I am her son, after all.'

'Good luck convincing her to move,' I said as I mixed the vegetables with noodles and chicken.

'I thought you might–'

'Look, I'm happy for her to stay with you, Garth, but I'm not going to waste my breath trying to convince her, especially when I know she doesn't want to.'

'Please.'

I walked into the living room where June was doing the crossword. 'June,' I said, loudly enough for Garth to hear, 'your son's on the phone. He wants to know whether you'd prefer to stay with him?'

'Only if he's staying here,' she said, then shook her head and went on with her puzzle. 'Now, where was I?'

I walked back into the kitchen. 'As I was saying.'

'Fine. I'll talk to her about it again tomorrow.' He sounded tired.

'Listen, I know you're trying to do the right thing, but she's comfortable here. Honestly.'

'It's just that all my family is at my house except me.'

'Garth, this is what you wanted. Besides, you have Amanda.'

'Yes,' he agreed, brightening. 'I do.'

I hung up and served dinner as everyone straggled to the table. I cut the noodles on June's plate to make it easier for her, but she ate slowly and with difficulty.

'Goodness me, you look like your father did when he was your age,' she said to Harry halfway through the meal.

'Yeah?' Harry mumbled.

'He was handsome, like you. I bet you have to fight off the girls.'

Hannah burst out laughing.

Harry glared at her. 'Shut it.'

'Garth was such a good boy when he was younger, so popular too. Girls were always ringing, badgering him about homework, dances, this, that and the other.'

'I think Harry's handsomer,' I said.

'Mum!' he groaned.

'Maybe,' June said, regarding her grandson thoughtfully. 'Pity he's dead.'

I put down my fork. 'Garth's not dead, June.'

'Metaphorically speaking, darling.'

I couldn't work out whether she was saying it to get a rise out of me, or whether it was the painkillers taking their toll.

'Vince and I were forever shooing the girls away,' she went on. 'I miss him.'

'Garth?' I asked. Why on earth? We'd only just seen him.

'No, Vince! He was such a strong ox of a man. Who would have thought his heart could give up like it did. He wasn't even doing anything extraordinary, just sitting in his chair reading the evening paper. One sip of beer, that's all he'd taken, and plop. He keeled over. The beer went everywhere. My poor carpet. It was never the same after that.'

I glanced at the kids, worried it would upset them hearing about their grandfather dropping dead. Harry and Hannah continued eating. They didn't flinch. Not one bit. Perhaps they'd tuned out, or maybe they were just used to their nanna's quirks.

I turned back to June. 'Vince was a great man.'

'Sometimes, I think I see him. When I wake in the middle of the night, he'll be sitting at the end of the bed. He doesn't say anything, just hovers, watching me. I'll look at him and say, "For God's sake, Vince, what is it? Is it the turbans? Because I'm not taking them off, you know." And then he disappears.' She snapped her fingers.

'Sounds a bit *Twilight* for me,' Harry said as he stood.

'Take your plate into the kitchen,' I reminded him.

'Your grandfather's not a vampire, Harry,' June said sharply.

'I think it sounds lovely, Nanna, having Granddad watching over and protecting you,' Hannah said, also standing.

Bless her. She could be so sweet when she wanted to be. Or wanted something!

'Spying, more like it,' June said. 'You know,' she said to me in a low voice, after the kids were out of earshot, 'Vince wasn't such a great man. He played around. He was a philanderer, just like Garth. I ignored it, but those years were hard.'

'Really? I never knew.'

'Why would you? We never broadcast things like that back then even though we all thought that the seventies was the "Me Decade" and the universe centred around our orbit.'

'Really? According to who?'

'An old author, you wouldn't know him, Tom Wolfe. Anyway, he had no idea what a "Me Decade" looked like! At least back then, your private life was still your private life if you wanted it to be. But Murdoch and social media changed all that. Don't even get me started on the Royals. Nothing's sacred these days. There are no secrets. Everyone knows everything about everyone.'

Tom Wolfe indeed. There were several copies of *The Bonfire of the Vanities* at the library!

Still, June was right. When Garth moved out, it seemed everyone within a ten-kilometre radius knew about it before his car had reversed out the driveway. Add in Facebook and Twitter, and even cyber-strangers knew about our personal situation. I kept telling the kids they had to be careful what they posted online, but apparently it wasn't them who'd spread the news; it was friends, and friends of friends. Almost immediately, my Facebook message page was filled with condolences and notes from people I'd never met. At first, I'd started responding, saying it was a mutual decision and that I was fine, but I quickly tired of that. After the tenth reply explaining our decision, I thought, what the hell am I doing? Who are these people, and why do I care? I deleted the posts and went about my business.

'Oversharing,' I said.

Long beat. June looked at me blankly.

'It's called oversharing,' I repeated.

June nodded. 'Some matters are better kept private. So what are we going to do about it?'

I was about to say, I don't think there's much you can do about Vince's nocturnal visits. If he wants to sit on the end of your bed and watch you, and you believe he's watching you, then so be it, when she went on. 'Garth could do so much better.'

'Pardon?'

'That Amanda woman! How are we going to put a stop to this nonsense?'

CHAPTER SEVENTEEN

I got out of the shower around ten thirty on Sunday night when the landline rang with an unknown number. The kids were always getting calls from their friends at odd hours (yes, even on the house phone), though I'd told them no calls after nine. They never listened. I didn't want to pick up. But I didn't want the phone to wake everyone in the house, so I answered in my gruffest mother's voice.

'Enjoy your weekend?' It was Steve.

I wrapped the towel tighter around myself. There was an uncomfortable silence until I said, 'What do you want?'

'You bitches have turned Jesse against me—'

'What? We haven't said a thing about what we saw last Thursday night—'

'And exactly what *did* you see?'

My hands were shaking. I wanted to hurl the phone to the other side of the room, but I also wanted to confront him, to tell him to back off and leave Carly and me alone.

'You know what I saw. You, playing dress-ups—'

'Your word against mine.'

'Your word against Carly's and mine.'

'That drunken flake? I'm not worried about her. But you say one word–'

'And what? If you don't tell Jesse what's been going on, I will. It's not fair.'

'Not fair? I'll tell you what's not fair. Having a wife who taps her foot, clicks her fingers, turns lights on and off–'

'No, this is about you and your X-rated parlour games. Do what you want with Jesse's consent but going behind her back is not okay. You're the one in the wrong here.'

'Think what you like, but know this – if you breathe a word to Jesse or anyone else, I'll destroy you.'

The phone went dead.

I sat down on the bed and released my grip on the phone. The indentation marks on my fingers remained. The smart me said I should call the police, or at least tell Jesse about the calls, but I had no proof that he'd threatened me.

I'd known Steve for over ten years. We'd never been bosom buddies, but we'd been to school trivia nights together, library Christmas parties. Hell, I'd done the chicken dance with the guy. Okay, so I'd always been a bit wary of him, but only because of what Jesse had told me. If I met him on the street or at a party – a standard party – independently, I'd think he was your run-of-the-mill forty-five-year-old man, even though he carried himself with an arrogance that shouldn't be the privilege of any person.

But the Steve I'd seen and heard the past couple of days wasn't the Steve I knew. No wonder Jesse had been exhibiting physical symptoms of her anxieties: the guy had a split personality. The worrying part was I truly believed he could be capable of anything and was definitely beginning to fear for Jesse's safety.

I texted her. *Everything okay at your end?*

Her reply was instant. *Good. At Mum & Dad's. You?*

I thought about telling her about June's arm, then launching into a tirade about her maniacal husband but thought better of it. *Yes, just thinking of you.*

I sounded like a deranged stalker, but at least she was okay, though it was odd she was with her parents on a Sunday night.

I considered calling Mike but stopped myself. I hardly knew him, and if we were going to start a relationship, I didn't want this to be our defining moment.

I could call Carly, but that would only confirm her worst fears.

Instead, I wrote down my conversation with Steve as accurately as I could remember. I also wrote down what I'd seen that Thursday night. It was midnight before I'd finished. I re-read my notes and wondered what to do with them. Send them to my lawyer in case Steve tried to bump me off? I didn't even have a lawyer.

It got me thinking. How long had Steve been involved in these sex parties? It obviously hadn't been his first time, so had it been months? Years? And then there were the people with him. I'd joked with Carly that they might have included the local teacher and butcher – but were we far off? A house full of people didn't spontaneously decide to have a night in the suburbs unless it was for a school fundraiser. They had to be locals. Or were they? Steve was, but did that mean the others were too?

I drifted off to sleep, a new mantra running through my mind: *I will not be bullied.*

I wasn't going to let Steve's harassment get the better of me. Given time, I'd figure out a way of dealing with him.

CHAPTER EIGHTEEN

JESSE

Jesse dreamed she was drowning, reliving a swimming accident from her childhood. She woke lathered in sweat. Eventually, she fell back into an uneasy sleep, and when she woke again, Steve had already left. Odd. Normally, he made a big song and dance about getting up so early while she had the luxury of sleeping in till all of 6:30am.

Before waking Ollie and Emmy, Jesse made herself a strong black coffee. She'd been worried about the twins lately; Emily was commenting on her habits and Ollie was turning switches on and off and counting his breaths. Ollie was a great kid – sensitive and quiet – but just the previous week, his teacher had told Jesse that he'd started tapping his pencil three times after writing a sentence.

'It's distracting for the other children,' she'd explained.

'I'll talk to him,' Jesse had assured her, trying desperately not to tap her foot as she spoke.

At school drop-off, after Emily had dashed off to find her friends, Jesse brought up the subject with Ollie. 'You know how Mummy sometimes taps her feet or checks to see that she's turned the light off?'

'Like a hundred times!'

'That's right. Do you ever do stuff like that?'

'Dunno.'

'Okay.' Jesse bit back tears. 'Please remember that if ever something's worrying you, or you want to talk about school or friends, you can tell me. You like school, don't you, Ollie?'

'It's okay.'

'Good.' She drew him close and hugged him.

'Can I get a new game for my DS?'

That was the extent of their mother/son chat. Jesse didn't want to make a big deal out of it if it didn't need to be a big deal. Everyone had quirks. So what if hers and Ollie's were a little more obvious than other people's?

She watched Ollie run off into the schoolyard before returning to her car and driving home. It was a sparkling sunny day. She should have walked. Maybe yoga was the answer. If she could control her breathing, then perhaps she could control other parts of her body. Often, it felt as if her hands and feet had minds of their own, minds she was powerless to master.

She'd only been home a few minutes when Steve rang.

'If you think I'm leaving, you've got another think coming,' he said.

'Pardon?' What the hell was going on? What had happened to the repentant husband who'd apologised for being moody and then made love to her? 'I thought after last night–'

'I'm reminding you that you have responsibilities: namely, the children and me. Or have you forgotten?'

'How could I forget? I love Ollie and Em more than anything–'

'Glad to hear it. You don't want to lose them then. Given your habits, you need to think very carefully about the consequences of any actions you might take, okay?'

He was making her sound like some mad woman who went

around with unkempt hair wearing caftans and mismatched shoes.

'I'm not crazy, you know.'

'Well, if you're not crazy, you'll know what's good for you, won't you?'

'I don't know how to respond to that, Steve.'

'You don't have to respond, simply think about what I've said.'

After he'd hung up, Jesse sat on the kitchen floor and cried. Steve could be so cold and manipulative. Sometimes she felt like a small animal trapped in a cage.

She needed to talk about this. She wasn't going to let Steve win. Drying her eyes, she stood and called her sister.

'Jesse, what's up?'

She always felt better hearing Louisa's voice. 'Steve phoned accusing me of all sorts of things and threatening to take the children away.'

'Why would he say that?'

'We had another argument over the weekend,' Jesse said, fighting back tears. 'I told him our marriage was hanging by a thread.'

'That'd probably do it.'

'But then last night I thought everything was okay again.'

'Don't let him get you down, Jess. You know Steve and his moods. You've lived with him long enough.'

Jesse let the tears flow. 'I'm teetering on the brink. I don't know what to do – I get so angry and then I get depressed. Sometimes I wish I could disappear forever.'

'You just need some help. Maybe Mum–'

'Mum's the last person I need meddling in my life. Besides, she has her hands full with Grandma Milly.'

'What about your friends?'

'Steve hates all my friends.'

'Gawd, Jesse! How many years has this been going on? He hates me too. If your marriage is hanging by a thread, why don't you leave him?'

'Where would I go? What would I do? It's not like I can take off and fly over to stay with you.'

The silence was almost unbearable.

'The kids have school for starters,' Jesse added.

'If you're going to come up with excuses all the time...'

'They're not bloody excuses. This is my life. My kids are in school. There are practicalities to manage.' Jesse took a deep breath. 'Sorry. I'm ranting. Everything's fine. It's Monday. Mondays are always stressful, everyone's cranky after the end of the weekend. I'm fine. Really. How's everything over there? How's Philippe?'

'He's good. We've had a lazy weekend so far: dinner Friday night, second-hand markets yesterday.'

'Sounds heavenly. Like I've asked you fifty times before, when do I get to meet this guy?'

Louisa didn't answer.

Jesse knew she shouldn't push. Sooner or later the conversation always got around to 'When are you coming home?' or 'The kids miss you. When can I tell them you're visiting?' She knew it made Louisa feel like she was being harassed. Besides, Louisa wasn't coming home anytime soon.

'I really miss you, Lou.'

'I miss you too. And I will come back, maybe your winter, like I said.'

'That's months away.'

'I'll do my best, okay? Maybe spring break.'

'And you'll bring Philippe?'

'Maybe.'

After the phone call, Jesse felt empty. Louisa couldn't do a hell of a lot for her on the other side of the world. She thought back to what Steve had said about her responsibilities. There was no way she was going to let her kids down, and she was damned if she was going to let Steve take them away from her. Jesse would suck up her unhappy marriage and live with it. She could do that. Countless other women did. In a few years, when the kids were older and she'd saved enough money, she'd fly away. One day, but not yet. Not while Ollie and Emmy needed her at home.

So, if she was staying, she needed to make the circumstances work for her. She thought back to the Secret Women's Business pamphlet. She was going to a meeting! She had to.

CHAPTER NINETEEN

STELLA

Monday didn't start well. After the threatening call from Steve, I'd woken at two to hear someone wandering around the house. Initially, I'd been frightened it might be Steve before common sense kicked in, and I got up to find June. She was disorientated and teary about not being at home in her own bed. I'd left it too long before topping up her painkillers.

'Pain,' she said through tight lips and gritted teeth, trying not to cry. Then, 'I don't like relying on others to take care of me.'

'June, I'm not an *other*. We're family.'

Poor old stick. I helped her to her room and watched while she downed a couple of Ibuprofen.

'My turbans, I need my turbans.'

Fifteen minutes later, June was asleep again. She looked mighty uncomfortable but obviously the pain had subsided.

By the time I walked into the kitchen for breakfast, things were improving. June was well into her second cup of Earl Grey and looking resplendent in a lemon and lime headscarf, a T-shirt that said *Grandmas Are Tops* and her favourite pair of blue jeans.

I kissed her cheek. 'You're looking bright.'

'Wish I could say the same about you. You look like death.'

'Thanks,' I said, pouring myself some tea.

'Hey,' Harry said as he made a beeline for the fridge. 'Are Will's parents getting a divorce?'

'Not to my knowledge. Why?'

'Nothing. Just something he said yesterday. I told him all parents get divorced eventually.'

'So much cynicism in one so young.'

'Marry an ugly girl,' June chimed in. 'She'll be so grateful she'll never leave you.'

I stared at my gorgeous fair-haired boy. He'd changed so much in the last six months. His two years of braces-wearing torture were over, so his teeth were perfectly straight. They were also white and hole-free, despite his love of all things sugary. His complexion was clear, and his body, so gangly and uneven the previous year, had filled out. He was as tall as Garth and tanned to boot.

'What are you staring at?' he asked.

I looked away. 'Nothing.'

He shook his head. 'Women!'

Moments after Harry stalked out, June spoke. 'There are an awful lot of paw prints and cat fur on the floor.'

'We're not perfect, June. Or perfectly clean.'

I followed June's eyes into the living room towards the fireplace, stained with smoke from winters gone by.

'A house needs to be used and loved,' I jumped in before she had a chance. 'There should be pets and fire.'

June nodded.

'Now,' I said, 'I've been thinking: why don't I drop you home today while I'm at the library? You might as well be in your own house as here.'

'Indeed,' she replied, tears pooling in her eyes.

'But you need to rest, okay? No climbing ladders or doing housework.'

She nodded obediently.

I'd barely done up her seat belt for her before she asked, 'Is your neighbour getting a divorce?'

I shrugged. 'Hope not. They're just going through a tough time.'

'What is it with young people? Don't you know the rules? You get married and you stay married. You don't get divorced. If you want out, you die. End of story.'

'Yes, well, that might have worked in the good old days, June—'

'Did you just hear yourself? Good old days. They were called the good old days for a reason. No one had any bloody time to think about whether they were happy or unhappy, they just were.'

'I understand, but—'

'But nothing. And speaking of no-good husbands, where's yours?'

'Garth's with Amanda, you know that.'

'Why can't he forget about that tramp and come home?'

'Because, darling,' I said, struggling to find a way to end this absurd conversation, 'we're separated.'

'I don't know why he had to go and break up a perfectly good marriage.' She stared out the window. 'It'll end in tears, mark my words. You know what you need, Stella? Fancy lingerie. Edible undies.'

'June!'

'What? I may be old, but I know a lot about a man's desires. Take off your Cottontails and slip into some satin. That'll bring him crawling home.'

'We'll talk more about it later,' I said, thankful to be pulling up outside her home and hoping to hell she'd have forgotten this conversation by the time I picked her up that afternoon. 'Call me if you need anything. I'm only ten minutes away. And remember what I said. Rest! No gardening and for heaven's sake don't lift anything or climb ladders. Oh, and don't overdo the painkillers.'

She nodded meekly.

I was at the library computer, pounding through overdue notices, when Carly rang.

'We've got to tell Jesse,' she said.

'Let me think about it,' I whispered, mindful that Manager Liz was hovering. I tried to hide my mobile by holding my hand over it, hoping she'd assume I enjoyed touching my cheek and ear at the same time. It was an awkward manoeuvre. 'We have to be careful about this. We've got no idea how Jesse's going to respond.'

Honestly, I had no desire to be the messenger. The messenger always got the blame and lost the friendship or her life. But as much as I didn't want to get involved, Carly had a point, especially after Steve's phone call the previous night.

'Stella, I don't understand why you're so wishy-washy about it.'

'I'm not wishy-washy. I just want to get our facts straight before we tell her.'

'The facts are clear, and HE is threatening us.'

'I know, Carls, but I have to go.'

I hung up and got on with my job, until Liz tapped me on the shoulder and demanded a word. 'In my office.'

I dutifully followed her and sat on the uncomfortable wooden chair in front of her desk.

'How's everything going?' she asked.

'Good.'

'How's Jesse doing?'

'Jesse?'

Liz sighed. 'Yes, Jesse. Remember exactly a week ago when I took her off the customer relations desk because she was taking too long with the patrons?'

As if I could forget that day. Liz had been keeping an eye on Jesse, monitoring how she was dealing with customers. Unfortunately, it happened to be a morning when Jesse had tapped her foot three times every time a customer handed her a book for scanning. If they were taking out ten or fifteen items, she repeated the process every time. Within half an hour, the line stretched back to the periodicals section and Jesse became increasingly agitated.

'You understand, I can't put up with her doing that.' Liz paused. 'And neither can the customers.'

'But Jesse loves working here.'

'I know she does, but I've been watching you too, Stella. Like last Thursday. You follow her around cleaning up her messes. I'm not saying she goes around stacking books according to height and colour, but it's touch and go.'

'I'll talk to her.'

'I'm not sure how that's going to help.'

I wanted to mention Jesse's idea for a monthly book club, but now didn't seem the time. 'Maybe she needs a holiday?'

'Yes, a very long holiday.'

I walked back to my desk feeling helpless. The last thing Jesse needed was more pressure at the library. But I had a feeling Liz was going to step in, which would mean a confrontation, one that Jesse wouldn't win. The minute Liz started talking to her, even if only to ask a simple question like 'How's your day going?' Jesse would start tapping her foot. I needed to keep the two of them apart, even if that only delayed the inevitable.

Despondent, I sat at the computer again, then noticed my mobile flashing. A text message, from Mike. My pulse leapt, and I was smiling even before I read it. It had been sent an hour ago.

Bored. What are you wearing?

Being a complete doofus, instead of texting back *Naked, apart from Chanel No 5* (which wasn't true, obviously), I told him what I was actually wearing – a navy wrap dress, pink heels. Idiot! I regretted it as soon as I'd hit the send button.

I was shocked when my mobile rang a moment later.

'Really? You couldn't do better than that, given what we saw the other night?'

'I know.' I laughed at my woefulness. 'I thought I'd never hear from you after that text.'

Mike chuckled. 'Takes a bit more than that to put me off. If you must know, I've been having librarian fantasies, so the image of you in a navy wrap isn't altogether unwelcome. But your hair needs to be tied up in one of those bun thingos and–'

'Let me guess, I'm wearing glasses and no underwear?'

'See! Now you're getting the hang of it. How's June?'

'A bit teary and lost. She's always been so independent.' I paused. 'About dinner–'

'Nope.'

'Pardon?'

'You're not backing out. I've made a reservation for seven thirty tonight at *Thai Tucker*. Know it?'

'Yes. Terrible name.'

'Great food though. I'll meet you there unless you want me to pick you up?'

Flustered, I said, 'All good. See you there.'

He clicked off, and I was left staring into space, excited I was seeing Mike, but mortified that I'd asked him to imagine me sans underwear.

A minute later, my mobile beeped and a text message popped up. *Am now imagining you wearing little more than horn-rimmed glasses. See you soon.*

I was still thinking of an appropriate response when Garth rang.

'What's going on?' he asked.

'Hi to you too. Can you give me a clue? Are we talking about your mum? Hannah? Harry's geography excursion? The lame Christmas present you bought me? What?'

'I've just spoken to Mum. She said you want me to come home. She also said you were going shopping to buy – I can barely say the words out loud – edible undies.'

'And you believed her?' I tried hard not to laugh.

'Well, no. That is, I thought ... Well, you never know. Women of a certain age, they decide they want a divorce and then change their minds again–'

'Pardon? It was a mutual decision. Besides, aren't you forgetting Amanda?'

Even after all these years, Garth could exasperate me. You'd think he'd be in heaven living with Amanda, far from his boring life in the suburbs with a wife and two kids. But he often made it sound like he was doing me a favour – that the only reason he was with Amanda was to make me happy. And I was happy he was occupied with her, but I wouldn't be for much longer if he kept pestering me.

Garth coughed. 'I didn't say I wanted to eat your edible undies.'

'Thank heavens for small mercies.'

'I only said that Mum said you were going to buy them and that you were getting sentimental about old times.'

'Really? I can see June saying something ludicrous about underwear but the getting sentimental part?'

'Yeah, okay. I made that up. So how is she?'

'Not bad, though evidently she's taking too many painkillers.'

'And?' Clearly, Garth wasn't in a jovial mood.

'Look, as much as she'd never admit it, I think she's lonely. It gives her a purpose being with the kids and me.'

'Jeez, I could never live with her.'

'No, *you* couldn't.'

'Are you saying you could?'

'Maybe.'

'You used to hate her. Said she was interfering.'

'A hundred years ago. It's different now. We're friends.'

'United against the common enemy?'

I laughed. 'Something like that.'

He snorted. 'She's been with you half a day. You'll feel differently by the end of the week, trust me. I lived with her for eighteen years, nine months, three days and fifteen hours. I know what I'm talking about. You'll be pleased when the week's up and you can drop her back to her villa, no questions asked.'

It was true that in the early days, long before Vince died, June could be a handful. She'd had very definite opinions on everything from toilet paper to chicken seasoning. Most of the time, I switched off. I didn't care what brand of toilet paper we used. If it made her happy that we used her preferred brand, so be it. I'd been less accommodating when it came to her suggestions about raising my kids. She was a self-proclaimed expert on breastfeeding, control crying, even banana puree. You name it, June knew all the answers. Dr Benjamin Spock had nothing on her. It was around that time I'd started making up excuses as to why I couldn't go to dinner with her or meet to see a movie in the city.

All that had changed when Vince died. The standard family joke was that Vince had died to escape June's nagging, but the truth was, June was lost after that. Gradually, she'd changed from being an overbearing matriarch to a caring, interested and loving grandmother. The more involved she became in our lives, the less she'd tried to interfere in the day-to-day running of the household. In the last couple of years, she'd been great. I really did enjoy her company, and I silently hoped we'd still be on speaking terms by the end of her stay.

CHAPTER TWENTY

After work, I picked June up and took her home with me. She'd packed another suitcase overflowing with turbans and scarves.

'You've been doing too much today. What about your arm?' I said as I unpacked them onto two rarely used hat stands.

'Nonsense. My arm's fine. I have painkillers.'

I raised my eyebrows. 'Anyway, when will you get time to wear all of these?'

She smiled. 'The ones I don't wear I like to look at. They're so pretty.'

I couldn't argue with that. She had exquisitely coloured silk scarves from India and Turkey, and turbans from Egypt. 'Where do you find them?'

'Mostly on eBay. I'm a very good shopper.'

I left June admiring her scarves and was preparing tacos for dinner, when Hannah wandered into the kitchen and told me she was thinking about applying for a job at the local supermarket.

What? My baby? 'Not until you're fifteen.'

'But Harry's got a job, and besides, I need the money.'

Harry had worked at a hardware shop over the summer,

doing five shifts a week, mad keen on saving for a car. I was happy about it. It kept him focused and off the streets. Plus, I knew where he was pretty much all the time. Now that school had started again, he'd cut back to one four-hour shift on Sundays.

'Hannah, let's talk about it when you turn fifteen.' That way, I still had a few months' grace.

My first job had been at Hungry Jack's when I was just a little older than Hannah. I'd dressed up for the interview, keen to impress. The manager, who was probably all of twenty-one, had taken me into a tiny grey room that smelled of grease and uncooked meat. I didn't have a resume, of course, but that didn't seem to matter.

'We can start you this weekend,' he'd said. 'Just to let you know, we put the good-looking kids out the back, cooking fries and assembling the burgers.'

I nodded.

'Yeah, customers get distracted if there's a stunning chick on the registers.'

'Okay,' I said, immediately thinking, yuck, not only do I have to wear the hideous uniform, I'll be covered in chip fat.

'So anyway,' he said, standing. 'Let's go out front, and I'll give you a quick lesson on the tills.'

All up, I'd lasted three miserable weeks working on a cash register I never mastered.

I looked at my daughter and thought about the years I'd spent sitting through dance recitals and flute concerts. When Hannah was five, I'd held my breath, tears in my eyes, as she pirouetted fleetingly across the stage, then I'd sat for a further mind-numbing two hours while all the other little sunbeams did their thing. One minute I was sitting at her first dance recital, and the next, she was getting a weekend job. Another blink of an eye and she'd be moving out on her own. I wasn't ready for that.

———

Before dinner, I did some Mike snooping – discreetly, of course – and found out he'd split acrimoniously from his wife several months earlier. She was restricting access to his three kids – two girls, and a son, Kurt, the eldest, who was a year above Harry at school. Mike only saw them every fourth weekend, and sometimes not even then because he was often on call seven days a week. It made me think how lucky I was that the separation was working out so far with Garth. Touch wood. We'd tried hard to keep things amicable for Hannah and Harry's sakes. Not that Garth should be narky, given his situation.

When I slipped out the front door a little after seven, no one blinked an eye. All five members of my current household had been watered and fed and were either chewing on a bone, curled up asleep or playing on their devices.

———

'Hey,' Mike said when we met at the restaurant entrance. 'Good timing.' He kissed me on the cheek and we were led to our table and seated. Graffiti wall art and colourful paper lanterns adorned the walls and ceilings of this bustling dining room, set up to reflect the buzzing atmosphere on the streets of Bangkok.

'Not wearing the navy wrap tonight? Shame.'

I blushed.

'It's BYO. I didn't know if you preferred red or white.' He opened a bag and pulled out a bottle in each hand. 'So I bought one of each.'

'I didn't know whether you liked gin or Scotch, so I bought a bottle of each.' I paused. 'Joking. Open the white.'

He laughed. 'Thank God it's a screw cap.'

He poured, and I swallowed a mouthful.

'Should we talk about food allergies or ex-partners?' I asked.

He grinned. 'They're both tedious. You choose. Then we can talk about diseases we've contracted and overcome.'

'I don't have any food allergies, but I have an ex-partner.'

'Don't we both. Diseases?'

'None that I can think of.' At that we clinked glasses and eased our way into a Bangkok-style street food menu of chicken satay, prawn pad thai and whole fish with coriander-chilli sauce.

We spoke briefly about June as more dishes arrived, crowding our tiny table. 'Way too much food,' I said. 'But I'm loving it all.'

A few minutes passed before we spoke. 'So' – I wiped my lips with a serviette – 'Are we going to talk about the elephant in the room or the party?'

'Was there an elephant in the room? There was certainly a lot going on, people crawling around with leashes around their necks.' He poured some more wine. 'How many of those do you know?'

'Just the one, I think, although who'd know?' I sipped my drink. 'Could have been anyone under those masks, a teacher, my chemist. It does my head in thinking about it.'

'Yeah, I haven't spoken to Pete yet, but I had no idea either.'

I had an incredible urge to touch Mike. I wanted to wrap my arms around him and hold him. I took a deep breath and tried hard to pull back and concentrate on our conversation.

'How's your friend?' he asked.

'We haven't told her,' I said, glancing down at my hands. 'But...'

'But?'

'Steve's been making calls to Carly and me. And he's sent emails.'

'What? Threatening you?'

'Yeah.'

'Stella, that's not good. You need to tell someone – if not the police–'

'No!' I shook my head. 'Jesse has a right to know, but–'

'Yes, she does. And once she does, she'll be able to deal with it. Something like this is almost impossible to keep secret.'

I nodded.

'It's a tough call, but I'm here if you need an ear.'

All too quickly, dinner was over, and Mike was walking me to my car. 'Can I see you again?'

I smiled. 'I'll be at the hospital with June tomorrow afternoon.'

'Excellent. A threesome.'

I smacked him on his shoulder. 'You wish.'

He kissed me on the lips. 'No I don't actually. I think you're enough for me.'

I stood on my toes and reached up to return his kiss. It had been a long time since I'd kissed someone new, and I wasn't disappointed. Despite sounding like a fifteen-year-old, all I could think was what a good kisser he was ... passionate, forceful, arousing.

'Okay. That works for me.'

CHAPTER TWENTY-ONE

CARLY

Carly waited until after Brett and Will had left the house on Tuesday morning before checking her emails. She was hoping Nicholas had replied. A phone call was out of the question. Nick didn't have a lot of money, and it was unlikely he'd spend what little he did have on an international call to his mother. She turned on the computer and drummed her fingers on the desk as it beeped into life. There were three emails, one from Nick. There was also one from Steve. That couldn't be good. And one from an address she didn't recognise. The other two could wait. Carly's boy had written to her.

Hey Mum,

What's happening? Freezing here. You'd hate it. Life's full-on but great. Had a mental with the head sports master but he's a freakazoid and getting bent out of shape about nothing. Everything's under control. I'm handling it so don't worry. How are Dad and the bro?

Carly wasn't sure what to read into that. Nick sounded fine, but what was the 'mental' with the sports master about? Was it something that warranted her calling him?

She looked at the other messages. What the hell was Steve doing emailing her? She opened it and quickly found out. One line. Eight words.

`I meant what I said the other day.`

What had he said? Something about keeping away from Jesse, or Stella and Carly would be sorry. The nerve of the guy! Carly trembled. She wanted to march over to Jesse's house and tell her everything! These threats had to stop. At least now she had proof – although was this proof? His words were ambiguous. He was too clever.

She rang Stella at work and barely waited for her to answer before blurting out, 'We have to tell Jesse what we saw the other night, or we'll end up being the bad guys.'

Carly could hear Stella tapping on her keyboard. 'Stella?'

'I got the same email.'

'Why are you whispering?'

'Because Liz is on the warpath. She runs this place like a bloody concentration camp.'

'Like you'd know.'

'It's a metaphor!'

'Okay, so what are we going to do about this? Steve's not going to let up.'

'I thought we'd decided not to say anything.'

'We agreed to wait until we had a plan,' Carly said. 'It's creepy now. Besides, don't you think Jesse has a right to know what her husband's up to?'

No response.

'Stella,' she snapped.

'It'll make things worse for her–'

'How much worse can it get? We'll be giving her more ammunition, surely. Besides, think about the diseases he's probably bringing home. Ugh! And you know how available Jesse makes herself. Even if she says she hates him, she certainly doesn't hate him from the waist down.'

Stella groaned. 'Carly! Trust you to say that. Gotta go.'

And with that, Stella hung up.

Carly had wanted to tell her about the notes she'd found in Nick's room, but Stella hadn't given her a chance. Probably a good thing. It wasn't fair to Nicholas. Carly needed to talk to him before she spoke to anyone else. Still, B must have meant something to Nicholas because he'd kept the notes. Nonsense, she argued with herself as she drifted back to the computer. What teenager willingly cleaned up his room and turfed out all the bits of unwanted paper and food scraps? That was what mothers were for.

Carly opened the third email. It was from the sports master Nicholas had mentioned in his email.

```
Dear Mrs Hindmarsh,
    I am writing to inform you that your
son has been suspended from duty as of
Monday 3 February due to inappropriate
locker  room  behaviour.  Pending  an
investigation,  it  will  be  decided
whether Nicholas stays on campus for the
remainder of the school year or is sent
directly home to Australia. Please feel
free to contact me on +44 1872 835694 to
discuss.
    Yours,
    Mr Evan Sinclair, Head Sports Master.
```

Inappropriate locker room behaviour! What the hell was going on with Nicholas? Carly's heart pounded. What had her son been caught doing? A thought popped into her mind, which she quickly wiped. She couldn't think like that.

She checked her watch and calculated the time in Cornwall – 10pm. Both emails had been sent eight hours earlier. If she woke up Nick, too bad. She dialled his mobile.

He picked up after a couple of rings. 'Yeah?'

'Nicholas, it's Mum. How's everything?'

'Great. At pub. Can't hear.'

'Is everything all right at school? I had an email from the sports master–'

'Crazy Stinky Sinclair? Everything's cool.'

Carly desperately wanted to believe him, to believe this was all a mistake, whatever 'this' was, and to know her son was safe. 'As long as you're sure...'

'Mum ... dropping out–'

The line was dropping out, really? The phone went dead and Carly was no closer to finding out what was going on. Nick had sounded in high spirits, but that was probably more to do with the number of beers he'd consumed.

She glanced at Evan Sinclair's number and considered phoning him. But it was too late. Besides, if Nicholas was at a pub, he couldn't be in that much trouble. If he'd done something truly awful, wouldn't he have been locked up or dispatched on the first plane back to Sydney?

She thought again about the kinds of things he could have been caught doing – fighting? Breaking some kid's nose? Stealing? None of those sounded like Nick, but she was trying to be open-minded. However, the more open-minded she allowed herself to be, the more outrageous her scenarios became.

She sat down and composed an email to Evan Sinclair.

Dear Mr Sinclair,

    Thank you for your email regarding Nicholas. It is very concerning. Can I ask what the inappropriate locker room behaviour was? Is there anything I can do? I know Nicholas is a good person by nature. I am sure he will have a reasonable explanation. (I have never condoned fighting but do understand that sometimes rough and tumble can explode into physical warfare.) I'll ring you tomorrow morning your time to discuss the matter further.

    Sincerely,

    Carly Hindmarsh.

She re-read the email, then pushed 'send', her mood plummeting further with every shallow breath.

Carly didn't have time to dwell because her mobile rang. Toby! Though he was a distraction she didn't need, she answered it.

'You've been avoiding my calls.'

'Not at all.'

'Really, Carly?' He paused. 'I'm seeing Stella and her mother-in-law in a little while.'

'Small world.'

'How's everything with you?'

She didn't answer.

'Your friend?' he prompted. 'Jesse?'

'So-so.'

'You told her?'

'No. Stella thinks we should stay out of it.'

'You don't agree?'

'How'd you guess?'

Carly padded over to the fridge, pulled out a bottle of wine and poured a glass. It was after midday. What the hell! She took a quick sip. Heaven.

'Have you thought any more about the other night?'

'Toby, I'm married. The other night I was hideously drunk.' She paused. 'And ... I don't think we should see each other again. It's not right.'

'I thought you might say something like that and I'm sorry to hear it. If you change your mind and want to catch up over a drink...'

Carly let out an audible sigh. She didn't need another friend.

'Okay, if you're ever at the Royal, don't be a stranger.'

'Thanks,' she said, making a mental note never to go anywhere near the hospital. 'It was nice meeting you.'

'Likewise.' He clicked off.

Carly shook her head. Crisis averted. All going to plan, their paths would never cross again.

She glanced at her glass. What was she thinking? She'd consumed over half of it. She tipped the rest down the sink.

What to do about Nick? Call Brett? He might tell her that the sports master was overreacting. On the other hand, Brett was particularly stressed about work these days. He didn't need the extra burden of knowing that Nick was in trouble overseas. There was little they could do about it except wait to hear more.

She poured herself another glass of wine and gulped half of it before tipping the rest down the sink. She didn't need alcohol. She needed to talk to Brett; tell him what was going on with Nick.

She dialled his number.

'Brett Hindmarsh.'

'Hey, big boy,' she said in a deep, throaty voice that she

hoped passed for sexy. 'I'm wearing nothing but black stilettos, and I'm alone in bed waiting for you to spank me! Hard!' As the words tumbled out of her mouth, she knew it was a huge mistake.

'Carly? Is that you?' Brett sounded confused and a touch concerned.

'Um, yes.'

'What the hell are you on about?'

'Sorry, I thought I'd try some sex chat to liven things up between us.'

'It's twelve thirty in the afternoon. I'm about to go into a strategy meeting. I don't need this now.'

'No, you never need it, do you?'

'We'll talk about this later.'

After she'd hung up, Carly closed the bathroom door and screamed at her reflection. Why had she rung? What had she hoped to achieve? If she'd been wanting to feel better, she was out of luck. Her stomach lurched and a red rash started spreading across her neck. Rejection gave way to bitter anger. Brett was never there for her. Not when she needed him, and she really needed him.

CHAPTER TWENTY-TWO

JESSE

Jesse double-checked the address on the scrap of paper she'd written it down on that morning. The scout hall was at 51 Station Street, several suburbs away from where she lived. She checked her make-up in the rear-view mirror. Satisfied, she hopped out and started walking down the messy yellow wildflower path.

This is a good thing, she told herself. A positive step in the right direction.

But she was nervous. Several times she went to turn around. Jesse kept thinking, *What the hell am I doing here?* But she forced herself to put one foot in front of the other and enter the building. Once inside, she exhaled deeply. After weeks of contemplation, she was finally here. She'd made it to a Secret Women's Business meeting. This could change her life, her perspective. She just had to be open to it. Go with the flow. Not so easy for a person like her, but she was determined to give it a try.

A woman touched her on the arm and smiled broadly. 'First time?'

Jesse nodded.

The woman, dressed in a casual white shirt and floral skirt, long red beads dangling from her neck, was welcoming but not gushy. She didn't invade Jesse's personal space, which Jesse appreciated.

'I'm Rebecca. Come and take a seat. We've all been through a first time,' she said gently.

Jesse did as she was told. Rebecca disappeared, returning minutes later with tea and Scotch Finger biscuits. 'Hope you like English Breakfast?'

Jesse nodded her thanks. It felt nice to be waited on. She drank her tea and surveyed the hall. The women were a mixed bag – some young, some older, some standing or sitting by themselves, others mingling. She felt comfortable, comfortably alone.

When it was time to start, Rebecca got up on the podium, obviously the group's leader. She spoke about commitments, prosperity, loving yourself and getting the mix right. About action plans, to-do lists and about revitalising one's spirit. 'It's time to embrace and celebrate who you are. Let us awaken the spirit within,' she boomed to her captivated audience.

Yes, thought Jesse, *that's exactly what I need to do: 'awaken my spirit and recharge myself in an atmosphere that nurtures my feminine energy and being'*. She completely understood what Rebecca was talking about; Jesse didn't want to wake up one morning and wonder what it had all been for.

'Isness is the business,' Rebecca shouted. 'Let us embrace the now and live consciously in the moment. Say it with me.'

'Isness is the business,' Jesse yelled, along with a room full of other women. Smiling, she relaxed for the first time in a very long time.

The hour flew by so quickly, Jesse could hardly believe it was over. She didn't want to leave, so caught up in the atmosphere of friendship, love and positive energy. But she didn't want to meet the others yet. It was too soon. Later, when she felt more confident, she might introduce herself to some women but not now. She was finding her way.

Baby steps, she told herself as she walked back to her car, broadly smiling. And they might have been baby steps, but she was feeling lighter and more energised than she had in months. As Jesse put her key in the ignition, she realised something else – not once during the entire session had she tapped her foot, clenched her hands or thought about her husband.

Jesse was optimistic – strong – as if she could take on the world and win. She felt confident she could find ways to handle Steve better, to nurture their marriage as well as the kids, and balance those responsibilities with her own ambitions and desires. This was definitely a turning point. Jesse was riding high.

CHAPTER TWENTY-THREE

STELLA

I was still elated by my dinner with Mike but had little time to think about him. The library was hectic, people everywhere, speaking loudly on their mobiles, letting their toddlers scream. I had a massive to-do list but had been stationed at the reference desk for most of the morning, dealing with customer enquiries. At one point it was so busy that the people waiting formed a huddle, inching ever closer to the desk as I tried to deal with them one at a time. One particularly rude man even tapped his keys on the desktop to get my attention. I wanted to ignore him, but Liz was nearby.

'I'll just be a moment,' I said and turned back to the elderly woman I was helping.

She wanted to know if the book she was holding, a 1969 out-of-print illustrated history of the magnolia flower, was for sale.

'It's not a bookshop,' Key Man barked.

I glared at him, then smiled at her. 'No, I'm sorry, madam, the book isn't for sale.'

She walked away, the book clutched firmly against her chest.

Key Man shook his head. 'Bet that book disappears before the end of the day.'

He was probably right.

At least Liz was having a good day. Her books order had arrived, and she was in her element, marvelling over jacket covers, making notes about guest authors to invite to speak at the library. She hadn't mentioned Jesse, and I hoped that meant she'd leave her alone when Jesse came in on Thursday.

After my stint at the reference desk, I got on with my other jobs.

By two o'clock, I was up to date and out the door. June and I had an appointment with Toby.

'I'm perfectly fine,' June, resplendent in a Pucci-inspired turban, said when I picked her up.

'I know, but your arm's still swollen and bruised. The doctor needs to see how it's healing.'

That was true. But I'd also phoned Toby to ask if he could discreetly run some preliminary Alzheimer's tests. He'd said it wasn't his area but had agreed to line up another doctor. Thinking about the possibility of June having Alzheimer's broke my heart, but we needed to get some facts. And then, hopefully, we could just put her memory lapses down to ageing and absent-mindedness.

Toby didn't keep us waiting. 'Mrs Sparks, how are you feeling today?'

'As I told my daughter-in-law, I'm perfectly fine. I wish everyone would stop hovering around me like I'm a cripple.'

'Excellent,' he soothed as he took her by her good arm. 'We're going to have a look at your arm and run a few tests–'

'What sort of tests?'

Toby glanced at me before continuing. 'Nothing to be concerned about. Standard procedure for over-seventies. Doctor Gordon is going to assist, but I'll stay with you.' He nodded to a woman nearby who looked even younger than he did.

'I'm not over seventy, I am seventy.'

'Come on, June,' I said. 'Stop being pedantic.' I suffered a twinge of guilt for not telling her the real reason for the tests, but I held my ground. They needed to be done, and she'd never agree. 'I'll be here when you're finished.'

I took a seat in the waiting room, cursing myself for not bringing a book. A few minutes later, Toby walked in.

'That was quick!'

'Sorry to disappoint you, we're just getting started.' He crossed his arms. 'I spoke to Carly a little while ago.'

'Ah.'

'Seems her declarations from last Thursday night won't be followed through. Pity. I thought we hit it off.' He looked over to the closed door of the room he'd taken June into. 'They'll be ready for me now. See you in a little while.'

I turned my attention to an ancient copy of *House & Garden* magazine. I'd almost dozed off when someone tapped me on the shoulder. Mike! I'd almost forgotten I'd told him I'd be at the hospital today. I ran my fingers through my hair and smoothed down my shirt.

'Hello, stranger,' he said, smiling broadly. 'I was told you were lurking around the second floor.'

'Nice to see you again.' I couldn't help grinning as I looked into his incredible blue eyes.

He sat down beside me, and our thighs touched. 'It's been too long, Stella.'

I blushed. 'Gosh, yes, at least fifteen hours.'

'How's June today?'

'Okay,' I said, feeling my cheeks glowing hotter.

'This isn't my area – trauma and emergency are my specialty – but Toby's filled me in today after our conversation last night.'

'Maybe I'm overreacting. June's been a bit forgetful of late, and then with her fall on Sunday, I thought it was a good opportunity to have her thoroughly checked out. I hope I'm wrong.'

Mike looked at me closely. 'I hope so too.'

I nodded. Despite the circumstances, I was happy. Nervous but excited, imagining Mike and me somewhere, anywhere, ripping each other's clothes off. His naked body and my pure lust driving me ... hard.

Mike took a moment. 'So, will we give texting another go?'

I nodded. 'Sorry about that. Don't get me wrong, I like getting your texts' – love getting them, actually – 'it's just that, well, I'm not used to flirting and sometimes don't know how to respond.'

He put his hand on my knee, and I shivered, hopefully not so much that he noticed.

'We can work on that. Because unless I'm reading this completely wrong – and tell me if I am – there's something between us. I just need to draw out your inner wilder Stella.'

'Hmm.'

'I'll take that as a "Yes, Mike! I totally agree. Do what you have to do." Am I right?'

I giggled nervously. 'Maybe.'

'Ahem.' It was Toby. 'We're all done, Stella.'

'Oh,' I said, standing and composing myself. 'How is she?'

'Still in a lot of pain, but she's a tough old bird, that one.'

'Who are you calling old?' June said, walking up beside him.

I'd have expected her to be more affronted by the word 'bird', but she didn't seem to mind.

'June,' I said, 'this is Mike.'

'Another doctor friend, Stella?' June's eyebrows were raised so high her turban wobbled. 'You seem to be gathering a collection.'

Mike held out his hand. 'Nice to meet you, June. Love your headgear.'

June smiled.

'You're in good hands with Toby here,' Mike told her, then turned to me. 'I'll be off. Let me know when we can catch up again.'

'Sure,' I said nonchalantly. But as he walked away, I suddenly felt deflated, like all the air had gone out of the room. When would I see him again?

June and I thanked Toby and headed towards the elevator.

'Are you going to tell me how you know all these handsome young doctors?' June asked as we stepped inside.

'From around.' A little flustered, I side-tracked her with a suggestion about stopping in at Flower Power.

Twenty minutes later, we were wandering amongst the herb seedlings at the nursery. It was a glorious afternoon. All around us, freesias, hydrangeas and lisianthus were in full and abundant colour.

'This was a nice idea,' June said as we breathed in the late summer orange blossoms.

'Should we stop at your house on the way home?' I asked as we made our way to the car park. I was loaded up with several pots of herbs, three flowering daisy plants and a standard lemon tree.

'No, thank you. I have all I need,' June said, as I helped her into the car.

I thought about Mike as I prepared dinner. Of course I did. He was creeping into my mind more and more. He was handsome but not drop-dead gorgeous. He had charisma though, buckets of it, and a great smile, piercing blue eyes. Not to mention he was charming and ... well, the whole Mike package made me swoon.

'Mum,' Hannah said, interrupting my thoughts and passing me the phone. 'Dad.'

'Are you seeing him soon?' I whispered.

She nodded. 'This weekend.'

I blew her a kiss. 'Good girl.' I placed the phone to my ear. 'Hi, Garth, how's it going?'

'Under the pump.'

Under the pump? What the hell did that mean? 'You're fixing a pool pump? Being pumped by a person or persons? Sounds painful.'

Garth exhaled. 'Busy with work.'

'Oh, okay. What's up? This is becoming a habit.'

'Aren't I even allowed to phone my family now?'

I shook my head. Men! 'Of course.' I wasn't up for a confrontation. 'What's news in the last six hours since we spoke?'

'Nothing. Just checking in.'

'You don't need to check in. You do know that, don't you? We're separated.'

I heard him sigh on the other end of the line.

'I took June back to the hospital for a check-up this afternoon,' I said. 'Her arm's healing but it'll take time.'

'Thanks for looking after her. I...'

Silence.

'What's up? You sound terrible.'

'It's Amanda.'

'And?'

More silence.

'Garth? I don't get it. You couldn't wait to leave me and hook up with her.'

'That was before.'

'Before what?'

'Before she wanted to get married.'

'Oh.' That took me by surprise. Garth marrying Amanda? The kids having a stepmother? Wow! Life really did move on quickly. I couldn't begin to imagine how June would take the news. Hannah and Harry would have a fit. They'd come around eventually, especially if he lavished them with gifts of iPads and holidays to Fiji, but I didn't relish the idea of sharing my children with another woman permanently.

'We're not divorced yet,' I said evenly, despite the lump at the back of my throat and the pain at the front of my head. It wasn't like I wanted Garth back; I didn't. And I wasn't jealous about his relationship with Amanda. But I didn't understand how he could re-partner so quickly. He'd moved from living with his mother to living with me, and now he was living with Amanda. Didn't he want any time alone to enjoy his own company?

'I know, so the longer we stay married, the better,' he said.

'You don't want to marry Amanda?'

'No! We're only in the getting to know each other phase.'

Okay, so Garth wasn't completely ruled by his penis, at least not yet. He still possessed a modicum of independent thought. I immediately felt twenty kilos lighter ... and the headache disappeared.

'Stella?'

'Mmm?'

'I thought I'd lost you.'

I blinked. What was he trying to tell me? 'Pardon?'

'The connection – I thought I'd lost you. Listen, I'd appreciate you not mentioning this to the kids.'

'Sure. Okay.'

Really? I felt like saying. *And why the hell would I?*

CHAPTER TWENTY-FOUR

I was finishing clearing the dinner plates and stacking the dishwasher when Jesse rang to ask if she could come over. I was a bit apprehensive. What would Steve say? Would he even let her come once he knew where she was going?

Thankfully, Jesse answered the question before I had a chance to ask. 'Steve's working late – again! And Mum's been pestering me about having Ollie and Em stay overnight, so I thought, why not?'

'Sure. Okay. Sounds excellent.'

'Good! I've had a great day, and I want to talk to you about the library and a bunch of other stuff.'

She certainly sounded in fine spirits, but talking about the library? Ugh.

Half an hour later, she bounded through the door holding a bottle of Chardonnay. 'I know it's only Tuesday night, but one glass can't hurt us, can it?'

I smiled. 'Absolutely! Should I see if Carly's free?'

'Why not? The more the merrier.'

Within minutes, Carly arrived, and soon the three of us were sitting on the outside deck, glasses of wine in hand.

'What's happened to you today?' I asked Jesse. 'Even your hair is bouncing.'

She beamed. 'I told you. I had a good day.'

'Did you win the lottery?' Carly asked.

'Nah, but I have been thinking about a lot of things, and I really want to apply for the full-time position at the library.'

'Okay,' I said tentatively. Liz would never agree. She wanted to cut Jesse's hours and including her fortnightly Monday and Friday shifts, Jesse was only doing ten.

'I know you're thinking Steve will never agree to it, but I have it all worked out. He'll come around. I'm feeling confident, so I may as well put my optimism to good use.'

Carly sipped her wine. 'Great.'

'But enough about me,' Jesse continued. 'How's June?'

'Mad as a cut snake,' I said with a grin. 'Feisty, determined and strong. But her fall was a huge shock. She's seventy, after all.'

'You're very good to take her in,' Carly said.

I frowned at her. 'Why wouldn't I? She's family.'

Carly shrugged and drank some more. 'Not for much longer.'

'June's part of our lives. She'll always be family, regardless.'

'Fair enough.' Carly paused a moment before clearing her throat. 'I'd like to apologise for my behaviour the other night. I don't know what got into me, fuck buddies and all.'

I laughed. 'How's that resolution coming along? You could have knocked me over with a feather when I realised Toby was June's doctor.'

'I'm confused,' Jesse said. 'What's this about?'

'Toby was one of the guys Carly met at the pub the other night.'

'And he's a doctor. Can you believe it? Small world, hey?' Carly said. 'He's a nice bloke though. So's Mike.'

'Mike being another guy at the pub?' Jesse asked. 'Also a doctor?'

I nodded. 'It's not as complicated as it sounds. In fact, I had dinner with him last night and saw him today at the hospital.'

'He seems like a decent bloke,' said Carly.

'Yes, but unlike you, I don't want a fuck buddy.'

'Are you seeing him again?' Jesse asked.

'Early days but yes, maybe.'

Carly smiled. 'Way to go.'

'You never told me what happened when you gatecrashed the party,' Jesse said. 'How was it?'

'Interesting,' I said.

'Yes! Interesting,' Carly quickly agreed.

'Come on,' Jesse persisted. 'Details, please.'

I glanced at Carly, who had her hand over her mouth. That's right, I thought. Keep it there. But in typical Carly style, she didn't.

'It wasn't your regular North Shore party,' she said. 'It was a dress-up kind of affair.'

Jesse looked confused. 'Like a Bollywood or Rocky Horror party?'

'Not quite,' Carly said. 'One of the doctors, Pete, is into bondage and fetish stuff, and he took us along with him to see if we'd be interested as well.'

'Carly,' I warned. 'How much have you had to drink?'

'Just a couple before I came over.'

Jesse snapped her fingers. 'Tell me more about the party. What was everyone doing?'

'There were people in dominatrix gear whipping each other,' I said dismissively. 'Standard stuff.'

'Plenty of naked or near-naked bodies in threesomes and foursomes,' Carly added.

'Oh my! And what were you guys doing?'

'Pete threw himself into a throuple, but the rest of us watched in disbelief,' I said.

Carly and I gulped wine. Jesse's glass remained untouched.

Carly nudged me. 'Go on.'

'Not much more to say, really.' I glowered at her.

'Come on, Stella,' Jesse said. 'Don't leave anything out. It's highly unlikely I'll ever get the opportunity–'

Carly burst out laughing. I glared at her, but she didn't stop. She was laughing so hard, wine dribbled from her nose.

'Carly, control yourself. Please.' I wanted to belt her.

'I'm sorry. I just can't get that image out of my head – the nappy, the dummy, the studded collar around his neck–'

'Carly! No,' I yelled.

'She needs to know, Stella.'

Jesse was pale, almost white. 'What do I need to know?'

'Don't do this, Carly,' I begged. 'It's nothing, Jesse.'

Carly snorted and guzzled the rest of her wine. 'Okay, here's the thing.' Her eyes were red-rimmed and wide as saucers, her cheeks flushed and full.

I willed her to stop. 'Now's not the time–'

'We saw your husband,' Carly blurted.

Jesse looked puzzled. 'Steve? At the party?'

'That's right, Steve. He was there and he was–'

'Stop,' Jesse said. 'This is a joke, right? Ha, ha. Very funny. Just as well I know Steve was working late last Thursday night.'

I glared again at Carly, who was now slouched back in her seat.

'Come on,' Jesse said. 'You're having a laugh, right? Well, you got me. I almost fell for it.'

I put my hand on her arm. 'Jesse–'

'No!' she said, closing her eyes as if to block out my voice. 'I don't want to hear any more. I don't believe you. Steve was working last Thursday night. He told me.' She hesitated, trying to get her breathing under control. 'There's no way...' She pushed her chair back and stood.

'I'm sorry,' I said quietly. 'But despite Carly's lack of tact, Steve was there. We saw him.'

Jesse shook her head. 'No.'

Silence. Even Carly didn't speak.

'Did he see you?' Jesse asked.

I didn't know what to say. I rose to hug her, but she shrank away.

'Just tell me,' she demanded.

I nodded.

Jesse scrunched up her face, trying to compose herself. 'I still don't believe you. You've always hated Steve, and now you're saying things that aren't true to push me to leave him. Well, guess what? I never will. I'm going to work even harder to get my marriage back on track. I don't need you. Fine friends you are, spreading vicious rumours. How could you?' Tears streamed down her face. 'Steve's a good man, a really good man.'

I tried to stop her from leaving, but she pushed past me.

'Just leave me alone,' she said. 'As for you, Carly, you might want to start on my glass next, seeing as you're on a roll. As usual.'

With that, she hurried down the deck stairs and onto the driveway.

'Jesse, please don't go,' I called after her. 'Let me explain.'

She got into her car and slammed the door shut. The engine revved, she put the gears into reverse and was gone.

'That went well,' Carly said.

I turned to look at her. 'You've got one hell of a big mouth.'

'She'll forgive us.'

'You reckon?'

'She has to. We're the ones who are going to get her through this nightmare. I don't know why you're being so shitty about it. We're only telling her the truth.'

I shook my head. 'Did you ever stop to consider that she might not want to know the truth? People bury their heads in the sand for all kinds of reasons. Maybe Jesse already had an inkling but chose to ignore it. Now we've forced her to face something she mightn't be ready to deal with. Couldn't you see her foot tapping as soon as we mentioned the party?'

'Yes, but–'

'Didn't it occur to you that we might be making her situation worse?'

'Her tremors, you mean?'

'If that's what you want to call them.'

'Look, I'm sorry. I thought–'

'Carly, sometimes your insensitivity astounds me.'

CHAPTER TWENTY-FIVE

Carly left when I told her I didn't want to open another bottle of wine. And she talked about other people being in denial! As soon as she was out the door, I rang Jesse, but her mobile was switched off.

'Jesse, I'm so sorry,' I told her voicemail. 'We shouldn't have said anything, and you're completely right, we were probably mistaken. Maybe it wasn't Steve ... Call me.'

I was so exhausted by the time I slipped into bed I could hardly move. It had been a long day. I'd just switched off my bedside lamp when the phone rang. I wasn't going to answer it, worried it might be Steve again. Then I saw the name.

'Jesse, are you okay?'

'Yes. No.' She was crying. 'Steve's not home. I've left a message on his mobile and called his office phone. No answer. I don't know what to do.'

'Do you want me to come over?'

'No, I'm okay. Sorry I freaked out. I was shocked. Still am.'

'I could kill Carly.'

'She was being herself.' Jesse took a moment and her

breathing calmed. 'Can you tell me exactly what you saw that night?'

'I'm not sure that's a good idea. The room was dark, there were loads of people–'

'Stop bullshitting and tell me. I don't need specifics. We can talk about that on Thursday at the library. I just want you to tell me whether the man you saw at the party was Steve.'

'I'm ninety-nine per cent sure. And since that night, he's left Carly and me threatening voicemails and messages.'

'No!'

'I'm sorry, Jess, but yes.'

'So it was definitely him. We can be one hundred per cent sure.' Jesse took another deep breath. 'Was he drunk or...' She paused. 'High?'

'He didn't seem drunk, but maybe he'd been taking drugs. I really don't know, Jess. If you want to take Thursday off, it's no problem.'

Jesse sniffed. 'I'll be in. Ten o'clock as usual.'

'You sure? You sound too calm.'

'Trust me, Stella, I'm fine.'

I wasn't. I hung up feeling decidedly shaky. Jesse was taking the news well, almost too well. She was too composed, her emotions overly controlled. It worried me. I thought about driving over to see her, but it was late. She'd be asleep before long. Besides, Steve was probably pulling into their garage about now. I didn't like to think of Jesse confronting him. She'd wither with a single well-placed gibe. I dreaded to think how he'd react when he found out Jesse knew what he'd been up to.

I couldn't imagine him saying, 'Okay, Jesse, you caught me. I was wrong, I'll do anything you want.' He'd never agree to a divorce if that wasn't part of his agenda. Jesse had told me once that their home and bank accounts were all in his name. He held all the aces: the money and the power. I found it odd, but that summed Steve up perfectly. He needed to control every aspect of Jesse's and the kids' lives. She had no money of her own aside from the small amount she earned at the library.

Besides, Steve wasn't the kind of man to give up easily. To him, image was everything. To the outside world, he lived the perfect life: the glamorous wife (even though he kept her apart from his colleagues so they wouldn't notice that she twitched in his presence), and the gorgeous twins, one girl, one boy. Steve would rather crawl naked over broken glass than admit he was wrong about anything. He'd probably enjoy it too.

CHAPTER TWENTY-SIX

JESSE

Jesse sat on her bed, hugging her knees to her chest, rocking backward and forward, tears streaming down her face. What to do? It had just gone eleven o'clock. She considered ringing Louisa, but she'd only spoken to her a couple of days ago.

Stella was her best friend, but Jesse couldn't continually burden her with her secrets, regrets and desires. She knew too much already. More and ... well, it would be too much for her to keep it to herself. Jesse couldn't ask that of her. She'd get what she wanted in the end. She just had to figure out how to make it happen – how to work it to her advantage.

She stared at the ceiling as she thought back over the evening. The humiliation and shame. And it had come from Carly, of all people! The least-qualified woman Jesse knew to be lecturing her about her marriage. She could kill Steve for what he'd done. She should walk out on him tonight.

She remembered a conversation with Louisa years ago. Lou was high on coke, and she'd blurted out something to Jesse about how her sex life with Steve 'must be pretty out there, given what he's into'. Jesse had pretended she knew what Louisa was talking about, so she'd continue.

'I don't know how you put up with it, all that nappy stuff, having to clean up after him when he shits in it.'

Jesse had thought Louisa was talking about Oliver. The next thing she knew, Louisa was packing her bags and leaving for San Francisco. Jesse had been stunned.

'Tell me what's happened?' she'd begged her sister.

'Nothing, Jesse,' Louisa had assured her, tears streaming down her cheeks. 'I just need a break. I'll be back.'

Famous last words.

Jesse had even resorted to questioning her mum. Dot's response? 'A silly misunderstanding with a friend that got out of control.' How silly could it have been if it forced Louisa to take off overseas?

Dot also told her that Louisa would be back. 'This is her home, darling. Besides, she loves Ollie and Emmy too much to leave them permanently.'

Six long years later, Louisa still hadn't stepped back onto Australian soil and Jesse wasn't a lot wiser about the reason why. Her parents didn't talk about it, and Louisa had never confided in her sister as to why she'd left the country so abruptly.

Jesse glanced at the clock again. Eleven thirty. Steve still wasn't home. She got out of bed and wandered the house, trying to ignore her shaking left hand. Usually she'd check on the twins – watching them sleep always calmed her – but tonight they were at her parents' place. She made herself a cup of green tea, retreated to bed and tried reading her book.

What if Steve had been in an accident and was lying in a ditch somewhere? For a moment, she wished it were true. But she knew it wasn't. He was at a sex party somewhere, snorting cocaine and possibly being infected right at this very second with an STD...

Stop it, Jesse!

She could barely control her raging anger. What kind of man did this to his wife? His kids? She had loved him. Loved her family. And now? Well, now her life was in tattered ruins. She took a sip of tea to calm herself before racing to the bathroom and vomiting into the toilet bowl.

Having emptied the contents of her stomach, Jesse flushed and rinsed her mouth. She refused to let despair defeat her. Working hard to rein in her thoughts, she calmed her breathing, because once the dark side took hold...

I choose to be positive.

Back in the bedroom, Jesse pulled out a bottle of valerian from the top drawer of her bedside cabinet, gulped two tablets, then turned off the bedside light. *I choose to be positive.* It was just after midnight.

Steve crawled into bed at three thirty. Did he really think she was naive enough to believe he'd been working until then? His boldness astounded her. She was seething. He'd ruined the life they'd built together. She shuddered to think what her parents would say when they found out – because eventually they would. Everyone would! Jesse's life as she knew it was over. It had been built on a lie. And it wasn't just one lie or one indiscretion. Steve had a separate secret life.

What else had Steve kept hidden from her? Another family? She'd read about that kind of thing: a seemingly straight-up family man, who, after being killed in a car accident, was found to have three other wives ... or boyfriends. She'd also read stories about sex parties going wrong and family men being murdered. It could so easily be Steve. For starters, Jesse wanted to murder him! It took every bit of strength not to roll over and knee him in the groin.

Instead, she shifted to the other side of the bed and lay there thinking as the hours ticked by.

CHAPTER TWENTY-SEVEN

Wednesday morning, Jesse dragged herself out of bed on autopilot and, after her mother dropped the children off, got them dressed and organised for school. Despite what catastrophes might befall you, life went on – in another country, there might be a tsunami, a suicide bombing, war – but in Jesse's world, the kids still needed to be fed, their homework completed, their teeth brushed.

The previous night, in between dozing, listening out for Steve and overthinking her wretched life, Jesse had had another weird dream. This time about Louisa leaving. It had started with Louisa calling her name.

'Louisa?' Jesse had replied. 'Is that you? I'm so happy. It's so good to have you back home. I missed you. Don't ever leave me again.'

Jesse was standing in the middle of the flower shop where she'd worked many years ago. Ollie and Emily were young, only three or so; they were tugging at pale pink tulips in a vase. 'Stop that,' Jesse told them. She handed them each two rolls of ribbon and a balloon to play with and they started rolling around on the filthy wet floor.

'I'm going,' Louisa said.

'But I don't want you to leave.'

'I have to. It's all blown up.'

'What has?'

Louisa wouldn't explain. 'I can never come back again.' She was crying, sobbing Jesse's name over and over.

Jesse reached out to put her arms around Louisa, but she couldn't seem to touch her.

'I hate all these flowers,' Louisa had screamed.

Then *pop!* Emily's balloon burst, making Jesse jump. She looked around for Louisa, but she'd gone. She'd left Jesse again.

Jesse had woken up feeling startled and unsettled.

When she dropped the kids at school, she found herself lingering longer than usual at the gate.

'I love you,' she called as they raced off into the schoolyard. Emily didn't give her a backwards glance, but Ollie turned around and ambled back to where Jesse was leaning against the car.

He hugged her tight. 'I hate seeing you sad, Mummy. Everything will be good, you'll see.'

She nodded through her tears. 'You have a good day, my darling. The best. I love you.'

Ollie kissed her cheek. 'I love you too.'

It took every bit of strength to let him go. She wanted to hold him, to tell him he could take the day off so they could hang out together and go to the beach or the movies. But she didn't. What was she doing to that beautiful boy? she wondered as she drove away. She swore he could see into her heart, that he knew what she was thinking, how she was feeling.

Once home, she forced herself to eat some toast and then dialled Steve's number. There was never going to be a good time for this. She didn't have all the facts, but she had enough.

'Where were you last night?' she asked. She tried to remain calm but her voice broke.

'Working,' he replied, not missing a beat.

'And last Thursday night?'

'Working.'

'Liar!'

She was pacing like crazy and switching lights on and off. Flick, flick, flick. In her mind, she saw him with a range of nameless, faceless women, stroking and kissing them, having sex on leopard-skin rugs, revelling in his adultery.

'I don't know what you're talking about.' Steve's tone was measured, superior.

'People saw you.'

'Which people? What exactly was I supposed to have been doing?'

Jesse couldn't believe he was carrying on the charade. He'd been caught, he knew he'd been caught, yet he still acted like he was God.

'I'm not going to dignify those questions with a reply. You're a sick man.'

'I'm sick? That's funny. What about you with your pacing and other obsessions?'

'This isn't about me, Steve.'

Silence.

'Look,' Jesse stammered, trying to erase the filthy images from her mind. 'I don't want you here. I want you to move out.'

'Who are you to tell me I can't live in my own house?' His voice was restrained. Overcontrolled. 'A house, I might add, that I paid for. If anyone should be leaving, it's you. You're not a fit mother. You're the one who's sick.'

'I don't want to argue with you, Steve.' Jesse felt faint. 'I just can't live with a man—'

'What? Go on. Say it!'

'I can't live with your infidelity. Our marriage is based on a lie. You're not the man you claim to be.'

'You're talking nonsense. Besides, it's not me you should be interrogating. It's those sluts you call friends!'

Jesse's hands shook and her chest tightened. 'How can you say that?'

'And as for your sister—'

She hung up before he could say another word. Arsehole.

Jesse was shaking so hard she could barely breathe. She needed to take a long, brisk walk around the neighbourhood, but she didn't think her legs would carry her that far. She was almost hyperventilating.

Steve was a prick, acting like he was the wronged one, like he hadn't been caught out. What more could she do? Show him photographic evidence? An ugly thought flashed into her mind: she prayed there weren't any incriminating photos of him on somebody's phone. Or worse, hard drive.

She contemplated taking the kids to her parents and staying with them until she figured out what to do next, but why should she have to move out of her own house?

Nausea overwhelmed her. She only just made it to the bathroom in time, threw up in the toilet, then collapsed on the cool tiles, lying silently for several minutes. She could feel the distress eating away her insides. All she wanted to do was sleep. She closed her eyes.

Sometime later, she woke feeling marginally better and slowly stood, walked into the kitchen and popped a couple of headache tablets.

Louisa? Where did she fit in all of this? Jesse felt a little jolt at the back of her throbbing head ... some distant memory trying to break free.

She dialled Louisa's number.

'Tell me what you know,' she said when Louisa answered. 'About Steve.'

She heard Louisa suck in air like it was in short supply. 'Pardon?'

'About the parties.'

Louisa hesitated. 'I wanted to tell you–'

'Really? You knew?'

Jesse's world collapsed. Even though Stella had said Steve had left her threatening messages, part of her had been hanging on to a hope that Stella and Carly had been mistaken. But now, with Louisa's words, it all became horribly real.

'Jesse? Talk to me. It was a long time ago. I was a different person back then.' Louisa was speaking, but Jesse couldn't comprehend what she was saying. 'And then six years ago–'

'When you left Australia?' Jesse said, trying to follow the conversation.

'Yeah. Dad's golf friend recognised me.'

'Hang on. What?'

'He told Dad that the last time he'd seen me, I'd been dressed in a black corset and suspenders and had been whipping his bare bum with a cane.'

'What's this got to do with Steve?'

'Everything. Isn't that what you're asking me?'

'I'm not sure.'

'Jesse, I knew years ago that Steve was into this crazy shit.'

The conversation was happening faster than Jesse could process it. Louisa and Steve? With the golf guy? It didn't make sense.

'You were in it together?' she asked.

'Not exactly,' Louisa said. 'I was being paid.'

'I'm confused. What are you telling me exactly?'

'I'm telling you that when I first met Steve fifteen years ago, he was into bondage and–'

'Fifteen years ago? But–'

'–then he met you and I recognised him, and he promised me he'd given all that up.'

Jesse took a long breath. 'And Dad's friend?'

'He'd been a client years before. I never expected to see him again. Then when he saw me with Dad, he assumed–'

'Jesus, Louisa! Which part of you decided it would be a good idea to keep this secret from me?'

'I was protecting you. Steve loved you, and I thought he was telling me the truth when he said he'd stopped living his fantasy double life.'

'You were protecting yourself more like it. So you were a … prostitute?'

'It wasn't like that. Look, it was a long time ago. How did you find out about Steve?'

'Friends saw him at a party.' Jesse paused, feeling her throat constrict. 'He was wearing a nappy.'

Louisa groaned but didn't say anything.

Jesse continued. 'As I thought about it more, I remembered a conversation we'd had just before you went away.'

'I'm so sorry. I really am. What are you going to do?'

Jesse couldn't answer. Her life was over. It was as simple as that. Soon everyone would know. She'd be the joke of the North Shore.

'Jesse! You've got to believe me – I got out of it years ago, and Steve promised me he'd done the same.'

'This is unbelievable. An unbelievable nightmare. You! Steve! I feel utterly betrayed. How could you have kept this from me? Allowed me to marry a man like that?'

Silence.

'Is that why you haven't been home all this time?'

'I couldn't trust myself not to tell you about Steve. I was protecting you.'

'How could you think that something like this could be kept secret? I can't forgive you for this. Why didn't you tell me?'

How could her life ever return to normal after such a revelation? She felt stupid, alone and thoroughly humiliated. 'My life's over.'

Her body began to shake and convulse ... she felt as though she was shrinking ... disappearing. Suddenly, it wasn't her body anymore.

Jesse dropped the phone as her mind went blank.

CHAPTER TWENTY-EIGHT

LOUISA

Louisa freaked out when she heard a thud – presumably Jesse falling. The rational part of her hoped she'd only fainted, but what if Jesse had hit her head on a table corner or had a heart attack? Ever worse scenarios clamoured for her attention as she dialled her mother's number. Jesse would hate her for getting Dot involved, but Louisa didn't know who else to call. She certainly wasn't going to ring Steve.

Dot called half an hour later to say that Jesse was okay. 'I'd like to know what brought this on,' she said to Louisa. 'Jesse says she didn't eat much breakfast–'

'So, there's a simple explanation. Can I talk to her?'

Dot huffed before handing the phone over to Jesse.

'I'm sorry,' Louisa started, knowing how much she'd hurt her sister.

'We'll talk about this later.' Jesse's voice was barely audible.

'Are you okay?' Dumb question. How could Jesse be okay given what she'd found out? Plus, Louisa had involved their mother who'd no doubt interrogate Jesse for hours once Louisa was off the phone.

'Fine,' Jesse said gruffly and hung up.

So now Jesse knew. She knew about Louisa, about Steve ...
A combination of nausea and relief flooded through her. She'd
meant what she said about telling Jesse anything she wanted to
know. Louisa would be honest. It was time. What did she have
to lose?

Louisa thought about that question some more. A lot more.
She'd already lost her father and was now on the brink of losing
Jesse if she didn't deal with this situation carefully. Dot was
oblivious, and Louisa hoped that could continue. Eventually,
Louisa would have to face her father again and that would be
torture.

Fifteen years earlier, Louisa had come across Steve in her
role as Mistress Lola, dominatrix. She'd loved studying at
university, but she had no money. Even though she was working
part-time as a waitress, she always spent more than she earned.
And she hated being poor. One afternoon, she'd spied an ad in
the local paper, and a week later she was hooked up in a black
leather corset brandishing a riding crop. Louisa was on her way.
It was the best of both worlds. She could stay at university and
indulge her love of the arts, earning top dollar while doing it. It
was fun in the early days, dressing up, being part of someone
else's fantasy. Before long, she'd done it all: spanking, caning,
whips, chains, handcuffs. She'd pretty much seen it all too: the
cages, leather-upholstered beds that doubled as coffins. Nothing
fazed her.

Steve was one of her occasional clients. She met with him
about three times before he moved on to private parties. She'd
never had sex with him – thank the universe! Louisa trembled at
the thought. He was a crazy bastard, one of those guys who
wanted his mummy to spank him when he shat in his nappy or
cried liked a baby.

Three years later, he'd turned up on Jesse's arm at a family
dinner – Father's Day. It had taken Louisa a while to recognise

him, but she never forgot a face. By the time her mother had wheeled out the crème brûlée, Louisa knew exactly who he was. But she didn't say anything to Jesse. She'd hoped he was a passing phase. Unfortunately, he'd hung around.

One night, after consuming several Scotches, he'd asked Louisa if she was still in the business.

'No,' she'd lied. 'You?'

He'd dismissed the question with a shake of his head.

She could tell he was scared when he'd realised for certain that sweet Jesse's older, wilder sister was the woman who'd seen him crawling around on the floor in a nappy. He must have been terrified that she might blab about his idiosyncrasies. But why would she? Exposing him would have meant revealing her secret as well. And she wanted to keep that side of her life hidden from her family.

She kept out of his way as best she could, which wasn't difficult given she was working six nights a week. Her social life was non-existent back then. But by that stage, she was tiring of the business: it was mentally, as well as physically, exhausting. She was fed up with spanking, whipping and humiliating middle-aged stockbrokers, solicitors and teachers. By the time Steve and Jesse married two years later, Louisa was done. She was earning enough money lecturing at university to give up her night job.

But six years ago, everything had blown up in Louisa's face. It had been an unfortunate coincidence that her dad's friend had seen Louisa with Bernard. He'd assumed Louisa was on the job and had bowled up to them with a sly wink and nod. Bernard, of course, had had no idea what was going on. When Louisa had been forced to explain it to him, he'd listened in a silent daze, not knowing where to look or what to say. Could it have been more embarrassing? Well, yes actually, but Louisa didn't want to think about that scenario.

'Why, Louisa?' he'd said, crying, humiliation, disappointment and despair written across his face. 'We would have given you money.'

She couldn't look him in the eye.

Bernard had begged Louisa not to tell Dot and Jesse, and she didn't. Why would she choose to shame herself further? But not telling them had meant she continued to protect Steve. At least she wouldn't have to do that any longer.

Six years was a long time to be away from her family, but disappearing had seemed the only answer. Life in Sydney, the revelations ... it had spun out of control. And Steve? He'd been beyond smug, telling Jesse that Louisa was a bad influence on the kids. Like he could talk!

'Promise me you aren't dabbling in these parties anymore, and I'll go quietly,' Louisa had said to him just before she left Australia.

'I don't have to promise you anything.'

And the bastard hadn't. Sometimes she could have kicked herself for not telling Jesse what she knew about him, but she'd believed it wouldn't help the situation. Ollie and Emily were three when she left. There was no way she could have told Jesse about Steve's past without destroying her family, and Jesse had been fragile enough at the time.

So Louisa had got the hell out of Sydney. Melbourne, Perth, even Hong Kong, weren't far enough away. Louisa had connections in San Francisco, so it had seemed as good a place as any. She'd got a job at the University of San Francisco and an apartment in Nob Hill. Before she knew it, she was settled, and life was comfortable, even if she was estranged from her family and didn't see her niece and nephew. She figured that when they were older, they'd understand. Then she met the professor and life had skyrocketed to sublime.

Louisa gazed from her sofa out across the large bay window

seat towards the harbour in the distance. This area was used for eating, writing, and sitting in the sun to read and write. The wind was howling. She'd always known the day would arrive when Jesse would discover the truth and Louisa would have to explain everything. She'd imagined it would be earth-shattering, a ticking bomb finally exploding. But she felt strangely calm. Once Jesse was over the shock and saw Steve for the dirtbag he truly was, she'd come through the experience stronger.

Louisa wondered if Steve was still doing cocaine. Back in the day, he'd snorted any drugs he could get hold of. He'd been a huge coke head. Soon after Jesse had started going out with him, Steve had offered her some. Jesse had been horrified. She'd only ever tried grass before – once – and hated it.

'I felt so out of control. Yuck. Do you think Steve might have an addiction?' she'd asked Louisa.

It had been the perfect opportunity for Louisa to warn Jesse, or at least plant a seed of doubt in her mind. But she hadn't wanted to rock the boat, and certainly hadn't wanted to incriminate herself. So, she'd said nothing. Jesse wouldn't have believed her anyway. Love is blind and all that. Besides, it was none of Louisa's business, and if Jesse wasn't being hurt, it was okay.

The trouble was, Jesse *was* being hurt. She just hadn't realised it, not really. Louisa knew lots of people who took drugs. They still had good jobs, led active lives. In hindsight, that decision was a cop-out. Another one of Louisa's fuck-ups she could have handled so much better.

CHAPTER TWENTY-NINE

Louisa's life was in San Francisco now. She shared her apartment only with Ziggy, her feline. Philippe, her boyfriend was a regular visitor. She'd only introduced him to a handful of her friends, and those who had met him had instantly teased her for being a 'cradle snatcher'.

'So it's just sex, is it?' one of them had asked.

'No ... and yes,' Louisa had replied.

Philippe made her happy. He massaged her toes, and she liked the feel of his young, unwrinkled skin against hers. He didn't have any of the bitterness that came with age and experience. He was free, unburdened. Louisa didn't question why he was with her. He was and that was all that mattered.

She wanted him the first time she saw him: when he walked into her Wednesday afternoon tutorial group five months earlier, at the start of the semester. He was late. Late and laughing, acting like everyone else in the room had just missed out on hearing the funniest joke. She kept her eye on him. It helped that he had a toned, muscular surfer's physique (those arms!), sun-bleached blond hair and a cheeky broad smile. He was late to other classes too but was always beaming and full of energy. How did people get to be that sparky? Louisa blamed his youth. Occasionally, he'd disrupted the class with his antics, but she never cautioned him because he was a good student, and his assignments were always handed in on time.

In October last year, however, he handed in a truly drab piece of research. There was nothing to it; it was transparent and juvenile. Louisa had failed him. To his credit, he'd come to see her in her office that same afternoon.

'Philippe,' she'd said, 'you can do better than this.'

He'd grinned at her. 'Really? Can you teach me? I don't have any experience, but I'm a quick study. If you want me, I'm available.'

Louisa didn't need to be asked twice. She'd locked the door and banged him on her desk right then and there. She'd never done it on a desk before. It was exhilarating. They'd been so frenzied, there was little time for foreplay. He'd whipped out his erect cock, Louisa gasping at the sheer thrill and decadence of it, and that was that!

Eventually, they'd moved from the desk to the carpet, and again the sex had been hurried, hungry.

Despite knowing she was risking her professional reputation, not to mention making a complete fool of herself with a student, Louisa had invited him back to her place.

'I can be there in thirty minutes,' he'd said, tucking himself in and zipping up his jeans.

'Better make it an hour,' she'd replied, doing her best to sound casual.

Fifty-seven minutes later when she buzzed him in, just on dusk, they'd barely made it to her bed, kissing, pulling and tugging at each other's clothes as if they might never see each other again – which was the way Louisa usually played her sex life.

When Philippe ripped off his T-shirt, she'd marvelled at his muscled chest. She'd had her hands all over it earlier, but now it was as if she was seeing him properly for the first time. She slid her fingers inside his jeans in search of ... ah! Her gaze dipped, taking in his tight, tanned body, his obvious arousal.

He pulled her close, slipping her black jersey dress easily off her shoulders. He released her bra and started gently exploring her nipples with his tongue, before moving down to lick her stomach playfully. 'You're perfect,' he murmured, before moving lower and finding her inner thighs ... He'd kissed and teased her, his tongue hot and nimble, bringing her to the edge of orgasm.

Dizzy with a desire she hadn't experienced in a long time, Louisa felt hot spasms coursing through her body. She groaned as his hands wrapped around her butt, pulling her closer.

He lifted his head. 'I think you're ready for me now.'

Louisa had let out a strangled 'yes' as he snaked his way up her body and kissed her with passionate force. She wrapped her legs around his waist as he thrust into her, loving the feel of him, all of him, deep inside her. She felt desirable, fuckable. Philippe was going to prove to be a distraction at work, no doubt about it.

And he was! He was all she could think about those first couple of months – his skin, his lips, his eyes, his touch. She practically orgasmed looking at him. He was extraordinary. Still, there was no way she was going to fall for him.

Several years before, when Louisa had first started working at the university, she'd fallen in love with an older colleague, an English professor, who'd wooed her with all the best lines from the Romantic poets. They had a brilliant two-year affair, right up until his announcement that his tenure was coming to an end, and he was moving back to New York City and his wife. Devastated, Louisa vowed never to fall in love again.

CHAPTER THIRTY

A couple of nights earlier over dinner at Fisherman's Wharf, Philippe had suggested he and Louisa move in together. She almost choked on her clam chowder.

'You know I love living on my own,' she'd told him.

She also liked it that Philippe came over for dinner and sex, then went back to his own apartment afterwards, leaving Louisa in her queen-sized bed to sleep uninterrupted. He'd known the deal when they got together. Yes, she adored Philippe, and there were times when she could almost feel their relationship evolving to the next level, but she always stopped herself. She couldn't go there again. The gut-wrenching anguish, devastation and betrayal she'd felt after the professor left was never far from her mind. The self-harm – Louisa didn't cut her skin, but she deliberately wounded herself by texting and calling him. She'd even flown to New York once. Stalking? If it wasn't, it was damn close.

Philippe had told Louisa many times how much he loved her. So far, she'd refrained from offering the same response. She hadn't told him not to fall in love with her – that would have been presumptuous, but she had said she was with him for a

166

good time, not necessarily a long time. Poor Philippe. He'd looked like a puppy rejected by his mother.

Having devoured a huge crab claw, Philippe wiped his hands on his bib. 'Don't you even want to talk about it?'

'I'm here with you now, aren't I?'

'But for how long?'

'As long as it's fun.' How more honest could she be?

'Don't you want more?'

'Like what?'

'Like knowing your partner is going to be there for you twenty-four seven. Someone who loves you unconditionally and forever?'

'I have my cat for that.'

Philippe shoved his plate away and swigged his beer. 'I'm serious.'

'So am I.'

As far as Louisa was concerned, these conversations were becoming tedious. They came up every couple of months. Philippe knew where she stood on this. It annoyed her that he was harping on about it again.

'Louisa, are you telling me that our relationship is going nowhere?'

'I don't know what you mean.'

'If you're never going to consider a future with me, then maybe we should call it quits before I get in too deep.'

'Stop. We're having fun. Don't spoil it.'

'You might be having fun, but I'm miserable. I want more.' He pushed back in his seat. 'Why does commitment frighten you so much?'

'It doesn't.'

'Bullshit it doesn't.'

Louisa noticed a couple of diners looking towards them. 'Keep your voice down.'

He ignored her. 'You're all about going with the flow until the flow stops suiting you. Don't you want to get married? Have kids?'

Louisa fumed, mortified. 'Calm down.' This was becoming a spectacle. Heads were turning and Louisa didn't like being the centre of attention, not anymore. She liked being discreet, in control, and squabbling like this, especially in public, was not how she wanted to spend her Saturday evening.

'Look at me, Louisa. I want everyone to know we're together.'

'You're my student.'

'I may be your student, but I'm also twenty-five.'

'Good for you. I'm pushing thirty-seven.'

'I don't care.'

'I do.'

'I want to be with you, Louisa, but if that's not what you want, so be it.' He stood and threw twenty dollars on the table.

People actively gawked as she picked up the notes and handed them back to him. 'I'll pay.'

He brushed her hand aside. 'Keep it.' And he walked away.

Perhaps he expected her to follow, but she hadn't. What would she have said if she'd caught up? *Yes, I love you, darling, can't live without you. Let's move in together right now!* She simply couldn't tell him what he wanted to hear.

Instead, Louisa swallowed, composed herself, and took in the stunning views of the Golden Gate Bridge. She breathed in the garlic aroma wafting through the dining room while she calmly finished her wine and scrolled through Twitter.

Louisa left twenty minutes later. She probably wouldn't frequent that restaurant again.

Give him a couple of days to calm down and he'd see that she was right. It couldn't be a more ideal situation for him: he had his freedom, Louisa didn't question what he did or where he went when he wasn't with her. Yes, she trusted him, but there was also a part of her that didn't particularly care what he did when he wasn't with her. That was his business. He had his friends and his family, and she preferred not getting drawn into that side of his life. Because once families got involved, they could trap you ... and getting trapped was not on her agenda.

Despite that, she'd met his family once, a few weeks earlier at Christmas.

'You can't spend Christmas Day alone,' he'd said.

'I'm perfectly happy on my own.'

'Come on. I left you alone at Thanksgiving, but my parents will never forgive me if I don't take you home on Christmas Day.'

'Philippe, I really don't want to. Look, maybe I'll come for dessert...'

'That's not going to work. Are you afraid?'

'Hardly!'

'Then what is it? Why don't you want to meet my family?'

'I do. It's just that Christmas is stressful enough without you introducing your parents to your much-older friend.'

'Is that what this is about? Your age?'

'No—'

'Good. Edna's met you. She adores you.'

Edna was Philippe's dog, and 'adore' might have been stretching the truth somewhat, but eventually, Louisa had given in. She had to eat, and at least when she spoke to her parents, they'd seemed pleased she wasn't spending Christmas alone.

Normally, she didn't tell her parents who she was seeing. Since the professor, her affairs never seemed to last more than a couple of months. But Philippe was hanging in there. As soon as she'd mentioned his name, her mother had wanted to know all about him.

'Where's he from?'

'He's American, Mum.'

'American? With a name like Philippe? Surely not!'

'Surely so!' Her mother could be so irritating.

'Work, Louisa? What does this gentleman do for a crust?'

'Student.'

'A student? At his age!'

Louisa didn't tell her mother that Philippe was significantly younger than her. She'd never hear the end of it.

'So anyway, I'm having Christmas with him and his family.'

'But not your own family?'

'Not this year, no.'

Louisa had wrapped up the conversation after that.

On his fur-covered soft chair, Ziggy yawned, stretched, and went back to sleep. That was one of the things she loved about him: he was always there, practically on top of her, but he still managed to remain aloof, his disinterest in her human affairs bordering on disdain. Louisa looked at the hefty box of assignments on the floor next to Ziggy's chair. She was tempted to forget about grading them and rewatch *Only Murders in the Building* instead.

Exhaling, she gazed round her compact living room, an explosion of bright orange walls with yellow skirting boards, architraves and cornices. Philippe had called it 'interesting and unexpected' when he'd first visited. She sat in her favourite red checked armchair, reached for the top assignment and started reading, but her concentration quickly waned.

Having mulled over Jesse's situation, the solution was clear: take the kids and leave the bastard. Now that Jesse knew the truth, would she?

Louisa sipped her wine and glanced at the sideboard and a photo of Emily and Oliver that Jesse had sent her for Christmas. Louisa didn't usually go in for sentimental mementoes, but the photo was sweet. Emily had handmade the red and green frame and sprinkled glitter on the border.

Staring out into the street, Louisa noticed that the sky had darkened; the forecast had warned of a wild storm. So far, only a couple of fat drops of rain had hit the windows. In the distance, she could hear the clackety-clack of the cable cars groaning up the hill. This was her home – small, cosy, happy and bright. She loved it. Loved the peace, the quiet, the total joy she felt at being in her own space. She loved her little herb pots on the kitchen and bathroom windowsills, loved the sunlight streaming through the skylight in her bedroom, the quirky Mexican tiles in her tiny bathroom. Why would she want to live anywhere else? She nudged Ziggy and stroked him under his chin.

She checked her phone for messages. Still no word from Philippe.

As much as she didn't want to admit it, Louisa missed him. A lot. And it wasn't just the sex. She missed his laugh, his warmth, the way his top lip curled when he smiled. Where was he and what was he doing? An image of his naked body popped into her mind. Just the thought of him grinding against her, skin to skin, was enough to get her burning with desire.

She shook off the feeling and checked her university schedule. She would head out to Australia and see her family, for sure. But she couldn't possibly go until the spring break, after Easter. For one thing, she couldn't let her students down, and for another? In three or four months, the dust would have settled, Jesse would have moved on, Dot and Bernard would be used to the idea that Jesse and Steve were finished ... Yes, by then life would be a lot calmer. In fact, she might not need to go back to Sydney at all. They'd all be so busy...

CHAPTER THIRTY-ONE

JESSE

When Jesse came to, her mum was shouting her name and knocking on the front door. She got to it just as Dot was letting herself in with the spare key.

After Dot had phoned Louisa, she fussed about the kitchen making tea, while Jesse sat at the bench. Her mum reminded Jesse of a sparrow – short, petite and darting about the kitchen at a hundred miles an hour.

Jesse touched two fingers to her temple as panic rose in her throat.

'Are you sure you don't need to lie down?' Dot said, eyeing her suspiciously.

Jesse shook her head. She felt queasy and could barely keep her eyes open, but she wanted to stay upright while her mother was there.

'All right, but Jesse,' Dot said, handing her a cup, 'I know what's been going on.'

Not her mother too. Jesse felt her chest tighten as she tried to suck in air. *Please don't tell me that Mum knows about Steve!* It wasn't right. She was so wound up, she'd gone beyond feeling embarrassed. All she could think of were the horrors that lay ahead: explaining to her children why Mummy and Daddy weren't living together, the divorce, coping as a single parent, Steve and his ... games.

'Don't look so surprised,' Dot continued.

'I ... I don't know where to start,' Jess stammered before bursting into tears. She could feel herself sinking into the stool, wanting to close her eyes and to forget about everything ... the conversation with Louisa, the last few days. To go back to a time when her world was still intact. Far from perfect but at least manageable.

'What made you think we wouldn't find out?' Dot asked.

Jesse shook her head. 'I really hoped it wouldn't become public knowledge.'

Dot raised her eyebrows. 'Hence the name, I suppose.'

'Pardon?'

'The name – the Secret Women's Business Workshop. I know all about it, Jesse.' Dot pulled a pamphlet from her bag and read aloud: *'Don't leave it until you wake up one morning and realise you've lived your whole life for everyone else and you no longer know who you are or what makes you happy.'*

Jesse jumped down from the stool. 'Where did you get that?'

'I found it.'

'In my handbag!'

And less than half an hour ago, Jesse thought, remembering the extra brochure she'd picked up at the meeting the other day.

Dot waved her hand dismissively. 'What is this? A cult?'

Jesse shook her head. 'Mum, really.'

'Wake up to yourself, Jesse. You have enough responsibilities. Secret women's business indeed.'

Jesse wasn't up for this conversation, but it was a hell of a lot better than talking about Steve's indiscretions. Her mother had been prying. Jesse wondered what else she'd found.

'The group sounds interesting,' Jesse said evenly.

'Interesting or not, you have enough going on in your life without adding this to the mix. Perhaps you should come to church with me? Bring the children.'

'Mum, you can't go snooping around in my belongings. It's none of your concern if I want to go to a meeting and–'

'And what?'

'Better myself.'

'Jesse, love. Look at you. You don't need more stress.'

It took Jesse a moment to figure out what Dot was talking about. She was standing by a light switch, flipping it on and off, while tapping her right foot on the floorboards. 'Mum, you don't need to be privy to every waking moment of my life–'

'Jesse, your mother's only trying to help. Aren't you, Dot?'

Jesse gasped. Steve was standing barely two metres away, watching her.

'I called him on my way over,' Dot explained, glancing at her watch. 'A good thirty minutes ago.'

'There was no need,' Jesse said.

Dot raised her eyebrows. 'No need? I had no idea what I might find when I arrived. I was scared, Jesse.'

Steve had a fake smile plastered across his face. He kissed Jesse on the cheek. 'You okay now?'

She nodded and turned away from him. Had he asked her that a few days ago, she wouldn't have doubted his sincerity. But now? She wasn't buying it at all.

'I'll leave you to deal with her, Steve.' Dot picked up her handbag. 'Maybe you can talk some sense into her.'

'I'll do my best,' he replied, smiling broadly.

Jesse wanted to vomit. 'Mum, you don't have to leave. Stay and have another cup of tea.'

Dot shook her head. 'Your husband's home now, darling. He'll look after you.'

Steve beamed. 'I always do.'

Jesse took her mother's arm as they walked to the front door, more because she was shaking than for any other reason.

'Settle down,' Dot said sternly. 'Put this nonsense about secret women's business out of your head. Focus on your family. You don't need any more stress or distracting influences.'

'Mum!'

'Come to church with me, or do some yoga, but for goodness' sake, get your act together. Steve will take care of you, but Jesse, you have to be reasonable.' With that, she waltzed out the front door and left Jesse alone with a monster.

'Smart woman.' Steve was standing beside her. 'Drives me crazy with her inane chatter, but she's all right. Knows when to leave.'

Jesse couldn't move or think. As long as the kids were with her, she could cope, but when it was just the two of them she wasn't sure what Steve might be capable of doing.

'We need to talk this through,' he said calmly, as if reading her mind.

She shrugged him off as he tried to put his arm around her.

'Jesse, you're not well. You need to see someone.'

'I'm perfectly fine. You're trying to pin your issues on me and make it my responsibility.'

'Sweetheart,' he said, moving towards her again. 'I don't have issues. You, on the other hand–'

'Stop it. Don't touch me. You're trying to make out that I'm crazy.'

Steve smiled. 'Why would I do that? You've had a bad fall. You need to see a doctor. At the very least, you need bed rest. Come on, I'll help you upstairs.'

'I don't want a bloody rest.' Jesse's head was spinning. Her stomach churned. She felt as if she was about to vomit, as she had earlier in the day. But there was no way she was admitting that to him. 'I spoke to Louisa.'

'Really?'

'She said she knew you years ago.'

'As if she'd remember!'

Jesse ignored him. 'So you were into this before we met?' She was determined to get him to admit it. 'I'm relieved it wasn't something I did, that I neglected you somehow, so you sought comfort elsewhere. You've always had an addiction. You were always into those games.'

Steve took a pace back. 'What if I was? What business is it of yours?'

First step.

'It *is* my business,' Jesse said calmly, 'because I'm your wife, your so-called life partner, and I deserve better.'

She wanted him to admit the truth. Her twitch was going wild, and it was his fault. She'd never tapped her foot or flicked light switches before she met Steve. She hadn't needed to triple-check that the iron or oven was switched off. She'd been happy, confident.

'And I deserve to be with someone who's not a nutter,' Steve said, pulling her back into their horrid conversation. 'Someone who doesn't switch lights on and off and retrace her steps over and over. That's what I deserve.'

Jesse hated him. How had she ever found him charming and handsome? He was a bully. Bile rose in her throat. She grabbed her car keys from a side table. 'I'm picking up the kids.'

'Come on,' he said, his voice even. 'Let's discuss this rationally, before it gets out of hand. I've made some possible errors in judgement–'

'You've done way more than that, Steve.'
'Hang on! We've both contributed to this–'
Jesse shook her head and pushed past him. 'I'm leaving.'
He crossed his arms. 'You'll regret it.'

CHAPTER THIRTY-TWO

Jesse was an hour early to pick up Ollie and Emmy, so she drove to a nearby café and ordered a skinny latte. She was all alone. There was no one she could ring who wouldn't judge her. Except maybe Stella. She'd support her. She always supported her, but was there anyone else who'd look out for her? Anyone else who had Jesse's best interests at heart?

She'd never been good at making friends. At best she had acquaintances. There was nothing wrong with that if she only wanted to talk about teachers, the netball roster and the tuckshop menu, but right now, Jesse needed more. That was one of the reasons she was so interested in the Secret Women's Business meetings. She was hoping to meet like-minded people – at a distance. She shook her head, remembering that her mother had taken a brochure when she left.

Jesse had always struggled to let people get close to her. When she married Steve, she'd let the few friendships she'd had slide, except for Louisa, of course. But when Louisa left, Jesse had felt let down, betrayed. Louisa was the person Jesse always turned to, so when she moved overseas, Jesse had had no one. Her best friend had suddenly disappeared.

Louisa's departure had affected her deeply, but Steve had been dismissive. 'She's gone. Deal with it.'

Now Jesse knew why. He'd had an ulterior motive for wanting Louisa to leave and never return.

After losing Louisa, Jesse had vowed she'd never allow herself to feel that vulnerable again. She had Steve and her children, whom she loved and trusted, so she began closing herself off from others, building a wall that stretched higher and higher as time went by. Now, apart from Stella, and occasionally Carly, Jesse rarely confided in anyone.

Even when she saw Stella and Carly, like the other night, she felt like she was somehow missing out. On what, she didn't know. A great joke, a funny exchange, life in general. Jesse couldn't pinpoint it, but it felt like she was being left behind.

And now, faced with the unspeakable revelations about Steve, her marriage was doomed. How could she ever trust him again?

She shook her head. The truth was, except for when she was with Oliver and Emily, Jesse felt heavy with loneliness and now, regret.

She lost count of how many times she'd stirred her coffee, but when she swallowed some, it was barely warm. Why couldn't she have had a simple life, one in which both she and her husband were normal? Happily in love and bringing up two adorable children? They'd got the adorable children right, just fucked up every other detail. Why did everything have to turn to mud?

The thought of spending another night in the same bed as Steve was abhorrent. She couldn't do it. But she also didn't want to run away and give him the satisfaction of knowing he'd triumphed. She'd rather walk barefoot over red-hot coals than admit defeat. Steve hadn't won, not by a long shot.

Tomorrow she'd be at the library. She could make it until then. Just. For now, she needed to play it smart.

CHAPTER THIRTY-THREE

CARLY

First thing Wednesday morning, Carly rang Jesse to apologise. She knew she'd behaved badly the previous night, all that stuff she'd blurted out. It didn't matter that it was true, what mattered was her delivery. Appalling. She needed to talk to Jesse, to square things off. But all she got was Jesse's voicemail. Maybe she was screening her calls.

Carly phoned Stella. 'Okay, so I'm an idiot and a shocking friend. I'm sorry. I've already left a message on Jesse's phone.'

'You said what you needed to,' Stella replied, not unkindly.

'I could have said it better.'

'Agreed, but listen, Jesse rang me. She knows we're telling the truth.'

The news took Carly by surprise. 'How was she?'

'Calm. Too calm.'

'What should I do?'

'You've left an apology. That'll do for now. I'll call you when I know more.'

Carly hung up, dizzy with remorse. She rolled her neck several times to ease the tension, but the action caused her stomach to churn. Poor Jesse. The phone rang again, almost instantly. Brett. Carly hadn't really spoken to him since the sex-talk fiasco the previous afternoon.

'Steve rang me,' he said. 'He kept going on about you and Stella interfering in his life. What does he mean?'

Carly gave him the first excuse she could think of. 'He's just annoyed because Stella and I told Jesse to stand up for herself.'

'Carly, Steve's furious. You don't want to aggravate him. Sometimes you women—'

'We women what?'

'You get carried away with other people's lives. Try not to get caught up in suburban gossip.'

'Really? You think encouraging Jesse to stick up for herself is gossip?'

'Whatever. Just don't take it on as a personal crusade. If Steve's in the wrong—'

'What do you mean, if?'

'I just mean, don't get involved. Let Steve and Jesse sort out their own domestics. It'd be in your best interests to give them some time alone.'

'But—'

'I don't have time to deal with this right now. I'm trying to run a company and keep you happy. I'd appreciate you pulling your head in.'

Carly wanted to argue, but Brett had a point. The last week had been an ongoing nightmare, and Brett didn't even know half of it. The previous night's behaviour at Stella's, the carry-on at the pub ... Carly was beginning to wonder whether she might be in the grip of a mid-life crisis.

'If you and Stella keep interfering, Jesse's situation, whatever that may be, is only going to get worse,' Brett said. 'And, Carly, I really don't need my wife's friends' husbands ringing me at work.'

'Okay, okay. Point taken.'

'Thanks. Steve sounded...' He stopped.

'Steve sounded what?'

'To tell you the truth, he sounded a little unhinged. Not normal.'

'Oh.'

'Carly?'

'Yeah?'

'Never mind. Have a good day, okay?'

She mumbled 'Yeah' again and hung up. So even Brett thought Steve sounded crazy. She took it as a good sign that Brett had called, it showed he cared about her safety.

All too quickly, she remembered her outrageous flirting with Toby and felt guilty. How could she do that to her husband? There was no way she could tell Brett why Steve was so furious with her. Brett would be horrified.

Carly watched as the clock ticked past midday. She couldn't wait any longer for Jesse to phone back. She called her again.

Jesse's mum, Dot, answered. 'Jesse's not well. She's resting.'

'Is there anything I can do to help?'

'No, thanks,' she replied, short and clipped. 'I'm here. Jesse will call you when she's feeling better.'

And that was the end of that! Dot was one very tough nut. She hung up and Carly was left worrying about why Jesse had taken ill. Maybe it was the business with Steve – her nerves had gotten the better of her.

There was nothing more she could do about Jesse now. Carly wandered over to the computer to check her emails. She was feeling rather poorly herself as she wondered if there was anything further about Nicholas and whatever debauchery and carry-on he was involved in on the other side of the world. She gulped as she saw another message from Nicholas's sports master.

Apologies if my previous email alarmed you.

It appears that some locker room high jinks got out of hand and one of the younger students complained. I understand the Australian reputation for exuberance, but when it comes to flicking wet towels on to naked boys' backsides (Carly winced at the words 'naked boys' backsides' and had to force herself to continue reading), *action needs to be taken. Nicholas is not the only one involved, and all have been suspended pending an inquiry. As sports master, I need to take all complaints seriously. Rest assured, this matter will be thoroughly investigated. However, I do anticipate a speedy and satisfactory resolution. I will keep you informed.*

She re-read the email several times. Nicholas had been cavorting with naked boys in the showers. It did her head in thinking about it. There was no way around it: she had to tell Brett. Imagine if he kept something like that from her? She'd kill him. But first, she decided to ring Nick and get his side of the story. She felt bilious with dread. She'd failed her son. She should have been more aware, more involved.

She took a few moments to compose herself before dialling Nicholas's number. Part of her hoped his mobile was switched off, but he answered after two rings.

'Hi, Mum. I was expecting your call.'

'So it's true,' Carly said, trying to keep her voice even.

'Which part?'

'The part about you being suspended for flicking towels in the locker room?'

'Yeah. Dumb, hey?'

'Nicholas, how could you?'

'It was a game. No big deal. But one kid went ballistic, overreacted and dobbed.'

'Do you need me to come over?'

'What? To Cornwall? Now *you're* overreacting ... It was a towel. A bunch of guys in a locker room rumble. What's the big deal?'

Carly dug her fingernails into her palms. The big deal was that he'd been harassed by his coach the previous year, or maybe even had an affair with him; the big deal was that he'd been suspended for coercing other boys into inappropriate behaviour. The big deal was ... Carly really needed a glass of wine. She checked herself. The last thing Carly needed was alcohol.

'Mum, are you okay?'

'Nicky, I'm just...' Her stomach cramped. 'You're so far away and I feel useless. I want to help you.'

'I can look after myself.'

'Is there anything else you want to tell me? I'm here for you. I'd totally understand–'

'What? No! Stop talking.'

'But, Nick–'

'Seriously, Mum. It's cool.'

He hung up and Carly felt even worse if that was possible. Nick was her son. Her mind returned to Mr Busby and those letters. Carly didn't care if Nick was gay. She did care if others were harassing him, or he was harassing others.

She got on with the housework and then some gardening, but she couldn't focus. Even though her head was pounding, every time she opened the fridge and caught sight of the Chardonnay bottle, she wanted to pour herself a glass. Guilt gnawed away at her. She had to speak to Jesse, to let her know how sorry she was.

As she dialled Jesse's number, she desperately wanted this day to be over, to get all this nasty stuff out of the way. Perhaps she could use a little help from Ms Cloudy Bay Chardonnay, then tomorrow would be a new and glorious beginning. A new, clean-living, happy Carly. But today? Well, today, she had a list of distressing activities to get through and Jesse was slap-bang at the top. Giving into temptation, Carly opened the fridge door, pulled out the wine and poured herself a glass.

'Jesse,' Carly said, relieved when her friend answered. 'It's Carly.' She reached for her wine glass and gulped. This was going to be an excruciating call, she could tell. 'I'm ringing to apologise for last night. I had no right–'

Jesse stopped her. 'Carly, I understand. You didn't want to be the bad guy, but you were.'

Carly didn't know how to respond.

'Steve's here now,' Jesse whispered. 'I can't talk.'

'But, Jesse, I'm so sorry. And your mum said you were sick. Are you okay?'

'Fine, thanks.' She sounded weird. Preoccupied. 'Anyway, Steve and I are sorting everything out.'

Really? Carly didn't buy it. Jesse sounded anxious. She heard shuffling in the background. 'Is there anything I can do?'

'You've already done more than enough.' It was Steve.

'Jesse?' Carly said. But the line went dead.

Carly skulled the rest of the wine and poured another glass. Her hands trembled. Should she ring back? Call Brett? She thought for a moment, then phoned Stella.

'What do you mean he eavesdropped on your conversation?' Stella asked after Carly had explained the situation.

'Exactly that, and then he said, "You've already done more than enough," and hung up.'

'And Jesse didn't say anything?'

'Not after that, no. I'm worried.'

'I'm sorry, Carly, but I'm going to have to go. Liz is eyeballing me–' Stella hung up.

Carly rinsed her empty glass. Nothing good could come from a third glass of wine. She already felt numb. Instead, she took two Nurofen Plus and went upstairs to bed. She doubted she'd fall asleep, but she needed to lie down and pull herself together. She was crawling under the sheets when her mobile rang. Now what?

'Instead of being so eager to gossip about my family, why don't you take a good long look in your own backyard.' Steve's voice was unmistakable.

'Pardon?'

'You heard me. I'm sure you've got a few family secrets you'd prefer remain secret.'

'Steve, I never meant–'

'I know what you mean, Carly, and all I'm saying is that before you go poking your nose in my business, perhaps you should look more closely at your own family.'

'I have nothing to say to you. I think you need help.'

Steve laughed. 'I need help! That's rich coming from you. Why don't you ask your husband what he gets up to when he's away on business – on those nights when you're stumbling into bed alone after a few too many chardies?'

'What are you implying?' Carly said, her voice breaking slightly.

'I'm simply saying,' Steve said calmly, 'that before you go gossiping about other people, you should make sure no one is gossiping about you. By the way, I can recommend the Oyster Bay Riesling this week. It's on special for a hundred and seventy bucks a dozen, and since you buy your liquor by the crate, you'll save a bundle. Or rather, Brett will.' Steve clicked off.

Carly felt an uncomfortable jolt of anxiety and guilt. Her breathing quickened and her hands trembled. Did she really drink that much? Had it become common knowledge?

As for Brett ... what did Steve mean? Yes, Brett travelled a lot and worked long hours – what banker didn't? There was no way she was going to let Steve make her paranoid about her marriage. This was about him and his wrongdoings, his debauched lifestyle, not about Carly and her husband. Fuck Steve!

On autopilot, she walked down to the kitchen, opened the fridge, pulled out the half-empty bottle and poured herself another glass. She deserved it after what she'd just been through. Her mind raced, darting in all directions. She needed the drink to calm her nerves.

Was Steve implying that Brett was having an affair? The thought had crossed Carly's mind, many times. But so far, it had been pure speculation. Did Steve have proof? Brett was still attractive, he had a great sense of humour, he was intelligent. He got on well with Stella and Jesse, and whenever Carly had seen him with his work colleagues, he'd seemed to get along well with them, especially the women.

Carly continued gulping wine as her mind went into overdrive. The trips away, the late-night phone calls and texts ... It all made perfect sense. And if Steve knew for sure that Brett was having an affair, that would explain why Brett had phoned her in such a flap that morning. He didn't want Steve revealing his secret to Carly.

She tried to compose herself. Perhaps if she sent Brett a text? Fumbling with her phone, she managed to type out *Spoke to Steve. Madman! Making all kinds of accusations about you. LOL! C xx*, before climbing into bed and passing out.

CHAPTER THIRTY-FOUR

Moments later, or what felt like moments later, Brett was above her, shaking her awake.

'What's going on? What do you mean Steve's been making accusations? I told you not to talk to him.'

Carly took some time to figure out what he was talking about. 'Brett?' Her mouth felt dry, and she had a throbbing headache. 'I don't–'

'Are you drunk?'

'No. I–'

Brett sat down on the side of the bed and Carly struggled to sit up and face him. 'What the hell is going on around here?'

'Shhh. Keep your voice down,' Carly pleaded. 'Steve rang me. He's a lunatic, he was raving on about all sorts of things.'

'Like?'

'Like, I don't know. Telling me to look in my own backyard before snooping around in his. Does he know you're having an affair? Is that what he meant?'

'Carly, I've no idea what you're talking about. Apart from Steve's call this morning, I haven't spoken to him since our Christmas get-together.'

'And the affair?'

'I'm not having one. Never have. What's going on?'

'He's threatening me because of what Stella and I know about him.'

'And what is that, exactly?'

Carly hesitated. Her head was swirling. She felt heavy, almost nauseous. Then she started crying. Not huge, racking sobs, but a continuous stream of tears running down her cheeks.

'Carly? What's up? Tell me.'

She shook her head. 'Nothing.'

'You don't normally cry over nothing.'

She looked at him. 'Is that right, Brett? Can you honestly say you know what I cry about?'

'I know you cry when you've had too much to drink.'

She waved him away with her hand.

'I know you cry over Nicholas, old movies, kittens in pet shops–'

'Stop it. You don't know anything.' She should have stopped there. 'You don't know that Stella and I saw Steve at a sex party.'

'A what?' That had shocked him. 'When?'

'Last Thursday. You also don't know that I sat on a guy's lap and told him I wanted a fuck buddy–'

'Carly, that's enough. You really are drunk.'

Carly ignored him. 'You don't know the half of it.'

'Why are you telling me this? Why do you do this to yourself? I saw the empty bottle in the kitchen.'

'Because I'm lonely.'

'You don't have to be lonely. I'm here. Will's here. Why don't you come to his basketball games occasionally, or watch TV with us?'

She shook her head. 'Why would you want me to? I'm old.'

'You're not old.'

'I will be soon, and it frightens the hell out of me – the wrinkles, the grey hair. My body ... ugh. I'm ugly.'

'You're only ugly because you've consumed an entire bottle of wine. Stop it. Drink some water, take a couple of headache tablets, and you'll be as good as new in the morning.'

Carly saw Will hovering at their bedroom door, deliberating whether to walk in. He watched for a moment, thought better of it, and disappeared down the hallway.

Carly let out a huge sob. 'What am I going to do with the rest of my life? You have your work, Nick's left and William will be gone in less than two years. Where does that leave me? Alone and old, that's where.'

'Instead of alienating yourself from us, why don't you join in? It doesn't have to be all doom and gloom.'

He disappeared into the bathroom and returned with a huge tumbler of water. 'Drink this.'

She propped herself up further against the bedhead and did as she was told.

'Feeling better?'

She nodded.

'Okay, start at the beginning. Last Thursday night, you, Stella and Jesse went to the pub where you cracked on to a group of guys–'

'I didn't crack on–'

'No? You told a stranger you were looking for a fuck buddy. Am I right?'

'Maybe.' Carly started tearing up again. 'I didn't mean it. I was being stupid.'

Brett rolled his eyes. 'Understatement. Then what? You went to a party where you saw Steve...?'

'It wasn't just any party; it was one of those swingers things, a sex party–'

'Go on.'

'We were standing there, totally gobsmacked, when we saw Steve–'

'Where was Jesse?'

'She'd left the pub ages before. Meanwhile, Steve was sucking on a dummy, wearing a nappy and being dragged about by a dominatrix.'

Brett shook his head. 'Excuse me?'

'He was wearing a black studded dog collar.'

'Sounds unreal.'

'It was. We tried to leave, but he saw us. Since then, he's been bombarding Stella and me with text messages and emails, saying that if we tell Jesse–'

'He's been threatening you?' Brett's voice was ice. 'Now it's all starting to make sense. Why didn't you tell me this before?'

'I was ashamed.'

Brett put his arms around her and kissed her forehead. 'Carly' – he shook his head – 'you really know how to get into trouble, don't you?'

She couldn't answer. She was suddenly very tired. 'That's not the worst of it.'

Brett sighed. 'There's more?'

'Last night at Stella's, I told Jesse about Steve.'

'You did? What was her reaction?'

'She ran off, after screaming that Stella and I had always hated Steve and now we were making up stories to cause trouble. I never should have blurted it out, even though I wanted her to know. It was wrong.'

Brett stood. 'I've heard enough for one session. We'll talk more about this in the morning when you're feeling better.' He paused. 'Sweetheart, you really should think about taking a break from the wine for a while.'

'Mmm,' she mumbled.

'Stay in bed and get some rest. I'll sort out dinner for Will. Do you have a busy day tomorrow?'

'Nup.'

'Glad to hear it, because I don't think you'll be up for much. I'll bring you some paracetamol.'

'Don't need them.'

'You might think you don't, but trust me, you do. They'll make you feel better.'

'Nothing could make me feel better.'

'That's what I don't understand,' he said, his tone serious. 'I'm really angry with you, Carly. We've built a life together, and sometimes I think you go out of your way to try to piss it up against a wall.'

'It's not that,' Carly said, finding clarity in her voice. 'It's just that we're so ... comfortable.'

'And that's a bad thing?'

'I thought it was,' she said, flopping back down on the bed. 'We used to be so wild. But now I don't know anymore. Are you sure you're not having an affair? Steve implied–'

'I'm not having an affair, Carls, and by the sound of it, Steve's a master manipulator. He's saying whatever he can to shut you up.' He kissed her again. 'Get some rest.'

———

Carly woke hours later and stared around the pitch blackness of the room until her eyes adjusted. Brett was asleep beside her. On the bedside table sat two headache tablets and a full glass of water. She swallowed the tablets and turned to Brett, nudging him in the side with her finger.

'Brett?' she stage-whispered. 'Are you asleep?'

He rolled towards her. 'Not anymore.'

'Do you ever feel the urge to dress up?'

'Carly!'

'Do you?'

'No. Go to sleep.'

'And group sex doesn't appeal to you?'

'Why?' Brett asked, now fully awake and propped up on his elbow. 'Does it appeal to you? Is this the kind of wild you think you've been missing out on?'

'No, just asking. Brett?'

'Yes?'

'Did I mention the fuck buddy thing to you tonight?'

'Yes, love. I'm afraid you did.'

'I'm going to be in big trouble tomorrow, aren't I?'

'No,' he said, kissing her shoulder. 'I was angry, but now I'm just sad. We have a good life together, Carls. You're not in trouble, but you're going to be nauseous and embarrassed.'

'I want to be a better wife.'

'I know you do, my love,' he said, rubbing her arm. 'But for now, just try being a quiet one.'

CHAPTER THIRTY-FIVE

JESSE

Against a backdrop of a beautifully bright full moon, Jesse held her newborn, marvelling at how perfect she was, how effortlessly her tiny fingers gripped Jesse's forefinger. She watched, mesmerised, as her baby gurgled contentedly. She was in love, so in love, and so happy. Her life was complete.

Suddenly, the baby was ripped from her arms. Steve was beside her, berating her for having another child. He was adamant. 'I told you, no more kids.'

'But having this baby will be good for us,' Jesse pleaded. 'She's the answer to our problems.'

'And what problems would they be, Jesse?'

'These days we hardly see each other. Our new baby–'

'You can't handle another child. You can barely manage the two we've got. It's out of the question. End of discussion.'

'But she's here. Maybe you'll love me again now we have another baby.'

'Get rid of her. You need to look after the twins, especially Ollie.'

'What do you mean?'

'Do I really need to spell it out for you? What happened to the shrink you were seeing?'

'That was years ago.'

'Well, maybe it's time you went back. And take Ollie with you. He's heading down the same path as you.' Steve's lips weren't moving, but Jesse could still hear his voice haranguing her. 'Why would I want another child with you, another lunatic to deal with?'

'Is that really what you think of me? Steve? Steve!'

Jesse woke up. It took her a moment to adjust, to realise she'd been dreaming. Holding the baby in her arms had felt so real, so right. Typical that Steve had come along to ruin it.

She glanced at the clock: 3am. On the other side of the bed, Ollie and Emily slept peacefully. Jesse sighed, rubbed her belly and drifted back to sleep.

'I wish we could sleep in your bed every night, Mummy,' Emily said when she woke on Thursday morning.

Jesse wished so too. She'd been awake for a good fifteen minutes, just staring at them, aware of their warm little bodies breathing contentedly next to her. She felt at peace, loved and strong when she was with them. Despite what she and Steve had become, they had created two perfect children.

'Where's Daddy?' Ollie asked, rubbing his eyes and sitting up.

'At work, darling,' Jesse said, aware that Steve hadn't come home that night.

He wasn't at home when she'd got back the previous afternoon with the children. A short message on the kitchen bench read *don't wait up*. She hadn't.

While the kids got ready for school, Jesse showered and

thought back to her dream. It had felt so real, she'd felt so connected to the baby. As she dried herself, she looked at her naked form in the mirror, her flat stomach. She thought back to her pregnancy with the twins. She'd loved it, right up until the twenty-eighth week, when she'd become so heavy and tired she could barely move. Those babies sure knew how to kick. She remembered the sensation as if it were yesterday.

'You look pretty, Mummy,' Ollie said when she walked into the kitchen.

That was all the encouragement she needed to guarantee a fantastic day. She didn't want to think too much about the future, about tomorrow or the day after that. *Isness is the business.* She needed to live in the now. It was all about keeping her head above water, putting one foot in front of the other and moving forward, no matter how slowly. If she thought about Steve, she started to twitch, so she needed to put him out of her mind, at least while working at the library. After work, she'd have the children to distract her and dinner to prepare.

Maybe they could have another movie night like the previous night when they'd watched *Luca*, eaten popcorn and shouted '*Silenzio, Bruno!*' together.

'What does that mean?' Emily had asked.

'It's what you say to silence the negative voices in your head, the ones telling you, you can't do something.'

'Like riding a bike, but then thinking you're gonna to fall off,' Ollie said. '*Silenzio, Bruno!*'

Jesse laughed. 'Exactly.'

Silenzio, Bruno! she kept repeating over and over ... Anything to keep her thoughts optimistic and her mind off Steve. As long as her outlook remained upbeat, she could get through this nightmare.

CHAPTER THIRTY-SIX

STELLA

My phone rang. I checked the caller ID: Mike.

'You're up bright and early. I haven't even eaten breakfast,' I said, aiming for nonchalance.

'Early shift, taking a break. Thinking of you. Thought I'd call. Too keen?'

I smiled. 'Nah. So what's up?'

'What's up is that I want to see you. Assuming there aren't any emergencies, I finish at noon, then I'm on call. Any chance you could meet up for coffee? Or lunch?'

I hesitated. Yes, I wanted to see him again. But ... I was sure there were buts; I was having trouble remembering them.

'Your silence isn't encouraging, Stella.'

'Sorry. It's just that–'

'You think too much. I'm not asking you to move in with me. I'm offering to buy you a Caesar salad in your lunch break, okay?'

I took a deep breath. I was getting way ahead of myself. 'Okay. Sounds great. Where will I meet you?'

'Diner Doll? Twelve thirty?'

Diner Doll was known for its classic old school neon signs and funky 50s décor. 'Good choice. See you there.'

I hung up, hands clammy, heart pounding. Clearly nervous. Excited as well, but nervous. Another date with Mike! I silently danced a little jig.

I glanced at the time. Arrrgh! Late! I dressed, hurriedly splashed on some make-up and bolted downstairs for breakfast.

'June,' I said, noticing her elaborate turban, 'what have I told you about wrapping your own turbans? Let me help.'

'I can do it. I've been on this earth seventy years – you adapt.' She paused. 'If you don't mind, I'll stay here for the day. Your garden, Barney and Shirley are looking decidedly neglected. They could do with some attention.'

I hugged her. Great! I wouldn't be late for work after all. I nodded at the animals. 'They'd love the company, and yes, the garden could do with some TLC. Please don't overdo it.'

It had started raining. Maybe June wouldn't need to water the garden or take Barney for a walk. Enforced rest! I liked the sound of that.

June regarded Shirley making a meal of Barney's ears. 'At least they have each other. Better hope they die together.'

I shrugged. 'You do look rather regal in your crimson turban and silver sequined blouse.'

'Thank you.' She beamed. 'I can still rise to the occasion of dressing myself and applying make-up. It's just a pity that the chemically laden dishwashing liquid you insist on buying is drying out my good hand and making my nails brittle.'

June! God love her.

'Mum, who are you meeting up with?' Hannah asked. She was staring into the open fridge, clearly hoping some new and previously hidden food delight would magically appear.

I took an imaginary step back. 'Pardon?'

'On the phone before? You were giggling and acting stupid.'

'I wasn't being stupid, Hannah. Anyway, he's just a friend.'

'A he?' June said. 'One of your doctor friends?'

Sharp as a tack! 'Yes, as a matter of a fact. Mike. You met him the other day.' I couldn't prevent myself from grinning like a fool.

June and Hannah's faces dropped.

'Mum! You've only just thrown Daddy out,' Hannah squawked, slamming the fridge door shut.

June nodded. 'Exactly! How are you supposed to win Garth back when you're cavorting with other men?'

'I'm not cavorting, and I didn't throw your father out, Hannah. He left of his own accord.'

'Because you pushed him,' she shrieked.

'Nonsense. What's happening at school today? How's Fiona?'

'Ugh! Don't ask! I'm not speaking to her. She stole my look.'

Harry walked into the kitchen. 'Is this about the feud with Fiona Hewson? Build a friggin' bridge.'

Now it was Harry's turn to stand and stare into the open fridge.

'I didn't realise you had a look,' I said to Hannah, watching as she buttered toast on the kitchen bench, spreading crumbs and butter everywhere.

Her hair hung over one eye, her uniform was a good ten centimetres too short, and her cherry lip gloss looked a lot like red lipstick. Definitely a school no-no. But she wouldn't listen to me. Let the teachers deal with her ... I'd endure her outraged complaints about the shocking unfairness of school rules later. Harry wasn't looking any tidier. His fringe was too long, his pants barely covered his behind, his white shirt wasn't tucked in, his tie was skewiff, and his black shoes were scuffed and unlaced.

Hannah glared at me and flicked her hair. 'The left side

part, sweeping over the right eye and ear? Fiona totally stole it from me.'

'Noob!' Harry shouted. 'Justin Bieber did the mop head years ago. So did Rihanna. You're such a loser.'

And Penelope Cruz before that, I thought, as several other actors' hair styles popped into my mind.

June sipped her tea. 'What is a noob, exactly?'

'You know, Nanna, a noob, a douche,' Harry replied.

Hannah started screaming at him, he screamed in return, and June, ignoring the teenage hysteria, struck up a conversation about laundry items with Barney. I left them to it and stepped into the pouring rain. People always went a little crazy in wet weather ... or was it windy weather? No matter. The people I lived with skated close to the mark pretty much all the time.

On the drive to the library, June's comment about winning Garth back played on my mind. I didn't want him, but was I ready for him to marry someone else? I was stunned that I could be replaced so quickly and with such ease. Wife number one to wife number two in the space of a couple of months. Not that Garth was keen on the marriage idea, but it was only a matter of time. With a cleavage like that, Amanda would wear him down eventually.

Then I thought about Mike and my stomach backflipped. Why was I so resistant to taking things further with him? Despite dinner the other night and agreeing to lunch today, I didn't want to get involved in all that relationship stuff again, at least not so soon. I couldn't imagine introducing Hannah and Harry to my ... what? Friend? Boyfriend? Lover? No, the more I thought about it, the more I realised I wasn't up for anything serious. But still, I couldn't help smiling whenever I thought about Mike, especially when that tingling sensation took over...

As I turned into the library car park, my mind returned to more pressing matters. What was I doing thinking about myself when Jesse's troubles were so much more serious? I'd called her again last night, and she'd seemed calm, but she'd only known about Steve's dalliances for twenty-four hours; surely that wasn't long enough to fully process the information? I doubted she'd formulated an action plan yet. On the one hand, it was a no-brainer that she should leave Steve. On the other, her kids were much younger than mine and still at primary school. They'd be confused, devastated ... And, as I'd already surmised, Steve wouldn't leave quietly.

Jesse had mentioned on several occasions that she intended applying for the full-time librarian position. I needed to warn her about Liz. Now wasn't ideal for Jesse to badger her about more hours. The problem was, I agreed with Liz that Jesse wasn't up to working full-time, at least not right now. Maybe in a few months, when things had settled with Steve, she'd be in a stronger emotional state to take on greater responsibility and longer hours. But today? I honestly didn't think so. Still, I was concerned about having that talk with her, given everything else that was going on in her life.

Liz was hovering by the entrance when I walked into the library.

'I don't think it's going to stop,' I said, shaking my wet umbrella.

She grimaced. 'I'm off to a meeting up the road. I've left a pile of paperwork for you to read through. And could you make up some signs saying the computers will be turned off fifteen minutes before library closing time? Otherwise we'll continue getting idiots like last night who won't get off even as we're turning the lights out and rattling car keys in our hands.'

'Sure. Enjoy. Beware of potholes!'

Liz was off and running to her car in the rain, seemingly stepping into every deep puddle along the way.

CHAPTER THIRTY-SEVEN

JESSE

Even though Jesse had left plenty of time to drop the twins at school and drive to the library, she was late, and she couldn't understand why. Maybe it was the rain. People always drove erratically in the rain. Then there were the roadworks. One lane was blocked, the others were moving torturously slowly, mostly due to branch debris on the streets. Even so, she should have been on time.

She banged her hands on the steering wheel, willing the traffic to move faster. The last thing she needed was for Liz to catch her coming in late. She didn't want to provide her with any more ammunition about her work habits.

As vehicles crawled forward, Jesse got increasingly agitated, so much so that she couldn't keep her foot still on the brake or the accelerator, and the car kangaroo-hopped. It took all her concentration to co-ordinate her feet and get the speed right.

To calm herself, Jesse thought back to the Secret Women's Business meeting and how uplifted she'd felt afterwards. 'I choose to be positive,' she whispered, reminding herself to stay focused on the present, the here and now. *Isness IS the business!*

The previous day, Rebecca from the meeting had left a phone message asking for feedback. When she finally returned the call, Jesse would only have good things to report. She was very much looking forward to the next meeting.

Jesse also liked the fact that no one there knew her or her husband or was likely to hear their humiliating secret. She was anonymous. This was one tiny part of her life that Jesse could quietly nurture alone. Some women chose Pilates or vodka; Jesse chose these meetings. She hoped they'd give her the strength she'd need to hold down a full-time job once she separated from Steve.

Separated. The word rolled around inside her head. She'd be like Stella. Amazing how quickly a person's life could change. Last week, Jesse couldn't have imagined walking in Stella's shoes. This week? Well, they were practically treading the same path. It was reassuring knowing Stella was on her side. Maybe she'd tell Stella about the Secret Women's Business meetings once she'd become comfortable with the women there and could hold her own. Stella might even attend meetings with her. A distinct possibility.

The recent hiccups at the library had been just that – hiccups. The worst had been a couple of weeks earlier when Liz had pulled her off the loans desk because Jesse's nervous habits had resulted in a line of borrowers that extended beyond the periodicals section. Jesse had been truly shocked to discover so many witnesses to her silly behaviour. She needed to check herself and make sure it didn't happen again. She needed to concentrate, to focus on her career as a progressive, caring, efficient librarian. Positive thoughts.

When the timing was right and Liz was in a charitable mood, Jesse would ask her about the full-time position. It wasn't as if she didn't have the qualifications. If Liz gave her a chance, Jesse was confident she could handle the responsibility.

Jesse pulled into the library car park twenty minutes late. She forced herself to breathe deeply several times before she entered the building. She was determined to have a successful day no matter what obstacles she faced.

CHAPTER THIRTY-EIGHT

STELLA

I'd been at the library an hour when Jesse rushed into the staffroom, Gracie covering the 'shop' floor.

'Sorry I'm late. Bad traffic, roadworks, wet weather, the lot.' Jesse locked her handbag in the cupboard. 'Where is she?'

'Relax. At a meeting up the road with the other library heads.'

Jesse nodded and disappeared into the bathroom. When she came out, I handed her a coffee. 'Tell me what's going on.'

She sipped her drink. 'Where to start? But first, tell me what I should be doing.'

'There's printing and filing to be done and a load of shelving. Are you up for it?'

I didn't want to sound patronising, but I also wanted to protect her. If Jesse wasn't up to shelving the books correctly, I'd prefer she didn't do it at all. There were plenty of other tasks that needed attention.

'No problem. Have you spoken to Liz about my idea for a monthly book club?'

I shook my head. I'd forgotten since the other day. 'Not yet.'

'Maybe we could talk to her later today?'

'Sure.' A monthly book club was a great idea, but the staff were already overstretched.

I left Jesse to get on with it while I continued organising Authors' Week, which was less than a month away. Liz had left me phone numbers for a dozen publishers' publicists, but I hadn't made a dent in the list by the time she returned.

'How's it going?' she asked, her eyes veering towards Jesse.

'Great.' But I didn't have any idea. I'd been so busy I hadn't checked on Jesse since she'd begun shelving.

'I've got a pile of reports to fill out by this afternoon,' Liz continued. 'I don't know why I'm surprised. It's the same after every meeting.'

She disappeared into her office. A good sign. She was too busy to pull Jesse aside and ask her twenty questions.

Later, Jesse and I crossed paths in the periodicals section.

'Fill me in,' I whispered.

'Steve didn't come home last night. He knows I'm serious about him leaving.'

'And?'

'And I think it's going to be really hard. I had no idea what he was up to ... I mean, when I force myself to think about it, I can vaguely recall snippets that might have suggested...' She shook her head. 'And then all the stuff with Louisa.'

'Like what?' I kept my voice low and pretended to tidy *House & Garden* magazines.

Jesse shook her head again. 'Louisa knew about Steve. I don't know the full story, but Louisa used to ... she used to be professionally involved in those parties.'

'No way!' I knew Louisa had been a wild child, but this?

'A dominatrix apparently. She knew Steve before I did. I'm so furious, I want to scream.'

I nodded. 'Preferably not here. But,' I said, thinking out loud, 'I've read about Rage Rooms springing up around the city.'

Jesse looked confused.

'It's a place where you go and smash plates, cups, microwaves, to de-stress and take out your pent-up anger. Hence the name.'

'Those places exist?'

'The world is full of angry and stressed people.'

Liz's voice interrupted us. 'Are you two doing any work?' She checked her watch. 'Stella, you can take your lunch break.'

I glanced at one of the wall clocks. It was almost time to meet Mike. I felt uneasy about leaving Jesse with Liz, but the way Liz was glaring at me, I had no choice.

'Fine,' I said, squeezing Jesse's hand. 'We'll talk more later.'

CHAPTER THIRTY-NINE

I was still processing the extraordinary information about Louisa as I walked to Diner Doll. A revelation like that would have knocked Jesse out. Louisa and Steve? I would never have guessed it. Had they ever...? I couldn't even finish the thought. Bizarre. It just went to show what people could hide from family and friends. Perhaps that explained why Louisa had left Sydney.

Mike was already seated at a booth when I arrived. He smiled, stood, and kissed me on the cheek. Part of me was disappointed he didn't go straight for the lips. He smelled like freshly cut grass. Swoon.

I couldn't stop smiling but perhaps that was because I felt like I was on the set of *Grease* about to rock 'n' roll. The interior was full on neon pink, red and blue with photos of old rock stars covering the walls.

'Nice to see you,' he said, stepping back self-consciously and taking his seat again.

I nodded, my cheeks colouring. 'You too. Short shift today?'

'Probably not. I'm on call. No doubt there'll be an emergency. There usually is.'

Mike's job would be demanding, never being able to relax and completely switch off. 'It must be incredible doing the work you do. Saving lives.'

He nodded, raking a hand through his hair. 'I don't always win.'

A roller-skating waitress dressed up as an extra from *Gidget* took our order and we made small talk while we waited for it to arrive: kids, travel and, of course, Steve and Pete.

Mike had a way of looking me directly in the eyes that made me nervous but was also very attractive. I wondered why on earth his wife had ever let him go. I wanted to touch him and wondered if it was just physical attraction or if it went beyond that, perhaps hoping that this might be something deeper.

Deeper? No! What was I thinking? I'd only just ended a marriage to a man I'd loved very much, who happened to be the father of my teenage children. I needed to take a huge step back.

Still, when Mike reached out and took hold of my hand across the table, I didn't pull away. 'What are you thinking?'

I glanced at my watch. 'That I should be getting back to work.'

'How disappointing.'

'No, I meant ... this has been nice.'

He raised his eyebrows. 'Nice in that it was totally boring and awkward, and you can't wait to escape? Or nice in that you wish your lunch break wasn't so short and perhaps if this was dinner...?'

I shifted in my chair. 'The second option, I think.'

'You think?'

'Stop it, Mike.' Heat rushed through me, warming my face. 'You know what I mean.'

'Let's have dinner again to find out what you really mean.' He reached out, pushing the hair back from my cheek.

I couldn't stop smiling on the walk back to the library. Was this really happening? Mike and me? Maybe I was getting ahead of myself, but I couldn't deny the attraction between us. I almost skipped through puddles like Debbie Reynolds in *Singin' in the Rain*.

I was locking my bag away when Jesse appeared looking visibly upset.

'Liz thinks I'm too slow stacking books and cataloguing DVDs.'

'I'm sure it's not that bad. You're meticulous, organised and thorough. The customers love you. I'll talk to Liz–'

'That's not the issue, and you know it,' Liz said behind me.

I wheeled round to face her.

'What is it then?' Jesse asked.

'It's about Stella covering for you when she should be doing her own job.'

'I–' I started, but Liz cut me off.

'Here's the thing, Jesse. I understand you like to have everything in order, and I'm not suggesting that you stack the books by height, colour and width. But you're too slow most of the time and, well, we're not running a charity.'

'I'm not slow all the time.'

'No, you're not,' I agreed.

'But you are when you're tired or having a bad day, like today,' Liz said, gesturing to where Jesse had been stacking shelves. She'd barely made a dent in the trolleys.

'Maybe you just need a break,' I said calmly. Jesse was about to have a full meltdown, and Liz was looking for any excuse to cut her hours, or worse.

Jesse turned to me. 'A break from the library is the last thing I need.'

'Good thinking, Stella,' Liz said at the same time. 'A holiday is exactly what Jesse needs.'

'No, I don't.' Jesse was practically screaming.

I felt ill. I'd totally put my foot in it. I back-pedalled. 'I meant a break as in a walk outside. To take you out of the situation so you can return refreshed.'

Liz rolled her eyes. 'I think Jesse knows the job is too much for her. She also knows we're trying to run a business.' She looked at Jesse and attempted a smile. 'Sometimes it's like you're living in a different...'

Jesse twirled her hair, becoming more agitated.

'That's not fair,' I said, but Liz held up her hand.

'Stella, Gracie needs relieving on the customer relations desk.'

'But–'

'Now.'

Not wanting to create a bigger scene, I did as I was instructed, but I'd let Jesse down. Who knows what Liz was about to say, but I had a bad feeling, and now I wasn't there to support her.

Minutes later, Jesse rushed past me in floods of tears. I went after her.

'Jesse?'

'I've been made redundant. Effective immediately.'

'No!' This was much worse than I'd expected. I felt responsible. I'd never wanted this to happen. Yes, maybe Jesse needed a rest and counselling, but to lose her job? This would kill her. Jesse loved the library.

'Why didn't you back me up, Stella? I needed your support.'

'I do support you – all the time. I'm so sorry this is such a mess. I'll sort it out with Liz. We'll work something out.'

'The library's the only thing I have that's mine, that makes me feel good about myself. Now I have nothing.'

'Jesse,' I said, putting my hand on her shoulder. 'We'll get through this.'

I didn't want her hurrying out, upset and angry. And I

meant what I'd said. I would talk to Liz and sort this out if I could. What did I mean 'if'? I had to, for Jesse's sake.

Her expression changed from despair to resignation. 'You might, but...' She shook her head. 'It's okay. I mean it's not the end of the world. There are plenty more libraries, hey?'

I nodded but didn't trust myself to look at her. I should have had her back and I hadn't.

'I've got to get out of here,' she continued, swinging her bag over her shoulder. 'If I've forgotten anything, can you keep it for me?'

'Sure. I'm so sorry.'

'It's all right.' She dried her eyes. 'Maybe a rest is exactly what I need. You never know, Liz might be doing me a huge favour.'

I started to walk with her to the door, but she stopped me. 'You have a job to do. Besides, it's raining.'

'I'll call you tonight.' I watched her run to her car.

CHAPTER FORTY

JESSE

Jesse sped out of the car park and onto the main road. Her mind was racing, leapfrogging from one thought to the next as rain lashed her car and the windscreen wipers whooshed furiously. With tears streaming down her face, the visibility ahead was practically zero. Jesse kept her eyes on the road as she mulled over the day's events. She'd been made redundant! The one thing that had been keeping her going, keeping her strong and focused, had been her job. Now Liz had ripped it from her. If it was just a matter of losing her job alone, Jesse might have coped, but coming on top of Steve's betrayal and infidelity...

What could she have done differently to hold her marriage together? To go back to how it used to be? To make Steve love her again? Where had that love gone? Had it simply vanished one day while he was drinking his morning latte and reading the *Financial Review*? Or had it eroded over time, chipping away until there was nothing left?

The more she thought about his double life, the more furious and upset she became. She'd been patient and kind. She'd loved him ... and for what? Reality felt like a sharp dagger slicing open her heart. What had made him go to those parties?

Boredom? With her, with their marriage? When Steve was at those parties, did he consider Jesse at all? How might she feel about what he was doing?

Then there was Louisa. Her own sister had been lying to her for years. How could she have let Jesse marry Steve, knowing what she did? Why hadn't Louisa warned her? Protected her from the hideous revelation that lay ahead?

Carly and her big mouth. If only she hadn't blurted it all out, Jesse would be none the wiser. And Stella! Jesse had practically begged her to talk to Liz and convince her that she'd be a valuable full-time employee, but Stella hadn't backed her.

Jesse couldn't control her thoughts or tears ... jumping from Steve to Louisa to losing her job, the Secret Women's Business meetings. Jesse wanted her old life back. Damn it! Why was this happening to her?

The rain came down in thick sheets. Yellow hazard lights flickered at the side of the road, warning of ditches prone to flash flooding. Jesse's foot tapped wildly on the accelerator and her hands clenched the steering wheel so hard they turned ghostly white. She needed to stop the car, calm down and get a grip. And she would, just as soon as she could see well enough to pull over.

CHAPTER FORTY-ONE

STELLA

I marched straight into Liz's office and slammed the door. 'How could you?'

Liz looked up from her computer. 'How could I what?'

'Retrench her. She's devastated.'

'What choice did I have, Stella? If anything, I should have done it months ago.'

'You have no idea about her family situation. This couldn't have come at a worse time.'

'I'm sorry if Jesse's personal life is challenging, but she's a liability. It was only a matter of time before we had real problems.'

'What, so we don't have real problems with her now? This situation could have been avoided.'

'Stella, you're being deliberately difficult. We don't have the funds or the resources to keep up with Jesse patrol.'

'On her good days, she positively beams, and she's always up to date with new releases. Jesse lives and breathes the library, and the patrons love her for it.'

'I'm sorry, Stella. My mind's made up.'

We stared at each other a few moments before Liz said, 'Anything else?'

'You can't do this.'

'I can. It's done. End of story.' She shook her head and went back to reading her computer monitor. I stood my ground until she looked up again. 'Seriously, I don't have time for this.'

'Neither do I. I quit.' I grabbed my bag and marched out of the library.

I shook my head as I walked to my car. What had I just done? My job! Fuck. I couldn't afford to quit. Besides, I loved the library. Yes, Liz was a pain, but she was a manageable pain most of the time. Nevertheless, I had to stick up for Jesse. Defend her, go after her and talk her down, which was exactly what I intended to do.

I swung out onto the road, still furious with Liz. The woman had no compassion. She was a cyborg, no doubt about it.

It was hard to hear my phone ringing over the downpour, but eventually I did. I fumbled through my bag and reached for it. 'Yes?' I said distractedly.

'Stella, it's Toby. I've got June's test results. She doesn't–'

I was having trouble concentrating, not to mention visibility was almost nil. 'Sorry. Could you repeat that?'

'June doesn't appear to have Alzheimer's. Doctor Gordon's only conducted preliminary tests, as you know, but it doesn't look sinister.'

Relief washed over me. 'Thank goodness.'

'We'll schedule her for further appointments so we can absolutely rule it out, but I'm confident...'

I could barely hear Toby over the rain, and the cars in front of me had come to a standstill. There was some sort of commotion up ahead. Looked like a car accident. Smoke was billowing everywhere.

'Stella?' Toby said. 'Stella, are you there?'

'There's been an accident.' I pulled up on the side of the road. 'Oh my God. It's Jesse,' I screamed, as I saw her car mangled against a huge gum tree. The front was totally wrecked.

'Stella?'

'We ... we need an ambulance!' I dropped my mobile, tripping over my feet in my frantic attempt to get out of my car.

Two men were trying to break open the front doors of Jesse's car.

'What happened?' I shrieked to the few bystanders.

'She drove into a tree,' someone said.

I walked closer to the wreckage.

'Don't,' a man said, grabbing me by the arm. 'Don't go any closer.'

'I have to. She's my best friend.' I trembled and struggled to remain upright.

The stranger continued holding me. 'We've called an ambulance. Shouldn't be too much longer.'

Jesse was slumped back against the driver's seat, bloodied, unconscious. Sirens in the distance grew closer.

'I have to talk to her,' I begged the man. 'She needs to know I'm here.'

He looked at me kindly. 'Let's wait for the paramedics.'

Close by a teenager struggled with an excited Labrador who was straining at his lead. They moved towards us. The man bent down to pat the dog, gently shushing him.

'I've got to help her,' I sobbed, but I did as the man suggested.

An ambulance parked near Jesse's car and two women climbed out. A third ambo, a man, directed everyone to take several steps back. It all seemed to be happening in slow motion.

The police arrived and the man with the teenager and dog approached them. In a daze, I followed.

'Did you actually witness the accident?' one of the officers asked the man.

He hesitated. 'Yes.'

'And what did you see?'

'I was walking with Charlie, my son, and Sam, here,' he pointed at the dog and continued, 'on the other side of the road. The driver was travelling in the opposite direction. She pulled her car over and slowed right down. Maybe even stopped. And then barely a minute later...' He paused.

'Go on,' the officer said, looking up from his notes.

'This is the unbelievable part. She accelerated straight into the tree.'

'No!' I screamed, suddenly dizzy. Not Jesse.

Someone led me away. 'Is there anyone we can call? Family? Your friend's husband, maybe?'

I shook my head, sobbing into my hands. Poor Jesse. This couldn't be happening. It just couldn't. The front of her car was completely twisted. It would be a miracle if she...

I couldn't think like that. Jesse needed me to be strong. I wiped my eyes and stood. 'Yes, of course. Her family. I need to phone her family.'

Somehow, I made it to my car, opened the door and retrieved the phone I'd flung on the floor in my haste to get out. I selected Steve's number.

The ambulance siren started up again as it sped away.

'Where are they taking her?' the man with the dog asked the police.

'Royal,' one of them said.

Mike, I thought, just as Steve answered the phone.

'What?'

'Steve?' My voice quavered. 'Jesse's been in a terrible accident.' The words tumbled out of my mouth. 'Car accident. They're taking her to the Royal.'

'If this is a joke–'

'Please hurry.'

Before he could say anything else, I hung up and dialled Carly's number.

'Hey, Stella.'

'Carly!' I sobbed. 'It's Jesse. She's been in a car accident. They've taken her to the Royal. I'll see you there.'

'But–'

'Carly, I don't know any more. Just hurry up and get there.'

As soon as I hung up, my phone rang. Toby.

'Stella, Mike's on his way in. He's had word to expect a patient who's been in a car smash near your work. Is it–'

'Jesse? Yes. She looks bad. Really bad. I don't know what to do.'

'At this stage there's probably not much you can do. Are you coming in?'

My mind went blank.

'Stella, are you there?' Toby's voice was firm and clear. 'We're getting ready to receive her. I'll talk to you when I can.'

I dropped the phone to my side. Over at Jesse's car, the police were taking photos, removing personal items and interviewing witnesses.

The man with the dog reappeared next to me. 'I'll drive you to the hospital,' he said gently, pointing at my car.

'No, I shouldn't bother you.'

'It's no trouble. Charlie will take Sam home. Please, it's the least I can do.'

I motioned towards the police. 'Don't you have to stay?'

'I've told them everything I know. They have my details. They'll be in touch if they need me. Come on, it's a ten-minute drive. Let me take you.'

I burst into tears again. I needed to be with Jesse, but I was a mess. I wiped my eyes again and nodded. 'Thanks.'

The man hugged his son and watched as the boy and dog walked away from us. 'Sorry, I didn't introduce myself,' he said as he helped me into my car. 'I'm Robert. Rob. And you are?'

I sat in the passenger seat in a daze, staring at the throng around Jesse's car. It still didn't seem real. 'Stella.'

Rob pulled out onto the road. He was driving at the speed limit, but we seemed to be crawling.

'Excuse me,' I said. 'I need to ring my husband, ex-husband actually. But we're still good friends. He should know.'

Garth answered after one ring.

'Jesse's been in a car accident,' I told him, sobbing again. 'They're taking her to the Royal. Meet me there?'

'Of course, love. On my way.'

CHAPTER FORTY-TWO

Rob and I arrived at the hospital seven minutes later and he guided me through the hospital's automatic doors.

I was in shock, unable to focus, so Rob asked for directions to the emergency department. Around us, doctors and nurses flew by in a blur. Finally we made it to the dull grey waiting room. I looked around hoping to see a familiar face. No one I knew was there yet.

'Can I get you anything?' Rob asked. 'Water? Coffee?'

I shook my head.

'At least take a seat,' he said, signalling to a row of chairs near the windows.

I sat, wringing my clammy hands. 'I don't know what to do. What do you think's happening? Where is she? Why isn't anyone else here?'

'I don't know.'

'My God,' I said, my voice sounding strangled and foreign. 'I don't know what to do.'

'I don't want to leave you here alone, but I feel like an intruder. I shouldn't stay.'

'Please do, at least until someone else gets here.'

'I'm sorry about your friend.'

I looked at him as if seeing him for the first time. 'Yeah.' I started crying again. 'How did it happen? The roads were wet and slippery, but Jesse's driven that road a hundred times.'

Rob was silent.

'You told the police that Jesse slowed down and pulled over to the side of the road?'

'That's what I saw.'

'Then what happened?'

'Look, Stella, maybe I didn't see things clearly. I'm not sure.'

'But you said she accelerated into the tree?'

Rob took a deep breath and sighed. 'Yes, to be honest, it looked like she slowed down almost to a stop and then sped into the gum tree. I'm sorry.'

I was sobbing again, shaking my head. 'That can't be true.'

Rob nodded. 'I hope you're right.'

The seconds ticked by as if they were hours. I distracted myself by thinking about the kids, the roast I was cooking for dinner, the storm and the flash flooding in the area. But there was only so much distraction I could manage before other thoughts hijacked my brain. The last time I'd been in a hospital waiting room – other than for June's sprained arm – was after Dad's car accident. Images of him in intensive care filled my mind: tubes everywhere, the burns ... Once the swelling and bruising had faded, it had looked like he'd had a facelift. His legs had borne the brunt of the impact and had required numerous skin grafts ... I shuddered at the memory, wishing Mum and Dad lived closer, not in Melbourne, a thousand kilometres away.

Carly came rushing into the room. 'I got here as quickly as I could. What happened?'

I stood. 'Jesse's been in an accident.'

Carly hugged me. 'I hope they've got the other bloke in custody.'

I stood back from her and wiped my eyes. 'That's just it. Nobody else was involved.'

I looked around for Rob, but he'd gone. My car keys were on the seat next to me. I hadn't even thanked him.

Carly gasped. 'But how is that possible?'

'Yes, how?' It was Steve.

It was the first time I'd seen him since last Thursday night. I went to hug him, but he backed away.

'Don't touch me. Just tell me what's going on.'

'She was in an accident,' I said.

'You were there?'

'No. I arrived a few minutes later. It happened just after she left the library.'

'That damn library! I told her I didn't want her working there.'

It's a little too late for that, I thought as the three of us stood there awkwardly.

'I'm so sorry,' Carly said.

Steve didn't acknowledge her. He strode over to the unoccupied nurses' station and rang the bell. 'Hello? Anybody here?'

I couldn't believe his attitude, as if he'd been inconvenienced and was doing everyone a favour by gracing us with his presence.

A minute later, Mike appeared. It was odd seeing him again so soon. But then, lunch seemed like years ago. Carly and I rushed over to him.

'I wish we were meeting under better circumstances,' he said. 'Stella, I'm so sorry. How are you bearing–'

'Ahem, doctor? I'm Steve Foster, Jesse's husband.'

'I know who you are,' Mike said calmly.

Steve seemed taken aback. 'Can I see my wife?'

'I'm afraid Jesse's had a severe head trauma,' Mike started.

'It appears–'

Both Carly and I gasped. My whole body was shaking.

'Is she alive?' Steve jumped in.

'Yes, Jesse's alive,' Mike said. 'But you can't see her. She's being examined for injuries.'

'But, Mike,' I said, my voice rising, 'she's okay, isn't she?'

Steve looked at me. 'How do you know his name?'

'Doctor Mike Thompson,' Mike said, not missing a beat as he stuck out his hand to shake Steve's. 'I have some papers for you to sign, Mr Foster. This way, please.'

He led Steve out of the waiting room and down the corridor.

Carly and I had been sitting there for what seemed like hours when Garth showed up.

'How is she?' he asked after hugging us both.

I shook my head. 'We don't know.'

'What happened?' He wrapped his arms around me in a gesture of comfort.

Briefly, I thought about the oddness of Garth and Mike both being here, but I was too worried to care about social niceties.

'It all happened so quickly. Jesse ran out of the library crying, I confronted Liz–'

'Why was she crying?' Carly asked.

'Liz retrenched her. Claimed Jesse's quirks had become too much of a distraction for her to continue working properly.'

'Poor Jesse,' Carly said. 'She'd have been devastated.'

I nodded. 'After my argument with Liz, I quit.'

'You what?' Garth said. 'It must have been quite a disagreement.'

'I got in the car and headed home. I'd only been driving a couple of minutes when I came across the accident. A witness says Jesse deliberately accelerated into a tree, but she would never do anything so reckless. She loves her kids.'

Garth shook his head. 'Nightmare.'

'A nightmare we're having to live through.' Steve was back.

'Steve, mate,' Garth said, 'I'm so sorry about this. But Jesse's one strong woman. She'll pull through, you'll see.'

'I wish I had your blind confidence,' Steve said.

'Do you want me to call Jesse's parents?' I asked him.

'I've already rung them.'

It felt like I'd been at the hospital forever, but only fifty-five minutes had lapsed. At this stage, we couldn't do more than wait. I phoned Hannah and Harry to fill them in and asked Steve if he wanted a friend to pick up Ollie and Emily from school.

He declined, telling me, 'It's all under control.'

A little while later, Toby walked into the room. Carly and I swooped on him.

'How is she?' My voice was little more than a whisper.

'Early days,' he replied, then saw Steve and went over to him. 'Mr Foster?'

Steve jumped slightly. 'Do I know you?'

'I don't think so. My name's Toby Mitchell. Together with Doctor Thompson, I'm attending to your wife.'

'What are you doing here then?'

'Keeping you up to date and informed,' Toby said evenly. 'At the moment, Jesse's undergoing a series of X-rays to assess for fractures of the skull and spinal instability.'

'Oh no.' Carly clutched my shoulder.

'Her brain has sustained significant swelling and bruising due to the trauma of the accident.'

Steve considered Toby's words for a moment. 'Right. So, when will she be better?'

'I'm afraid that's like asking "how long is a piece of string?"

The truth is, we really don't know. As long as it takes, I'm afraid.'

'As long as it takes? Really? That's your professional opinion?'

Toby nodded. 'I'll let you know more as and when we have news.' I had to hand it to Toby: he had grace under pressure. If I'd been him, I'd have wanted to punch Steve.

Before disappearing through the doors to attend to Jesse, Toby pulled me aside and spoke briefly about June's test results and the possible explanations for her behaviour.

I was processing the information when Garth tapped me on the shoulder. 'There's nothing I can do here, why don't I go home, check on Mum, see the kids after school and organise dinner? Looks like you're in for a long night, and I can be more helpful doing something practical.'

I hugged him, tears rolling down my cheeks. 'Thanks, I appreciate it.'

'It'll give me some time to spend with Mum alone.'

'She doesn't have Alzheimer's. I knew you were worried, so I had Toby—'

'The doctor here? The one from last Sunday?'

'Yeah. I had him organise some preliminary tests, and he just spoke to me about them. He said that once people get to a certain age and start forgetting things and becoming increasingly absent-minded, their children assume they have dementia, but it's often not the case.'

'That's a relief.'

'Yeah. It's more likely a combination of old age, grief over Vince—'

'Still?'

'Still. And stress.'

'About?'

'Our separation, getting older, not being able to do what she wants when she wants to. The fall the other day wouldn't have helped.'

'I guess I should have trimmed the hedges like she asked.'

I nodded. 'And maybe you could also take a more softly-softly approach with her regarding Amanda.'

Garth rolled his eyes. 'Amanda! I need to tell her I'll be home late.'

He kissed me, then walked over to Steve and shook his hand. Garth was a good bloke. I was glad he was the father of my children.

Jesse's parents arrived and made a beeline for Steve.

'My baby,' Dot cried. 'Where is she? What happened? Somebody tell me what happened!'

'Jesse's been in a car accident,' Steve said. 'She's being attended to.'

'Is it bad?'

'We don't know yet,' he said, and for the first time since he'd walked in, I sensed vulnerability, his confident veneer slipping.

'Dot,' I said, walking over and hugging her. 'I'm so sorry.'

'Stella, were you with her?'

I shook my head. 'No, but I do know she's in the best hands. These doctors are miracle workers. Jesse's going to be fine.' I said it for my own peace of mind as much as for Dot's.

Jesse's dad, Bernard, had hugged Steve but hadn't said a word. Tears fell as I watched him walk towards the windows and stare out on to the drab multi-storey car park. Dot joined him and took his hand.

'What should we do?' Carly whispered to me. 'I feel useless sitting here.'

I nodded. 'Let's wait until we hear more and then decide.'

CHAPTER FORTY-THREE

It seemed like forever before Toby and Mike reappeared.

Mike was carrying a clipboard with several pages of notes attached. He cleared his throat. 'Because little can be done to reverse the initial traumatic brain damage, our primary focus is on stabilising Jesse to prevent further injury.'

Brain damage? The words pulsed through my mind, and I barely heard the rest of what Mike was saying.

'We've been able to stabilise her and we're now ensuring proper oxygen supply to her brain and body. We're also maintaining blood flow while controlling her blood pressure.'

'But how is she?' Dot asked. 'When can I see her?'

'Not yet, I'm afraid,' Mike replied. 'We've done X-rays and a CT scan to assess damage to the brain. What we do know is that Jesse has suffered a severe blunt head trauma, but the good news is that, despite swelling and bruising of the brain, we've ruled out any other mass lesion or compression of the brain stem.' He paused. 'However, Jesse is unconscious and has broken her right foot. She's being prepped for surgery now.'

'Unconscious?' Steve said, speaking for the first time. 'She's in a coma?'

Mike nodded. 'That's correct. I'm sorry I don't have better news for you.'

Carly and I turned to each other, unable to speak.

Bernard stepped forward. 'Bernard Buckland, Jesse's father. When do you think you'll have a prognosis?' he asked in a choked voice.

'It's hard to tell,' Mike replied. 'But we're doing everything we can to make sure she's comfortable. We'll give her medications like steroids for swelling as well as anti-epileptic drugs in case of seizures. In the meantime, we have to wait until the brain recovers from the initial trauma.'

'Jesse fainted the other day,' Dot blurted out. 'Could that have had anything to do with the accident? Did she blackout? I told her she needed to slow down, that she was taking on too much stress and wasn't taking care of herself or her family. But she doesn't listen to me. No one listens to me.'

Bernard rubbed her arm tenderly.

'It's true,' she continued, shaking him off. 'She didn't listen to me. I knew something like this would happen. It was a matter of time.'

'Do you have anything you can give Dot?' Steve asked, clearly agitated by his mother-in-law's ramblings.

Everyone turned to look at him.

'Well?' he said impatiently, staring at Toby and Mike. 'Do you?'

What was he suggesting? A quick shot to the temples?

Bernard took Dot nearby to sit down, but she continued babbling at a hundred miles an hour. Everyone had different coping mechanisms. Talking was Dot's.

I closed my eyes briefly as I leaned against a wall for support, wishing the day would come to an end. Toby and Mike were talking in hushed tones to Steve, and Carly paced the waiting room. I called her over to join me.

'This is my fault,' I said. 'If I'd supported Jesse more at the library, none of this would have happened.'

'That's not true,' Carly said, tears trickling down her cheeks. 'It's my fault. Me and my big mouth.'

I shook my head. 'It's not you. I should've helped her more at work. I knew Liz was angling to sack her.'

We took seats at a table and stared over at Steve and the doctors.

'How do you think he is?' Carly asked.

I shrugged. Who knew with Steve?

A few minutes later, Brett arrived. He hugged Carly tight and stroked her hair. 'It'll be all right,' he soothed. For all of Carly's complaints about Brett, he certainly appeared loving and caring towards her.

Turning to me, he said, 'How are you holding up? Carly said you saw the scene.'

'Okay,' I whispered, then shook my head. 'It's like a bad dream. I keep pinching myself, hoping I'll wake up.'

'And Steve?'

We turned to look at Steve again, who was alone by the water dispenser. Brett walked over to him and tried to hug him. Steve resisted, then shook his head and started talking. I couldn't hear their conversation.

Toby came back into the room.

As Carly and I made our way towards him, I heard Steve say to Brett, 'Those women.' Brett glanced at us briefly before turning back to Steve.

'How is she really?' Carly asked Toby.

'The next twenty-four to forty-eight hours will be critical.'

'And?'

'And if she pulls through, we'll hold our breath for the next day and then the one after that. I'm sorry I can't tell you more.'

Carly sniffed back tears. 'It's okay. You're doing your best.'

He hugged her.

'Hey! You guys are acting a bit too familiar,' I whispered.

Carly broke free and shot a glance at Brett, who was staring straight at her. Steve looked at us too, and his eyes widened. No doubt, the pieces were rapidly falling into place in his mind.

'I think he recognises you,' I said to Toby.

Toby glanced towards Steve, who was still staring straight at us. 'You could be right. I'll see you both soon.' He left the room.

Moments later, Brett was beside Carly. 'Who was that guy you were all over?'

'Pardon?'

'It doesn't matter. I'm just curious.'

'He's a doctor, Brett. I'm upset. He was comforting me.'

Brett raised his eyebrows. 'Okay. It's a tough time for everyone.'

'How's Steve doing?' I asked.

Brett paused. 'Not good. Having a hard time. It's to be expected.'

Doubly so, given that the two attending doctors had already met him under dubious circumstances.

'Maybe if he'd treated Jesse better, none of this would have happened,' Carly said.

'Keep your voice down,' Brett told her.

'Why? It's what everyone thinks.'

Brett glanced around the room. 'I'm going in search of coffee. Can I get either of you anything?'

Carly shook her head.

'No thanks,' I said. 'I should go and speak to Dot.'

Brett kissed Carly lightly on the forehead. 'I'll be back soon.'

I went over to Dot and Bernard at their table by the window. 'How are you?'

'How do you think I am?' Dot said. 'Distraught. I'm not even allowed to see my own daughter. It's not right.'

Bernard reached across the table to hold her hand. 'Come on, love.'

'Is there anything I can do?' I asked. 'Phone Louisa for you?'

Dot wiped her eyes. 'Bern's already called her.'

Bernard nodded. 'She'll be on the next flight out of San Francisco.'

'Did I hear right?' It was Steve. 'Louisa's coming here?'

'Yes,' Bernard said, taking a deep breath. 'Our Louisa's finally coming home.'

I glanced at Steve. He looked pale, and the can of lemonade shook in his hand.

When I got home late Thursday night, June was asleep, but Hannah and Harry were waiting up for me. I explained what had happened.

'What's a coma?' Hannah asked, pale with worry.

'It's like a deep sleep where the person can't be woken up and doesn't respond normally to pain, light or sound,' I said, having memorised Mike's spiel. 'When Jesse hit her head on the airbag it would have felt like a mighty kick. Her brain had a severe traumatic injury, and she went into a coma straight away.'

'But she'll be okay, won't she?' Harry said.

'I don't know,' I whispered. 'I really don't know.'

I said goodnight to the kids and made myself a cup of peppermint tea before stretching out on the sofa. I tried closing my eyes but kept opening them to stare at a photo of Jesse, Carly and me on the side table taken at a Robbie Williams concert a few years back. We all looked so animated, joyful ... alive.

After a restless night's sleep, I spent most of Friday at the hospital. Not that I knew what to do. Mostly, I just sat with Jesse when her mum, dad and Steve took a break.

In the afternoon, I had a longer chat with Mike over coffee in the hospital cafeteria.

He told me that although Jesse was stable, it was still touch and go. 'It might be days, weeks, maybe even months, before she recovers.'

'You don't have even an approximate timeline for her improvement?'

'I wish it was that simple.'

'Can't you do something? Anything? We're all just waiting around. Aren't there any drugs you can give her to make her better?'

'If there was a magic bullet, we'd have tried it. I'm sorry, but we're doing the best we can.'

I teared up. 'Well, your best isn't good enough.'

Mike sighed. 'Do you know how often I hear that? For all the good we do, when a patient dies–'

'Are you saying–'

'No, but it always comes down to the ones who don't make it, the ones we can't fix.'

'But Jesse's my best friend.'

He held my shoulders, forcing me to look at him. He had dark circles under his eyes. 'Do you believe in prayer?'

I shrugged him off. 'Not really.'

'Do you believe Jesse can hear when you talk to her?'

I nodded.

'Good. Then that's what you should do. Talk to her.'

'I'm sorry,' I said, wiping my eyes. 'I know you're doing everything you can. You must be exhausted.'

He placed his hand over mine. 'I could say the same about you.'

It was at that moment that Steve walked up to us. 'You two disgust me. I don't want you seeing my wife,' he said, glaring at me. 'And as for you–'

Mike stood. 'As for me, Mr Foster, I am your wife's primary doctor, and I will thank you to respect that.'

Go, Mike!

Steve looked taken aback. 'Whatever,' he muttered before walking away.

Mike resumed his seat. 'That went well.'

'He's such a charmer.'

'Clearly not pleased Toby and I are on the job.'

'Yeah, he hoped he'd never see you again.'

Later, I saw Jesse, despite Steve's directive. Still, I was careful to keep out of his way. She didn't look like Jesse – so many bandages and tubes. It was frightening. Her poor kids. Dot told me that when they'd eventually been allowed to see her that morning, Emily had been reserved and quiet, but Oliver had been beside himself, in floods of tears, not wanting to leave his mum's side when visiting time was up. Heart breaking.

As banged up as Jesse looked, now that she'd made it through those crucial first twenty-four hours, I was confident she'd pull through. She had to. She was surrounded by the best medical care in the country. As for the ridiculous talk that she'd deliberately done this to herself, it was cruel. I knew Jesse well enough to know that even though Steve was a prick, she'd never leave her children voluntarily.

CHAPTER FORTY-FOUR

LOUISA

'How are we ever going to get through this?' Louisa's dad, Bernard, asked when he'd rung with the news about Jesse's accident.

Louisa had been over the question dozens of times since he'd called. Now, she was slouched in a hot taxi which reeked of overpowering aftershave, on her way from Sydney airport to the hospital where Jesse was lying in a coma.

The taxi wound through streets clogged with peak-hour traffic. Familiar shops and street names sprang up in front of her, as though it had been months not years since she'd left. There were more buildings and certainly more pedestrians and cyclists weaving their way along the roads. Sydney was a clean city, a sunny city, she'd give it that. As for crossing the Sydney Harbour Bridge? Magical.

Russell Crowe summed it up nicely: 'There's an ease that I have living in Australia. The best things about Sydney are free: the sunshine's free, and the harbour's free, and the beach is free.' Louisa was in tears. She couldn't disagree.

She examined her nails. Bleeding and sore, she'd absentmindedly chewed them all. What if Jesse died and Louisa never got to say goodbye? They'd been close once, best friends, but Louisa hadn't been part of her sister's life for a long time. There were phone calls, sure, but that wasn't the same, was it? Louisa had left family life behind when she'd bought her ticket to freedom.

What if she hadn't told Jesse all those things? What if she'd continued to keep them secret? Would Jesse be in this state now? The guilt was agonising. Louisa could barely face herself, let alone her parents and Jesse. If only she hadn't had that horrible conversation with Jesse. If only...

'Here do?' the taxi driver asked.

'I guess.'

Louisa stood outside the main hospital entrance. To her right, orderlies and nurses crowded together, smoking, laughing. When the enormous glass doors silently slid open, she hesitated. The anticipation of seeing Jesse in a coma was frightening. Perspiration trickled down Louisa's forehead. Thirty degrees and it wasn't even 9am.

The antiseptic smell hit her as soon as she walked in, and she suppressed the urge to vomit. The entrance area had a dull grey carpet, cream walls and a huge Australian landscape painting on the wall, with white lilies in a glass vase on a white marble table below it. The flowers were on the turn, their scent more odorous than fragrant.

Louisa was wasting time, and she knew it. Avoidance therapy, her analyst called it. But she wasn't in a hurry to move. Besides, her feet seemed incapable of carrying her towards the reception desk.

'Louisa?'

She turned to see a tall, slim woman walking towards her. Pretty face.

'Stella. Stella Sparks, remember?' the woman said, extending her hand to shake Louisa's.

Louisa remembered Stella as having dark hair, cut in a neat bob. Now it was blonder and longer, kind of messy and easy. She still had the same generous smile.

'I'll take you upstairs if you like. Your mum and dad are waiting. How was your flight?'

'Long.'

'How are you feeling?'

'I'm not quite sure. How's Jesse?'

'No change, I'm afraid.' Tears trickled down Stella's cheeks. 'But she's hanging in there.'

Louisa followed her along a corridor lined with breakfast carts and linen trolleys. *Hanging in there*: she repeated Stella's words in her mind. It had been four days since the accident. She'd hoped her father had been exaggerating the extent of Jesse's injuries, but it didn't seem so.

'At least she's been moved to a private room,' Stella said, as they took the elevator up to the third floor.

When they arrived at Jesse's door, Stella spoke again. 'I should warn you, she's pretty messed up. I'll be downstairs at the café if you need me.' She hugged Louisa and walked back in the direction they'd just come.

Louisa flinched. Her heart was pounding. Blinking away tears, she knocked and opened the door. She saw her dad first and fixed her eyes on him. She didn't want to look beyond. Didn't want to see her sister. To face reality.

Bernard walked to her, arms outstretched. 'It's been too long,' he whispered, enfolding her in his arms, his eyes wet with tears.

Louisa had only seen her father cry once. It was beyond painful. He looked so much greyer than when she'd last seen him. And older. Much older.

Dot was sitting in a grey hospital chair leaning against a grey steel hospital bed. A bed that Louisa quickly turned away from. Dot rested her left hand against Jesse's arm and extended her right hand towards Louisa. Louisa walked over, took it and squeezed hard.

'You're here now.' Dot took a deep breath. 'I feel so weak, like He might take me at any moment.'

'Who, Mum? Who might take you?'

'You know,' she replied, looking heavenward. 'God.'

'She's not good,' Bernard said, staring down at Jesse.

Louisa forced herself to look at her sister. Once she did, she found she couldn't turn away. This was real. Jesse was lying in a bed barely a metre from where Louisa stood. Her head was bandaged, and her cheeks were bruised, discoloured beyond recognition. Tubes ran from her mouth and nose. Other than her right foot, her body was concealed under white bedcovers, hidden from view. In addition to the IV pole, various machines beeped and whistled at short intervals. Louisa only knew it was Jesse because her name was printed in large black type on a white cardboard sign stuck to the bedhead.

She closed her eyes. 'What happened?'

'Freak car accident,' Bernard started, 'resulting in–'

'Severe blunt head injury,' Dot finished.

'How?' Louisa asked.

'I know what you're thinking,' Dot said. 'You're wondering what we could have done to stop her. Why didn't we do more to help her?'

Louisa hadn't been thinking that at all. 'Mum, it was an accident. It was no one's fault.'

Tears slid down Dot's face. 'Jesse was ... is ... troubled. You know that. It's always been there, of course, but lately it's been getting worse.'

'Don't, Dot!' Bernard said. 'This was an accident, nothing more. Jesse's a good girl.'

'Tell me more about the accident,' Louisa prompted.

'It seems Jesse pulled over to the side of the road. Stopped her car and then...' Bernard wiped his tears with a damp blue handkerchief. 'A witness said she accelerated into a gum tree.'

'What sane person does that?' Dot asked.

'Her foot must have slipped,' Louisa said.

'That's what I said too,' Bernard agreed. 'The way she's been tapping her foot of late, it makes sense.'

'So she's stressed?' Louisa asked. This was her fault, no doubt about it. Jesse had found out about Steve, on top of that, Louisa had dropped her bombshell. It had been too much for Jesse to cope with.

'The accident looked suspicious,' Dot said.

'For Christ's sake, you weren't there, woman.'

'But the police, Bern–'

'The police?' Louisa said. 'Why are they involved?'

'The police are investigating,' Dot said quietly. 'There were no skid marks...'

Bernard shook his head. 'It's not true.'

This was unbelievable. There was no way Jesse would have deliberately driven into a tree. She loved her kids too much to do something that reckless. Louisa just didn't buy it.

'What were you talking about the other day when she collapsed?' Dot asked.

'I can't remember,' Louisa lied.

'Think, Louisa,' Bernard encouraged. 'It could provide an important clue. Maybe she fainted again behind the wheel.'

'What with her fainting and foot tapping,' Dot said. 'I told you she wasn't well, Bernard.'

Louisa looked at Jesse again. 'How are Steve and the kids taking it?' She was relieved Steve wasn't here. It was going to be hard facing him, knowing what she did about him and how he'd treated Jesse.

'You know Steve; stoic, as usual,' Bernard said.

Yeah, right.

Louisa took a seat on the other side of Jesse's bed. *Wake up,* she willed her. *Please wake up.*

CHAPTER FORTY-FIVE

CARLY

Carly was running through the streets, listening to music on her iPhone, trying not to think about anything except the moment, the pretty gardens, the barking dogs, the other early morning joggers. All she wanted to do was keep running, to forget about the last couple of days ... weeks. Tears streamed down her face as she repeatedly told herself to focus, to push through the sadness and pain. Though she kept running, not even slowing for the many hills in the area, the image of Jesse in her hospital bed, helpless, unconscious, covered in bandages, tubes sticking out of her, crowded her mind.

It was Carly's fault. That much she knew. The last few days she'd operated on autopilot, not really knowing what to do with herself. She'd burst into tears in the supermarket, composed herself enough to buy bananas, bread and milk, then burst into tears again at the chemist buying Vitamin B12. She'd been a mess all weekend and was no better today.

Somehow, she made it back home. She didn't even realise she was on her street until she was practically at her front door.

Will was eating breakfast. He looked up when she walked into the kitchen. 'Hey.'

Carly smiled. She was exhausted, but at least she'd run five kilometres. That had to be more productive than lying curled up in bed crying. She flipped on the kettle. 'How's my boy?' She blinked at threatening tears.

'Okay.' Will looked away, choosing to watch Norman the cat destroying his chicken wing instead of his mother's distress. 'You know how I've got my learners,' he said, still staring at Norman.

Carly sighed. 'I'm sorry, Will. I haven't been taking you out as much as I should've been.'

'No, that's okay,' he said. 'We've been watching road-safety videos at school, seeing crash sites and stuff. Anyway, with Jesse's accident, we're all thinking that maybe sixteen is too young to drive.'

'I understand what you're saying, Will, but you'll be okay. We'll take it slowly and by the time you're ready to take your test, you'll do brilliantly, I'm sure.'

He smiled. She could tell that was exactly what he needed to hear.

Carly had showered and was figuring out what to wear to the hospital when Brett phoned.

'How are you doing this morning?'

'Okay. I managed a run.'

'That's encouraging,' he said brightly. 'Will and I have been worried. You've been so exhausted and shaken the last few nights.'

'I'm doing okay,' Carly replied. 'It's Jesse who's in trouble.'

With Carly, it was one thing or the other: exercise or alcohol. As much as she'd wanted a glass of wine the previous night and the night before, she knew she shouldn't. If she had one, she'd end up drinking twenty-one, and that scenario was too depressing to contemplate. Instead, she'd focused on sleep and running when she wasn't visiting Jesse.

The previous night was the first night she'd been home for dinner since the accident. She, Brett and Will had sat in silence in front of the TV, eating takeaway Thai curries, and she'd fallen asleep soon after an early episode of *Modern Family*. They made it look so easy on television: even when the characters were facing mayhem, they still managed clean, blow-dried hair, immaculate make-up and, most importantly, a happy ending. But at least the show had taken her mind off Jesse for twenty-two minutes.

After she'd hung up, Carly realised she still hadn't spoken to Brett about Nick. In fact, she'd barely thought about his situation since Jesse's accident. Not only was she a shocking friend, but she was a terrible mother. Guilt swamped her, eating away at her insides.

'Any news?' she asked Stella as soon as she arrived at the hospital.

'Louisa's here. She's in with Jesse.'

They found a bench in the sunshine near the hospital café.

'Her parents will be relieved,' Carly said, taking a seat.

'Yeah.' Stella paused. 'Before the accident, Jesse told me something about Louisa and Steve.' Stella told Carly everything she knew.

'Wow! I didn't see that coming.'

'Me neither.'

Carly thought for a moment. 'I was aware Louisa left Sydney suddenly, but I had no idea ... And now she's back.'

Stella nodded. 'That'll make for an interesting showdown with Steve. I haven't seen him yet this morning.'

'Count your blessings. Have you seen Jesse?'

Stella shook her head. 'No, but Bernard said she's had a couple of mild seizures—'

'What?'

'It's okay. I've spoken to Mike about them but...' Stella hesitated.

'But what?'

'I get the feeling he's not telling me everything. I feel like there's more we could be doing.' Stella frowned. 'Look who's here.'

Carly followed Stella's gaze. It was Pete from the pub. An image of him nude, cavorting on a sofa with several other naked people popped into her head.

He saw them and walked over. 'Ladies, I'm sorry we're not meeting again in better circumstances.'

Carly couldn't help herself; she giggled nervously.

He glanced at her. 'Not those circumstances.' He indicated their bench. 'Do you mind?'

Stella and Carly shuffled along to make room.

'I want to apologise for taking you to that party,' Pete said. 'I knew what was going on, but Mike and Toby had no idea. I'm sorry for dragging you both there.'

'No one dragged us,' Carly said. 'We went freely.'

Stella punched her in the arm. 'Speak for yourself.'

Carly nodded. 'Okay, I dragged Stella, but Pete, you didn't drag me anywhere.'

'Still, you weren't expecting that sort of party, and then seeing your friend's husband ... It's not good.'

'Do you have any updates on Jesse?' Carly asked.

'I'm not her doctor. I think she's stable though.'

Stable was better than unstable, Carly thought.

He stood. 'Nice seeing you both again.' And walked away.

'That must have been hard for him,' Stella said.

'I guess. I keep wondering where we'd be today if we hadn't gone to that party. If we'd gone home like you wanted to.'

'I doubt we'd be here,' Stella said, 'but you can't change what's happened.'

Carly glanced through the café window and noticed Bernard and Dot. 'I don't want to intrude, but we should go in and talk to them.'

CHAPTER FORTY-SIX

JESSE

Jesse shifted uncomfortably in her sleep, pictures and thoughts racing through her mind. It dawned on her that she could hear her father crying. He never cried.

'Dad, what's wrong? What's the matter? Are you hurt? What's happened?'

He didn't answer.

Dot was there too; she called out Jesse's name.

'I'm right here,' Jesse said.

'How did this happen?' her mother was asking, her voice shaking with anger.

Her dad replied that he didn't know.

Jesse could see herself; it was weird. She was seven, lying beside the river in the spot where her family used to go camping. Gradually, the picture became sharper, though the gloomy area remained very dark. Gum trees towered above her, and the cool breeze practically froze her skin. Jesse was wet, her clothes soaked. Her parents were hunched over her, both crying.

Louisa and Jesse had been playing a silly game. Their father was supposed to be keeping his eye on them, but he'd fallen asleep under his newspaper. They were daring each other.

Higher, they screeched as each took it in turn to jump from tree branches into the water below. Higher and higher they climbed, taking greater risks each time.

Jesse jumped and missed her mark, hitting her head on a submerged rock. The current dragged her downstream, pulling her under the water. Her head hurt; it was bleeding when her dad eventually pulled her out of the water. Jesse could see herself lying very still. Then she started coughing, vomiting, shivering...

'She's going to be okay,' her dad was saying. 'She's fine. Our little girl is going to be fine.'

'I knew she'd be all right,' Louisa said, her voice no more than a whisper.

Louisa was beside her and Jesse felt comforted. Her big sister was home, and everything would be okay. Jesse smiled. She just needed to rest a little longer.

CHAPTER FORTY-SEVEN

LOUISA

'I thought they'd never leave,' Louisa said to Jesse.

Bernard had taken Dot for a walk and some fresh air. Louisa sat in her mother's vacated chair and took Jesse's hand in hers. It was limp and warm. 'If you wanted me to visit, you could have asked. You didn't need to go to such extremes.'

Four years. It had been four years since Louisa had seen her sister.

'I've been thinking about that time you, Ollie and Emily visited me in San Francisco,' she went on, deliberately keeping her voice cheerful. 'Remember how we hired that red convertible Mustang and drove down the coast to Los Angeles and Disneyland? Magic.' She stroked Jesse's arm before holding her hand again. 'We had so much fun. Ollie and Em didn't want to leave Disneyland even though it was almost ten o'clock at night and they could barely keep their eyes open.'

Louisa thought back to how the holiday had ended ... waving them goodbye at the airport. She remembered Jesse saying, 'Come home soon, darling. We miss you.' And she'd blown Louisa a kiss before the three of them had disappeared behind the departure gates.

'I loved that holiday,' Louisa said, tearing up. 'Come on, Jesse. Say something. Anything.' She kissed her sister's hand as tears streamed down her cheeks. 'I'm so sorry I haven't been here for you. That I left you. I'll make it up to you, really I will. Just wake up, okay?'

The room was strangely calm and quiet, apart from the machines whistling and beeping. Louisa felt powerless. She let go of Jesse's hand, and it lay where she'd left it, red and creased from Louisa's vice-like grip. Walking around the room, she examined the flowers, reading the two dozen or more cards that had been sent. November lilies mostly, a bunch of cream lisianthus and a box of colourful gerberas with a bright pink helium balloon encouraging Jesse to *Get Well Soon*.

Louisa sat down again. 'Jesse, it's really strange being back. Mum and Dad ... well, they don't look like our parents. They're so sad. It's like they've given up. We need you, Jess. Come back to us. We all love you, darling girl. Wake up! Tell me you're okay. I won't neglect you again.'

A noise came from behind her, and Louisa glanced up to see Steve in the doorway – the first time she'd seen him in six years. She stood, fighting to control her emotions, resisting the urge to physically attack him. He was responsible for this tragedy.

Steve didn't look too pleased to see Louisa either. 'Ollie, say hello to your Auntie Louisa,' he said, rather than greeting her himself. He turned back to the corridor. 'Where's he gone?'

'It's okay,' Louisa said. 'I'll find him.' She rushed past Steve into the corridor.

It didn't take her long to spot her nephew hiding behind a trolley of dirty linen. 'Hi, Ollie,' she said brightly. 'Look at you! You're so tall.' She gave him a hug, even though he resisted. Her arms felt heavy and awkward around his slight frame. 'I'm so sad about your mum. Will you come in to see her?'

He shrugged. Louisa was struck by how much he looked like Jesse: her olive skin and green eyes. The same sandy hair.

'Come on, I'll hold your hand.'

He hesitated for a moment before allowing her to lead him inside, towards Jesse's bed.

'It's like she's sleeping,' Louisa said.

'Mum doesn't sleep with hoses coming out of her mouth and nose.'

'Oliver!' Steve barked.

'No, he's right. It was a silly thing for me to say. Where's Emily?'

'Downstairs with her grandparents.' Steve shook his head. 'Ollie wanted to kiss his mum good morning before he goes to school.'

'She's getting better, isn't she, Dad?'

'I hope so.'

Louisa thought it odd that this brave little boy, with his perfectly ironed grey shirt, shorts, and navy and red striped tie, had to go to school and spend the day mastering fractions and comprehension while his mother lay here in a coma.

Ollie kissed Jesse hesitantly on her bruised puffy cheek, and ran out of the room shouting, 'I'm going to find Emmy at the shop.'

'Should we go after him?' Louisa asked.

Steve sighed. 'He and Emily are doing it tough.'

'Steve, I'm so sorry,' Louisa said, forgetting her anger and focusing on the children.

'I bet this isn't the homecoming you had in mind.'

'No, but Jesse's going to be okay. I know it.'

'It doesn't seem real. Four days ago she was fine ... and now this.' He appeared bemused. 'Why?'

Louisa shook her head. 'Accidents happen. She had a lot on her mind.'

'Like what?'

She couldn't believe what she was hearing. Hello? 'Are you forgetting any special parties you've been to lately?'

'One lousy party. Anyway, this isn't about me. It's about Jesse. We need her to get better, so we can move on from all of this' – he waved his arms in the air – 'and start over fresh.' He shook his head and stared at Jesse's still body. 'Why did she do it?'

'It wasn't on purpose.'

Steve didn't respond.

'Mum mentioned something about–'

'Your mother! She hasn't shut up since she got here.'

Louisa wanted to tell him to leave her family alone, but she wasn't in a place to criticise; she'd moved to another country and rarely spoke to her parents. 'Before all of this happened, Jesse told me she wanted to have another baby, and you said–'

'It's none of your business what I said.'

'She's wanted another baby for a long time.'

'I don't have to listen to this.'

'You told her that it was "fiscally irresponsible to bring another child into this unpredictable world".'

'Does she tell you everything?' Steve shook his head. 'And so what if I did? It's the truth.'

'Jeez, Steve, you're unbelievable! No wonder she's nervous.'

Steve stared at Jesse. 'You're saying she did this to punish me?'

'I can think of better ways to punish you than by slamming into a tree.'

Why had she said that? This was too awful. Louisa couldn't face Steve any longer. She needed to get out of the room and breathe fresh air. She turned to leave and almost bumped into a man in a white doctor's coat who was hovering in the doorway.

He moved closer and Louisa read his name tag: *Dr Mike Thompson.*

'How's she doing?' Steve asked him.

'Not responding as well as we'd hoped.'

'But she's all right, isn't she? I mean, it might take a while, but she'll be okay?' Louisa asked.

'This is Louisa, Jesse's sister,' Steve said.

Doctor Thompson nodded in her direction. 'It's taking longer than is ideal.'

'What does that mean?' Louisa asked.

'No two coma patients are the same. By this stage, some people display movement and make sounds; some, like Jesse, don't. The hard truth about coma is that we don't know how well, or even if, the patient will recover. Recovery from any brain injury, especially one as significant as Jesse's, takes time.'

'Can we do anything to help her?' Louisa asked.

'You're doing all you can by being here and talking to her. You could also try playing her favourite music, maybe even reading stories. It all helps. But right now, we need to continue our tests.' He turned to Steve. 'We're going to raise Jesse's temperature to see how her brain responds.'

Steve nodded and Doctor Thompson ushered him and Louisa from the room. As they walked away, the 'Do not disturb' light outside Jesse's door flashed in red neon.

Doctor Thompson's words played through Louisa's mind: *The hard truth about coma is that we don't know how well, or even if, the patient will recover.* Any scenario other than Jesse waking up and walking out of the hospital unaided didn't bear thinking about. She was going to be fine. Any minute now, she'd wake up and wonder what all the fuss was about. Louisa could imagine how horrified Jesse would be that her family and friends had spent days grieving around her.

The last thing Louisa wanted to do was hang out with Steve, but he was heading to the cafeteria to meet up with her parents, Ollie and Emmy. And strangely, Louisa wanted to be near her family.

CHAPTER FORTY-EIGHT

At the cafeteria, Dot and Bernard were sitting by the window, watching Ollie and Emily, who were outside in the playground.

'Coffee?' Bernard asked Louisa.

'Thanks. Strong. Black.'

'Two sugars, right?'

'No sugar, thanks.'

'Of course,' Bernard replied.

'We'll go home soon, Louisa, so you can rest,' Dot said.

Emily came inside. The image of Steve, she had dark brown eyes, straight brown hair, thickset, almost the opposite of Oliver's build and complexion.

'Hi, Emily,' Louisa said. 'Remember me?'

Emily ran behind her father's back. Half an arm reached out to snatch the remains of a muffin Dot had been pulling apart. Dot didn't notice; she was staring out the window at a man sitting in a wheelchair in the morning sunshine.

Bernard returned with a coffee, which he placed in front of Louisa. He watched while she took a sip. 'Okay?'

Louisa nodded. 'Perfect.'

Everyone was tired. Worn out. Trying to make sense of the

last four days. But still, Louisa itched to have a go at Steve. How he could stand there like he'd done nothing wrong was incomprehensible to her. She glared at him, but he took no notice.

'Go and play on the swings with Ollie,' he told Emily, 'while I have a word with Nanna and Pop.' She obeyed him, and he turned to his in-laws. 'The doctors say Jesse's not doing as well as they'd expected.'

'She has internal injuries,' Dot said. 'It was only the airbag that saved her. She drove so fast into that tree. Why?' Dot banged her fist on the table.

'Easy, love.' Bernard grabbed her hand and pulled it towards him.

'She's going to be fine, Mum. You'll see,' Louisa said, struggling to keep her voice calm. The last thing they needed was her mother's theatrics taking centre stage.

'I knew something was up with her, Louisa. I knew it. She hasn't been herself.'

'Leave it, Dot,' Bernard said, glancing at Steve.

Louisa closed her eyes as her mother continued talking.

'I could see it. Whenever she dropped a pen on the floor, she had to tap her right foot three times before she bent down to pick it up. And what about her checking all the locks on the house before she went out? She was stressed. I should've stepped in and done something. I should've known it would end like this.' Dot started crying. 'Goodness knows how she got on at the library.'

'Come on, Mum,' Louisa said, putting her arm around her. 'From what Jesse told me, she loves working at the library.'

Steve snorted. 'How would you know? I told her the job was too stressful.'

'It wasn't the job causing her stress,' Louisa said pointedly. 'She wanted to be at the library. She looked forward to it.'

'True,' Dot agreed.

'Whatever,' Steve said.

Dot turned to him. 'What about you? Did you notice her habits getting worse?'

Steve puffed out his chest. 'Of course. Even Ollie's picked up a few of them.'

'And did you do anything to help her?' Louisa asked, unable to stop herself. She'd had enough of her brother-in-law and was more than ready to reveal some significant truths about him.

'Obviously I tried to help her,' Steve replied, indignant.

'Did you really?' Dot said. 'Because I never saw it.'

'Dot,' Bernard cautioned.

'You must have seen she wasn't herself – or were you too busy to notice?' Dot's tone had a sharp edge.

'I noticed, Dot. I told her to get help. Just the other afternoon, in fact, when she had the fall.'

'And where were you then, Steve? I was the first to reach Jesse even though I called you straight after Louisa phoned me. I was at your house for a good thirty minutes before you turned up, and your office is only fifteen minutes away.'

'Thank you, Dot, but I can't leave work mid-meeting. Our company is involved in top secret strategic movements right now. It's non-stop. I can't just up and leave every time there's a crisis at home. My staff rely on me. And, yes, I noticed something was up with her. That's why I told her to get help. I can't watch over her twenty-four seven.'

'Told her, yes. But did you actually help?'

'What are you implying? And, by the way, what did you do to help?' Steve glared at Dot. 'Jesse always seems particularly stressed after talking to you.'

'Let's stop right there,' Bernard said. 'This isn't helping anyone.'

Steve looked towards the playground. The kids, oblivious to

the adults' conversation, played on the see-saw. 'I'm sorry,' Steve said. 'But her behaviour was affecting the children, Ollie in particular.'

'So, you agree it's gotten worse in recent months?' Dot said.

Steve nodded.

'There you go.' Dot raised her eyebrows. 'There has to be a reason. Once we find the source of her worries, we'll have the answer to why she's been so stressed over the past few months.'

Bernard nodded.

'I don't understand why she didn't talk to me about it,' Dot went on. 'I'm her mother.'

'Maybe she tried,' Louisa said.

'I know what you're all thinking,' Steve said. 'It's my fault. I'm the bastard responsible!'

Louisa couldn't have put it better herself.

'I can hear you lot from inside the chapel.' Milly, Louisa's elderly grandmother, walked towards their table.

Louisa got out of her chair to hug her. 'Grandma!' She kissed her on both cheeks. 'I'm so happy to see you.'

Louisa loved Milly. Her fondest memories of growing up involved her grandma: Christmas drinks when Milly got slaughtered after two tumblers of sherry, Jesse's seventh birthday party where Milly gave a pink piglet piñata such a ferocious beating all the other parents had looked alarmed.

'Despite the metre in height I've lost?' Milly said.

Louisa smiled. 'You're just as I remember.'

'Don't give me that nonsense, Louisa. I wasn't born yesterday. When did you fly in?'

'A little while ago.'

'Seen your poor sister then?'

Louisa nodded.

'And your niece and nephew?'

She nodded again.

Milly looked around the table. 'Couldn't spare a few moments to pray to our Lord? Even short prayers find their way to heaven. You're all too busy for that, I see.'

Dot rolled her eyes. Bernard squirmed in his seat. Steve half-smiled.

'But you've got time for coffee and cake!' Milly was on a roll. 'Am I the only believer here? I'm in the chapel, praying, asking for guidance, and I walk out and what do I find? You lot huddled together, caterwauling and sipping cappuccinos. The Lord should be our caffeine at this time.'

'Okay, Mum, that's enough,' Dot said, helping Milly into an uncomfortable plastic chair. 'I'm surprised you'd pray in a chapel anyway, given your new-fangled ways. Would you like a tea?'

Milly nodded. 'Yes, I think I would.'

'Well,' Steve said, standing, 'I'd better take the kids to school.'

'What about Jesse and the doctors?' Dot asked.

'I'll go up now before I leave.'

'I'll come with you.' As much as Louisa abhorred being alone with Steve, she needed to hear first-hand Jesse's doctor's report. Then, armed with the most up-to-date knowledge, she and her parents could formulate an action plan. With or without Steve's help.

CHAPTER FORTY-NINE

'Steve,' Doctor Thompson said as soon as he saw Steve and Louisa, 'I'm afraid I have bad news.'

Louisa's hand flew to her mouth. *Please let her be okay.* She wanted the doctor to get on with it and tell them the news, but when he started speaking again, his words were fuzzy. Louisa stumbled.

The doctor caught her. 'Are you okay?'

She closed her eyes to compose herself. 'Yes. Go on.' But Louisa still had trouble focusing. Jet lag. Her mouth had a strange metallic taste, and the room was spinning. Maybe if she sat down...

'Pregnant?' Steve spat out the word.

That got Louisa's attention. Jesse, pregnant? Man, that sister of hers was good at keeping secrets – rather like Louisa herself.

'There must be some mistake,' Steve went on. 'Jesse can't possibly be pregnant.'

'I'm sorry, your wife *was* pregnant but she has miscarried.'

Steve didn't seem to hear. 'We had this talk only last week. She's not pregnant. It's impossible.' He sounded livid.

'Calm down,' Louisa said, regaining some strength. 'Maybe

she didn't get the memo.' She turned to the doctor, light-headed but focused. 'How pregnant?'

'Approximately six weeks.'

'Six weeks!' Steve fumed. 'This keeps getting better. I don't–'

'Is she okay?' Louisa asked. 'How will this affect her recovery?'

'The miscarriage won't affect Jesse's physical recovery. But any time a woman suffers a miscarriage, there's inevitable emotional trauma.' He looked at Steve. 'I'm sorry. If you'll excuse me.'

'She must have known she was pregnant all this time,' Steve said after the doctor had left the room. 'Did you know?'

'Me?' Louisa said. 'I knew she wanted another baby, but no, I didn't know she was pregnant. Maybe Jesse didn't know either.'

'Ha! She'd have known! And when the hell was she going to tell me? On the way to the delivery room? Despite everything we talked about, she went and got herself pregnant. Again.'

Louisa sat down beside Jesse. 'Under the circumstances, it doesn't really matter.' Steve went to say something else, but Louisa pointedly ignored him and took Jesse's hand. 'Jesse, can you hear me? It's Louisa. I'm with you. Can you hear me, sweetheart?'

'Of course she bloody well can't. Look at her.'

'We're supposed to talk to her,' Louisa said.

'Oh yeah?'

'Yes, actually. To let her know we're with her. Talk to her about what's happening in our lives. Ask her questions, include her.' She stroked Jesse's hand. 'We're not going to leave until you get better, Jess.'

'Great,' Steve said. 'When she starts answering and tells you why she got pregnant, let me know.'

'She's not pregnant anymore, Steve.'

'No ... well when she wakes up–'

'What? You're going to abuse her for not obeying your orders?'

Steve rolled his eyes. 'Jesse knows she's in the wrong. I just want her to admit it. Then we can put all of this nonsense behind us.'

Louisa glared at him, unable to speak.

He glanced at his watch. 'It's after eleven. I've got to drop the children at school and get to work.'

'Aren't you forgetting something?' she said as he moved past her towards the door.

He stopped and turned around, looking puzzled. He checked his pockets for his wallet and keys. 'No, I don't–'

'Don't you want to kiss your wife before you leave?'

Steve did a for-fuck's-sake eye roll and walked over to the bed. He bent and kissed Jesse's bandaged forehead. 'See you soon, darling.' He straightened and glared at Louisa. 'Happy? It's not as if she knows I'm kissing her.'

'I can see this is really tearing you up.'

'Don't you dare talk to me about compassion, Louisa. You waltz in here, holier than thou, after an absence of six years, expecting everyone to fall at your feet. Don't you dare think you're better than me. If Jesse wasn't in this state, you'd still be on the other side of the world basking in your debauched lifestyle.'

'How can you say that?'

'You've never had any intention of coming back.'

'What would you know? I love Jesse.'

'Yeah, of course you do, Louisa. She's got all of your letters to prove it.' He pushed past her and out into the corridor.

CHAPTER FIFTY

STELLA

Carly and I were about to enter the hospital cafeteria when Liz phoned. She sounded distraught. I turned and walked outside to our familiar bench in the sunshine. Carly followed and sat down. I paced as Liz talked.

'Gracie told me the news. I've been trying to get hold of you for days. I can't believe it. How's Jesse? Is it bad?'

I filled her in as best I could.

'You don't think I caused this, do you?'

What was I supposed to say? Yes, Jesse was so upset over losing her job, she got distracted by the rain and her tears and drove into a tree. I wasn't that heartless. Liz was suffering enough. 'No, Liz, it was probably a combination of bad weather and bad luck.'

'I've sent flowers.'

'She'll appreciate that.'

'Stella, you're not really quitting, are you? We need you.'

'Thanks, but I can't really think about the library right now. My priority is Jesse. I can't think beyond the next hour, let alone the next day or week.'

'Of course. Take your time. We've got a couple of casuals filling in.'

'How did that go?' Carly asked after I'd ended the call.

I shrugged. 'Liz feels responsible.'

'We all do.'

'Yeah, except Steve. I know Jesse wouldn't want me quitting, but I'm still furious with Liz.' I sighed. 'Eventually, life will have to return to some kind of normalcy. We can't wait at the hospital all day and night for weeks on end.'

Carly nodded. 'But I feel so guilty getting on with the everyday while Jesse's here. It all seems pointless.'

'I know. Every time I think about leaving the hospital, I panic. I don't want to leave Jesse alone. She needs us, especially when she first opens her eyes.'

The last few days had passed in a blur. All the waiting ... and then, when we were allowed to see her, the reality that this wasn't some minor bump to the head. The woman lying in intensive care, battered and bandaged, hooked up to tubes and machines, didn't look like Jesse.

'At least Louisa's here now,' Carly said. 'That'll make Jesse happy. Coffee?'

I nodded.

Inside the café, we found Dot and Bernard.

'Great news that Louisa's arrived,' I said.

Dot nodded.

'Any other news?' Carly asked.

'There's never any news,' Dot said sadly.

'She's...' Bernard faltered. 'She's had another seizure, but they've given her medication.'

'The doctors say that's not out of the ordinary,' I said, trying to sound encouraging.

Bernard nodded. 'You're right. For now, there's nothing we can do except wait, but it's so frustrating.'

That was what we were all doing. Waiting. And I'd never been good at that.

Carly and I left Bernard and Dot and walked to the counter.

'You know what? I don't think I can face another coffee,' Carly said.

'Me neither,' I agreed. 'So now what?'

'I feel like I'm in the way. I might–'

'Look,' I whispered. Louisa and Steve were standing just outside the cafeteria, glaring at each other.

We joined them. 'How is she?' I asked.

'In a coma,' Steve replied.

I stood there, appalled, not knowing where to look, afraid of bursting into tears at any moment.

'Hi,' Carly said, extending her hand to Louisa. 'You must be Jesse's sister. I'm Carly.'

Steve rolled his eyes and pushed past us.

Louisa shook her head, then smiled at Carly as she blinked back tears. 'Nice to finally meet you.'

I put my arm around her. 'Jesse'll be okay.'

'I know,' Louisa sniffed. 'She has to be. But it's so sad. Thank you both for being here. Now, if you'll excuse me...' She went to join her parents.

'I'll get going too,' Carly said, glancing at her watch. 'Maybe go into the city. Walk in Hyde Park. Meet Brett for lunch.'

'Sounds nice.'

'It does sound nice, doesn't it? I can't remember the last time I was at Brett's office.' She paused. 'Brett's always telling me that I take no interest in his work, so I'll surprise him. Show him that I can be an involved and interested wife.'

'Lunch with Brett might be just the boost you need.'

I spotted Mike down the corridor. 'I'll be leaving soon too, but I'll just have a quick word with Mike.'

'Okay,' Carly said. 'Let me know if there's any news.'

'Will do.' I dashed down the hall. 'Mike!'

He turned and waited for me to catch up.

'How is she?'

'I wish I had better news,' he said, giving my arm a gentle rub.

'Have the seizures been bad?'

'No. Still...'

'Still, what?'

'Our biggest concern is that she's still unconscious; she hasn't opened her eyes once since the accident.' He paused, and I could almost hear him deliberating over what to say next. 'Stella, I'm afraid it's up to Jesse now whether or not she wakes up. The best thing you can do is talk to her – tell her what's going on in your life, your friends' lives. I know how hard this must be for you, but unfortunately, it's a waiting game.'

'And the odds?'

Mike grimaced. 'I don't give odds.'

'Even? Sixty–forty? What?' I hesitated for a moment. 'What about her brain?'

He glanced down at his hands before answering. 'We're hoping for a one hundred per cent recovery, but there's no way to tell what her brain is going to do. I'm sorry, but there's no magic shot and no surgery option. Only time will tell.'

I shook my head. It was hard to take in.

'Talk to her,' he said again. 'Tell her how you feel. And, Stella, whatever happens, don't neglect your own family. It's easy to get caught up with what's happened to Jesse, but, as harsh as it sounds, life goes on, and your children need you as much as ever. Don't forget that.'

I nodded.

'I need to check on other patients, but I promise I'll let you know if there are any changes to Jesse's condition.'

After Mike disappeared into an elevator, I stood rigid for a few moments, deciding what to do. I wanted to see Jesse, but I was starting to feel I'd outstayed my welcome. Maybe if I just peered in on her? I wouldn't stay long. I just needed to check in and say hello.

Arriving at Jesse's room, I peeked in and was relieved to see only Louisa there.

'Sorry, I don't want to interrupt.'

'Not at all. Come in.'

I pulled up a chair and sat on the other side of Jesse's bed. 'Any change?'

Louisa shook her head. 'Did you know she was pregnant?'

'Pregnant? She'll be so happy.' Then I realised what Louisa had said. 'Wait. *Was* pregnant?'

Louisa nodded. 'She miscarried.'

'No!'

'Yeah. She was about six weeks along. You didn't know?'

I shook my head. 'Maybe Jesse didn't know either.'

'That's what I thought.' Louisa gripped her sister's hand tighter. 'Are you in there, Jess? I'm sorry about the fight with Steve. Despite what that asshat says, I do love you, darling.'

We sat in silence until Louisa spoke again. 'I've got so much to tell her, but it feels weird talking to her when she can't respond.'

'I know the feeling,' I said quietly. 'Would you prefer me to leave?'

'No, stay. We can both talk to her.' Louisa took a deep breath. 'I'm sorry I called your husband an asshat, Jess. But fuck! He's a massive asshat. And to think you had sex with him not once but twice. Really. You're a braver woman than I could ever be.'

'She's brave, all right.' I smiled at Jesse, then looked at Louisa. 'Just before the accident, Jesse told me you'd known Steve a long time?'

'Back in the dark days, yeah. You must think I'm...' She trailed off.

'I don't think anything. Truly.'

'I know it hurt Jesse, finding out about me and what I used to do. I should've told her sooner.'

'I can understand why you didn't.'

'Part of me didn't want to acknowledge it. If I'd told her about Steve's involvement, it would have meant telling her what I'd been up to as well, and I couldn't bear the thought of disappointing her. I chose to believe I was doing the right thing by not interfering in Jesse's life.'

We sat silently for a few moments, both gazing at Jesse. Two clear plastic prongs extended from her nose as she breathed oxygen in and out. A bank of machines monitored her vital signs, flashing red and green on a digital display. The tube to Jesse's mouth had been removed and her facial swelling had subsided.

Louisa said, 'So, Jess, after you get out of here, you've got to stick to your guns and leave him. I might even stay in Sydney for a while. You can teach me how to cook, because I suck big time. I'll let you in on a secret: I've always been jealous of your culinary abilities. Remember Mrs Beetle's home science class and the end-of-year bake-off? She was so pissed off when your double chocolate mud cake beat her saggy sponge. Remember? I'm sorry I've missed out on so much. The kids ... Holidays ... Christmases ... Birthdays. Time we should have spent together now forever lost.'

She stroked Jesse's hand, then looked over at me. 'How do you really think she's doing?'

I shook my head. 'Who knows? It's hard to take in, isn't it?'

'Impossible. Jesse's always been so full of energy.'

'Yeah, she's always so vibrant. So alive.'

'But she was struggling before the accident, right?'

'Yeah, even before the Steve bombshell, she wasn't doing great, dealing with her anxiety. She'd been working hard to keep it in check. Steve's controlling behaviour didn't help. And on top of that, she'd just lost her job.'

'No! She didn't tell me.'

'It happened right before the accident.'

'Poor Jesse.'

'The manager at the library couldn't put up with Jesse's quirks any longer so she made her redundant. I was furious. Still am.'

Louisa looked stricken. 'And there I was on the other side of the world, completely preoccupied with my own life. Too busy to fly back to Sydney to see her. And for what? I wish things could be ... different.'

'You're here now, Louisa. That's what's important.'

'It shouldn't have taken something like this for me to come back and see her and the twins. She's going to be devastated about losing the baby. Do you think she knew she was pregnant?'

I shook my head. 'I really don't know. She talked about wanting another baby, but whether she knew or not, I have no idea. I do know that a pregnancy would have symbolised a new beginning for her. New life, new hope.'

'And now that's been taken away from her.' Louisa leaned over Jesse and whispered, 'Jesse, are you there? Wake up, sweetie. Stella and I are here, waiting to talk to you.'

We sat in silence for a long time, watching Jesse and listening. Outside the room, staff wheeled trolleys and medical equipment up and down the corridor. I heard muffled conversations of people making their way to visit friends and relatives.

'Jesse mentioned you were seeing someone?' I said, wanting to break the silence.

'Philippe, yeah. He's great, but it's nothing serious.'

'Do you want it to be?'

'Nah. I tend to move on when things get too cosy. I mean, marriage and commitment is fine – just not for me.'

Even though my marriage hadn't worked out, Louisa's outlook seemed calculated to ensure she didn't get too close. Okay, so I didn't want a commitment with anyone right now either, but I knew what it felt like to be in a long-term loving relationship, and when it worked, it was heaven.

Thinking about long-term relationships led me on to Mike ... and how the idea of taking our friendship any further frightened me. The proper thing to do was have some time on my own and grieve the end of my marriage. But what if the feelings I was developing for Mike were real? An intense connection like that didn't come along often. I'd been with Garth seventeen years, and Mike was the first person I'd met since then who'd made me stop and think, what if?

Just then, the man himself walked in with two other hospital staff I hadn't seen before.

'We're going to run more tests now,' he said gently.

'Of course,' Louisa said.

'We'll keep you posted,' Mike added, holding my gaze for longer than he needed to.

Filled with warmth, I turned to Jesse. 'We'll be back soon, sweetheart.'

Louisa and I caught the elevator to the ground floor, along with a heavily pregnant woman and her partner, who was flustered and fussing over her. We let them out first and watched as she waddled towards the gift shop. I thought about Jesse and her miscarriage. So sad.

'Stella, can I ask you something?' Louisa said.

I turned to look at her. 'Shoot.'

'Mum said there'd been talk that Jesse might have deliberately...' She didn't finish.

'One of the witnesses said he thinks that's what happened. But I can't believe Jesse would do that to Ollie and Emily. She'd have needed to be deeply depressed to do that, no longer in control of her actions. I saw her practically every day, and I don't think she was in that state.'

The more I considered the idea, the more resolute I became. There was no way Jesse deliberately drove into a tree. And if she'd had the slightest inkling she was pregnant, I was doubly sure that self-harm would have been the last thought on her mind.

CHAPTER FIFTY-ONE

CARLY

Truth be told, Carly couldn't wait to leave the hospital. It was depressing seeing the devastation on Jesse's parents' faces; watching Ollie and Emmy play on the see-saw, knowing something was terribly wrong with their mother but not quite understanding the gravity of the situation. Not to mention how hard it was being around Steve.

Regardless of how many times Stella argued otherwise, Carly felt responsible for what had happened to Jesse. If she hadn't blurted out what they'd seen at the party the previous week, none of this might have happened.

And then there was Toby. Every time she saw him at the hospital, it gave her an ugly reminder of her ridiculous behaviour. Carly was embarrassed she'd flirted with him so madly. She really was a Jekyll and Hyde.

Carly dropped her car at home, caught a train to Town Hall station and walked towards Brett's office. It was three years since she'd last visited. Both boys had come along, and they'd all had lunch at the revolving Summit Restaurant, forty-seven floors above the city with breath-taking 360-degree views of Sydney and beyond. Then they'd climbed the Harbour Bridge.

A great day. It was hard to believe it had been three years. Time flew.

Over the past few days, Carly had made the decision to try to revitalise her marriage. Jesse's accident had made her realise how precious life was; it could be snatched away in seconds. Will and Nick deserved her full attention and a strong commitment to their father, and she was going to do her best to deliver.

As she walked down Elizabeth Street towards Brett's office, she wondered what was happening with Nicholas. She still hadn't heard back from Evan Sinclair, the sports master. Nick hadn't called or emailed either. If Brett was in a relaxed mood, she'd bring it up.

She glanced at her watch. Almost one o'clock. She was hungry and totally coffeed out. An image of Jesse lying in that horrid hospital bed, machinery whirring around her, flashed through Carly's mind, and she shuddered, silently praying that that afternoon there'd be an improvement in her condition.

When she arrived at Brett's building, Carly momentarily forgot which floor he was on. Ninth, that was it. Inside the elevator, she checked her reflection in the mirrored walls and watched the numbers change as they ascended. She was a little nervous. At the ninth floor, the elevator pinged, and the doors opened. She took a right towards his office. As she approached, she saw him leaning against the wall talking to someone, a woman. Colleague? Secretary? He was animated. It was good to see him smiling, enjoying office banter. Carly's heart skipped a little.

'Carly,' he said when he saw her. 'What a nice surprise.' He kissed her on the lips, then introduced her to his colleague, Nell, before she walked away.

He led Carly inside his office. 'Everything okay?'

She nodded. 'It's been a while, hasn't it?'

'Better late than never. I'm happy to see you. Any change with Jesse?'

Carly shook her head and stared out the window. 'It's horrible. Devastating. I feel useless.' She turned back to face him. 'Then there's us. I'm sorry for everything.'

'Carls, it's not just you. I haven't been doing my bit either. I need to pull back on my work commitments and spend more time with you and Will, especially now with Nicholas away.'

'About that,' Carly said, feeling tears sting her eyes. 'Nick's in a bit of trouble.'

'What kind of trouble?'

'He's been suspended from his coaching job because he and some other boys were fighting in the locker room.'

'That doesn't sound too bad. I'm sure–'

'Wait. There's more. Nick ... the boys were naked, flicking towels around.'

Brett raised his eyebrows. 'So? They were in a locker room. It's not like they were streaking through the school grounds. I'm sure it'll all be sorted.'

'But the suspension?'

'If it makes you feel better, I'll ring and see what I can find out.'

Carly nodded, fresh tears streaming. They were already talking about Nicholas so now was the time to bring up the matter of the letters. 'There's something else...'

Brett half-smiled and motioned for her to sit down. 'This is certainly the week for it.' He pulled up a chair beside her. 'Okay, I'm listening.'

'It's about Nick. I don't know where to start. I found some letters ... I think he might have been having a friendship with a teacher, a male–'

Brett sighed and put his hand on Carly's knee, stroking it gently. 'I'm going to stop you there.'

'No, I need to tell you this. I'm not making it up.'

'I know you're not. I already know about the letters.'

Carly blinked. 'What?'

'Mr Busby. Nick spoke to me about him. I went to the school, and we sorted it out.'

'You kept this a secret from me?'

'Nick didn't want a fuss. We were both worried you'd blow it out of proportion. Anyway, I fixed the problem.'

'Why didn't you tell me?' Carly said, brushing away his hand and standing. 'He's my son.'

'Carly, calm down,' Brett said, rising too. 'You're creating a drama out of nothing.'

She had to get out. Take herself for a long walk so she could think. On the one hand, she was relieved Brett already knew about the letters and the matter had been dealt with, but on the other, she was furious with him for not telling her. So furious she could barely look at him.

'I need to go,' she said, striding towards the door.

'Stop. Calm down. Let's have lunch and talk about this rationally.'

'Don't tell me to calm down.' She kept walking, only stopping when she reached the elevator. She jabbed the button with her finger. 'Hurry the fuck up.'

'I can explain,' Brett said, trying to step between her and the elevator.

Carly put her hand up in front of his face to stop him. 'Please don't.' The elevator doors opened. Several suits moved to the side to let her in. 'I don't want to know.'

The doors closed on Brett, a look of resignation on his face.

As she stepped out of the lift on the ground floor, her phone rang. An older woman standing beside her touched her on the arm. 'Don't answer, love. Give it time.'

She nodded and turned the phone off without checking the caller identification.

Once out of the elevator, Carly put her sunnies on and fled down the street, not looking back. She walked all the way down to the Opera House, along the foreshore and into the Botanic Gardens, tears flowing. Finally, she took a seat on a park bench and, in a daze, watched the ferries bobbing along the harbour.

By the time she checked her watch again, it was nearly four. She had no idea how it had got to that time but didn't really care. She turned on her phone to find several messages – all from Brett. The rational part of her knew he must have believed he had good reason to keep the matter from her, but she was hurt. All these years, she'd believed that she and Nick were close. Why couldn't he have confided in her?

Carly caught the train home and walked straight to the fridge in search of wine. It had been four days since her last glass. She'd give up drinking again, tomorrow.

As she drank the chardonnay, everything fell into place: the devastation and betrayal she felt at Brett not confiding in her about the problems Nick was having at school, his assertion that he'd preferred to fix it himself rather than discuss it with her, his belief that she'd overreact and turn it into a huge drama. Who was she kidding? This wasn't a marriage. She couldn't lie to herself or to Brett any longer.

She remembered back to when she'd told Brett about her desire for a fuck buddy. He hadn't seemed fazed. Oh, he'd said he was angry, but he wasn't. Not really. Carly gulped more wine as thoughts dashed in and out of her head. And what was the story with his colleague, Nell? They'd certainly seemed very chatty and friendly when Carly had arrived unexpectedly at the office. He was having an affair, she knew it.

Carly heard the key in the door turn as she reached for the bottle. It was empty. She'd drained it in less than an hour.

'Carly, I've been so worried,' Brett said when he found her propped up at the dining table. 'Are you okay?'

'Couldn't be better,' she trilled. 'But Brett, our marriage is over. Finito. Done and dusted.'

'What are you saying?'

'I'm saying that Blind Freddy could see that we haven't been getting on for a very long time. Why can't you?'

'Carly, stop.'

'No, it's over. You and I don't fit together any longer. We don't do anything together. We're a joke. You have your business and golf and that's it. When you're not working, you're playing golf–'

'I haven't played in months.'

'Or fucking your lady friend. Who knows?'

'You've been drinking. You're not making any sense.'

'I'm making perfect sense. Besides, I don't have a problem with any of this. It's great you've got other activities to distract you.'

He shook his head. 'Distract me from what exactly?'

'Haven't you been listening? Our marriage, Brett!'

He reached out to hold her, but she pulled away.

'How could you? How could you not tell me about Nicky? I feel so hurt and betrayed.' She shook her head. 'The fact you couldn't confide in me tells me everything I need to know about the state of our relationship.'

'That's not true. We were trying to protect you–'

'Protect me? Please!'

'I'm sorry,' he said, looking sad and beaten. 'I am truly sorry.'

'Can't you see?' Carly said, struggling to compose herself. 'We've ended up like Stella and Garth.'

'No, we haven't.'

She took a step back. 'How can you say that? I've been thinking that with Nicholas overseas it might be good to take a break.'

'A break?'

'Yes, as in you and me taking a break from each other, exploring other paths.'

'But I don't want to explore other paths. I'm happy on this path.'

'You aren't.' Carly burst into fresh tears.

'Carls, this is a passing phase, trust me. You're upset because you're missing Nicholas. That's the problem. Why don't you call him? You'll feel better once you've spoken to him. Then, tonight, we can eat out, just the two of us, or see a movie. Why don't we do that?'

She groaned. 'Brett, no.'

'You're being emotional because of all this talk about Nick. I'll never leave you, ever. This is my home, my life. This is where my family is.'

'But I don't even know if I'm still in love with you. We've had a good run–'

'We're still having a good run.' Brett's eyes began to well up too. 'I love you. I love my boys. I can fix this, really.'

Carly went upstairs and took a shower. When she came back downstairs half an hour later, Brett had prepared marinated steaks and a Greek salad for dinner, and was fixing a leaking tap in the laundry.

'At the weekend, we'll have a clean-up,' he told her. 'Time to get stuck into some odd jobs around the house and the garden I've been neglecting for months. Make a list and I'll get on with them.'

'Brett,' she said, but Carly couldn't think what to say next. The fight had completely gone out of her. She nodded. 'Okay, sure. Sounds like a good plan.'

CHAPTER FIFTY-TWO

LOUISA

Stella insisted on driving Louisa to her parents' house, and although Louisa invited her inside, Stella declined.

Louisa stood at the front gate, looking around, seeking familiar sights. Where there used to be paddocks, and horses had grazed across the road, there were now five blond-brick monstrosities. Ugh! The gravel street of her childhood was a bitumen road with cement guttering. There was even a cement pathway for pedestrians.

Overgrown camellia trees lined the fence of her parents' home, and the huge liquid amber she and Jesse climbed as kids was losing its leaves. Ancient agapanthus crept along the driveway. The house itself was as Louisa remembered, though weathered and badly in need of painting. The once-dark-green woodwork was pale and flaky, and the window frames looked dated and worn.

'Come on, Louisa. I've made a pot of tea,' Dot called impatiently from the front door.

Louisa nodded and walked towards her.

Dot's outstretched arms captured Louisa as soon as she made it up the steps onto the wooden veranda. 'Welcome home.'

A cursory glance around inside revealed that most of the furnishings remained the same, but the framed photos were different. They used to feature Jesse and Louisa at various ages; now they were mostly of Oliver and Emily. Then there were all of Dot's churchy ornaments: a crucifix, the Madonna – no change there.

Louisa followed Dot into the lounge room to find her father and Grandma Milly. Bernard's favourite brown chair had survived but looked worn and tattered, despite having obviously been patched up umpteen times. Dot had given it to him as an anniversary gift many moons ago and no one else had dared sit in it, ever.

'Ah, Louisa, you're home,' Bernard said, folding his newspaper and putting it down on the side table. 'Any news?'

'The doctors were doing more tests when Stella and I left.' Louisa wasn't ready to talk about Jesse's pregnancy. 'I hardly recognised the street. It's changed.'

'A lot of things have changed since you lived here, Louisa,' Dot said, handing her a cup of tea. In this house, tea fixed many ills.

'I'm surprised Steve didn't stay longer at the hospital this morning,' Louisa said, turning the subject away from her prolonged absence.

'Steve's Steve. He works hard and expects everyone else to fall in line,' Dot said.

'But given the circumstances...'

Bernard stood. 'Everyone copes in their own way.'

'He's an arrogant prick if you ask me,' Louisa said.

Grandma giggled into her tea. 'No change there then.'

'Louisa, really,' Dot said. 'What about you? How's university life?'

'Busy,' she answered truthfully. 'There are always new

courses to teach, assessments, student dramas ... never a dull moment.'

'Seeing anyone?' Grandma asked.

'I am, actually. His name's Philippe and he's ... at university with me.'

'Do I hear wedding bells?' Grandma probed.

'I don't think so.'

Dot clicked her tongue. 'You're not getting any younger, Louisa. Maybe this Philippe character is your Prince Charming. It's high time you settled down, don't you think?'

Great. Louisa had been home all of five minutes, and her mother had already given her the settling-down lecture. Following Grandma's lead, Louisa pretended Dot hadn't spoken. 'What about you, Grandma?'

'Don't be ridiculous. No more weddings for me.'

'I didn't mean that. How are you?'

'You know me, love. Fit as a fiddle.'

'Why don't you tell Louisa about the newfangled church you're going to, Mum,' Dot said, raising her eyebrows.

Milly sighed. 'Dotty, the traditional church doesn't work for me right now. Simple as that.'

'Doesn't work?' Louisa wanted to talk about something other than Jesse's plight ... Her grandma's new church was as good as any other topic.

'I've been at it for eighty years, Lulu-Bell – kneeling in pews and praying to the Almighty. Still not getting any answers, so I've moved onward and upward. It's wonderful. We sing songs and have outings to bowling clubs.'

'Sounds like fun.'

'It is fun, Louisa! Jolly good fun. We sing, we clap–'

'It's a cult,' Dot said. 'Last week, she brought home an evangelical Christian surfer from Cronulla. He was all of twenty-five–'

'I'll have you know he's a delightful young man,' Milly said. 'A delightful young man who's teaching me guitar, by the way. Imagine learning to play an instrument at my age. It's wonderful. Perhaps someday, I'll be the one playing the music at song time.'

If I had to put up with this on a regular basis, I'd go mad, Louisa thought. Aloud, she said, 'I'm sure you'll both be saved.'

'That's not the point,' Dot said. 'We should be united, praying as a family, especially at this time, not running off joining cults and chanting and clapping.'

'I'd hardly call it a cult,' Milly said, sipping her tea. 'Besides, I go to the old-fashioned church if there's no alternative, like I did this morning. I didn't see you praying there, Dot.'

Bernard walked to the front door. 'Might do some gardening before we head back to the hospital.'

Louisa's gaze followed him outside, where he stopped and deadheaded several agapanthus. 'Is he okay?' Because to her, he didn't look well.

'Obviously he's not okay, Louisa. Your sister's in a coma. He can't bear the thought that she might have ... that we could have done more to help her, and we didn't.' Her mother took a deep breath before continuing. 'That she's been suffering all this time. Whenever I asked Jesse how she was managing, she always said she was fine, even though recently she's been fussing – all that foot tapping, turning light switches on and off. It was breaking my heart. And when I think that she might have driven into that tree on purpose...'

'You don't know that,' Louisa said. 'Everyone I've spoken to thinks it was an accident. And if she did do it deliberately, then she was likely very depressed and not able to reason properly.'

'But no other cars were involved.'

'Dot, stop talking nonsense!' Milly said. 'I think I'll do a turn of the garden with Bernard.'

CHAPTER FIFTY-THREE

Louisa watched her elderly grandmother slowly make her way outside, then turned to Dot. 'Is Grandma okay?'

'She's been bereft since she lost her driver's licence and independence.' She scratched her temple. 'How often did you say you speak with Jesse? You rarely call us.'

'I'm sorry.' Louisa wasn't proud of her lack of contact with her parents but being at home again made her feel seven years old.

'We manage. I wanted to talk to you about something else – something your sister's been up to. I caught her out just days ago. Look at this.' Dot reached inside her handbag and pulled out a brochure, which she thrust into Louisa's hand.

'Secret Women's Business Workshop,' Louisa read out loud. 'And...?'

'Louisa, this is serious. Jesse was getting involved in all manner of things that aren't normal or healthy for a woman like her. A mother. A married mother.'

'Says who?'

'Don't keep asking me questions like that. I just know it's not healthy. These clubs are known fronts for brainwashing cults. They make people do strange things and take them away from their families.'

'You and your obsession with cults. Mum, I don't think Jesse was about to join one.'

'I wouldn't be too sure of that.'

'How do you know?'

'Because I confronted her about it. Told her to wake up to herself, that she had responsibilities and who did she think she was kidding? Secret women's business indeed.'

'How did she take it?'

'Told me to mind my own business.'

Louisa grinned. 'Fair enough.'

'Don't look at me like that, Louisa. I was shocked. She said the group sounded interesting. I said to her, interesting or not, she had enough on her plate without getting messed up in that kind of thing. I suggested she come to church with me–'

'She'd have loved that.'

'Would you stop sneering for one second?'

Louisa tried to assume a neutral expression. 'How did you find out about this anyway?'

'I found the leaflet in her handbag.'

'You were snooping?'

'I was not. I didn't have to look very hard to find it. We had a terrible fight – Jesse said I was invading her privacy. I thought we shared everything, but she went crazy. Told me it was none of my business if she wanted to go to meetings and better herself. I said she could better herself by getting her tics under control. That girl can be a walking convulsion. I told her she didn't need any more demands placed on her.'

'No, of course not. Not after you've just told her she's a walking bloody convulsion–'

'Louisa! Please don't use language like that.'

'This family has more pressing issues than the misuse of language, Mum.'

'It makes me wonder. If she was hiding this from me, what else was she keeping secret?'

'She's entitled to secrets. We all are. I can't believe you were prying–'

'I was looking for headache tablets and happened upon it.'

'Jesse might have a different take on the situation. When did you talk to her about it?'

'The day I went round to her house after the fall.'

'After she'd been on the phone to me?'

'That's right. She didn't seem herself. And now...' Dot started to cry. 'And now my little girl's in a coma in hospital.'

Louisa could see how devastated her mother was and suddenly felt ashamed. Ashamed she hadn't been there to support her, sad that she'd missed out on six long years. When she'd left Australia, her father was still working full-time, her grandmother resided in her own home and held a driving licence ... And now? Well, now, they were all so much older. Louisa was starting to realise that no one lived for ever.

'Mum,' she said. 'I'm sorry. I never meant to let you down.'

'Hey,' Dot said, drawing Louisa in close and hugging her. 'Where's all this coming from?'

Louisa blinked back tears. She was so incredibly tired.

'You turned out all right,' Dot said, patting her affectionately on the arm. 'More than all right, Louisa. Why do you think I was so hard on you and Jesse? I didn't want you making the same mistakes I did. I didn't want either of you to go through the pain.'

Louisa immediately wondered what mistakes her mother had made but was secretly pleased she was admitting to being hard on her daughters.

'Now that I'm older, I realise everyone must travel through

life on their own path,' Dot said. 'For all my nagging and interference in yours and Jesse's lives and my bickering with Mum, I realise that people need to make their own mistakes and find their own way home. Don't think for one moment I'm happy about it. I'm not. But I know that's the way it has to be.'

With that, Louisa burst into tears. 'I'm so sorry. I never wanted to stay away so long. It's just that...'

'You didn't want to talk to an old fogey like me about your troubles?'

Louisa nodded through her tears.

'Fair enough,' Dot said. 'I'd have wanted to clip you around the ears and lock you in your bedroom for months. Instead, you flew away. Don't ever do that again. Your father and I are old.'

A collection of family portraits hanging on the wall snagged Louisa's attention. Her breath hitched. There was a glorious photo of her mother and Grandma Milly taken probably thirty years earlier. They both looked beautiful.

'As for Mum,' Dot said, 'God in His wisdom has deemed that she live with us. Divine punishment, if ever there was one.'

'Grandma's cool,' Louisa said. 'And she keeps you on your toes.'

'I guess.' Dot turned back to Louisa. 'You're home now, Lou. Please stay. We've missed you.'

Dot and Louisa hugged for a very long time before Dot finally pulled away. 'Come on then, dear. Upstairs and shower while I make peace with my mother.' She glanced outside to where Milly and Bernard were talking animatedly beside an azalea bush. 'You know, the young man from Cronulla she brought home the other week was a thorough gentleman, and to tell you the truth, I don't actually mind the songs they sing.' She rolled her eyes. 'But if you tell Grandma I said that, I'll deny it.'

Louisa smiled. Families. 'Love you, Mum.' She kissed her on the cheek.

'You too, darling.'

Louisa picked up her bags and walked upstairs, still holding the pamphlet that promised to change women's lives by helping them to *let go of guilt and fear and grow into our authentic selves*. She thought about Jesse's doomed pregnancy and wondered what other secrets her sister might have.

Grandma Milly had taken possession of Louisa's old room, so she made her way into Jesse's room instead, which now housed bunk beds for Ollie and Emily. Louisa had always thought Jesse had the better room because hers overlooked the paddocks and the horses. You could see for miles out the window, almost to the ocean. Although Louisa's room was slightly bigger and had a built-in wardrobe, it overlooked the garage. Jesse's was definitely the pick: it was so much lighter and further away from their parents' room. Even now, she could see why, growing up, they'd fought about it.

Louisa unzipped her bag and peered inside. Just as she'd thought: she'd packed with her eyes closed. There weren't many clothes, and nothing suitable for a Sydney summer. But she'd make do. There was no way she was borrowing any of her mother's clothes. Or her grandmother's, for that matter.

Louisa flopped down on the bottom bunk and closed her eyes for five minutes before she had a shower. Her mind wandered to Philippe. He'd been so understanding when she'd called him, frantic after her father's phone call about Jesse. He'd come straight over, calmed her down, arranged the flight to Sydney, and promised he'd take extra special care of Ziggy and her plants.

'You'd do all that for me?' she'd sobbed.

'Of course,' he'd replied. 'I love you, babe.'

He'd stayed with her the next couple of days and nights, feeding her, loving her, until the time came to drive her to the airport. Any fool could see he was a keeper, but their age difference worried her. How could she fall in love with someone eleven years younger?

To her complete surprise, lying there on the bunk, Louisa began to cry again. Who was she kidding? She was in love with Philippe and had been since that crazy, frantic afternoon in her office. This wasn't just an affair. She thought about him all the time. She loved him. He loved her.

She texted him. *Home. Jesse hanging on. Too sad. Miss you.*

CHAPTER FIFTY-FOUR

'Could we drive past the accident site?' Louisa asked her father half an hour later as they were getting ready to go back to the hospital.

'I don't know, Louisa. I'm not sure your mother and grandmother–'

'We'll have to face it sooner or later, Bern,' Dot said. 'It might as well be now.'

Bernard shook his head. 'A bit grisly, don't you think?'

Louisa completely understood her father's reluctance. If you'd asked her two hours earlier, she wouldn't have wanted to go to the accident site either. But she needed to see the place to try to piece the jigsaw together.

'It might give us some insight into what really happened,' she said gently.

'Louisa's right,' Dot said. 'It's time we looked for ourselves, rather than relying on second- and third-hand reports.'

'But we promised the kids we'd stop in at Jesse's and pick up her iPad. It has all of her music on it,' Bernard said. 'We'll be late picking them up from school.'

'We will not,' Dot said irritably. 'We'll have plenty of time if we leave right now.'

'Why hasn't Steve already taken her music into hospital?' Louisa asked.

No one responded.

It was a silent five-kilometre ride.

'I don't know why you want to do this,' Bernard grumbled as he parked near the crash site.

'Just to see,' Louisa said.

The flat gentle landscape combined with the stark wilderness and scattered arrangement of gum trees. One in particular.

She got out and approached the gum. It grew on a straight stretch of bitumen road, a single carriageway with a 70-kilometre-per-hour speed limit. No blind spots, and the tree itself was huge. Huge and in plain view. Bush scrub and long grass were all around, but there were no other trees in this direct line. Louisa could clearly see where the front of Jesse's car had smashed into the trunk. The bark had been ripped away and broken glass and metal lay underneath and nearby.

The fog and mist of the previous week with heightened conditions of stormy, wet and windy, had been replaced by brilliant blue sky; a windless and pleasant twenty-five degrees. It didn't seem real.

'It's impossible to tell if she braked,' Bernard said, after examining the grass for several minutes. He stood and wiped his eyes.

'I'm sure she did, Dad,' Louisa reassured him. 'I'm sure Jesse slowed. It was just a terrible accident.'

Dot and Grandma Milly watched silently. Dot made the sign of the cross over her chest. Louisa wasn't used to them both being quiet for longer than two minutes and yet it had been almost fifteen.

'I don't understand,' Bernard said as they climbed back into the car. 'Why did she stop here in the first place? To accelerate into the tree, she had to be well off to the side of the road, on the grass.'

'Jesse drives this road most days,' Dot said. 'She'd know it blindfolded.'

'When she wakes up, she'll tell us everything we need to know,' Louisa soothed. She had a thought. 'What about a car malfunction? Brakes? There has to be a reason she pulled over.'

'We won't know about the car until the police examiner gets back to us, and Steve said that could take a week or more,' Bernard replied.

Jesse's house looked so normal, suburban. The garden was messy and green, a couple of bikes lay haphazardly on the veranda. Staring at the bikes, it struck Louisa how much she'd missed in the last few years – birthdays, Christmases, school plays – the truth was, she didn't know her own niece and nephew. They'd feared her when she saw them at the hospital. It was beyond sad.

As for Jesse, Louisa hoped it wasn't too late to prove they could be close friends again.

'What are you waiting for?' Dot said as Louisa hovered inside the front door. 'Come on.'

Louisa followed her mother down the hall into the kitchen. An open packet of bread, a tub of margarine and a jar of Vegemite sat on the bench. She put them all in the fridge while Dot stacked dirty plates and cutlery into the dishwasher.

'Where would Jesse's iPad be?' Louisa asked.

'In the TV room, I think,' Dot replied, pointing to a room off to the side.

The top of the entertainment unit was covered with framed photographs of Jesse and the kids at various ages: Ollie in soccer garb, kicking a ball; Em in a black and white netball uniform lunging at the hoop. Jesse's kids were so adorable ... and far too young to lose their mother.

Outside, Bernard beeped the car horn. Shaking off her fear, Louisa grabbed the iPad and charger that also sat on top. Hopefully it was Jesse's, not Steve's. She pressed the on button and scanned the apps – Healthy Weekly Menu Plan, Happy Homemaker, Clean Foods, Stay Calm, Your Best You – yep, Jesse's iPad for sure.

Five minutes later, they were waiting at the school pick-up zone.

'Let's try to be happy for Ollie and Emily's sake,' Dot said when they saw the twins appear.

'Are we going to see Mum now?' Ollie asked as he and Emily clambered into the back seat.

'Sure are.' Louisa held up Jesse's iPad. 'Now we can play music in her room.'

Dot attempted some chat about the twins' day, but they responded in monosyllables. Like the rest of them, they were clearly anxious to get to the hospital and see Jesse.

As they drove, Louisa watched people going about their daily business: walking in and out of the butcher's shop, the chemist, the newsagency. It seemed weird that for everyone else, life went on as normal. Meanwhile, their world had fallen to pieces. And they had questions ... so many questions...

'Nanna, what happens when you die?' Emily asked as they walked through the hospital doors. 'The kids at school say it's like a big black hole that goes on forever.'

'Who said that? What a load of rubbish. Heaven is a beautiful place, full of gardens and nature.'

'What about Hell?' Ollie asked as they rode the elevator to the third floor.

'Hell's only for bad people.'

'Mum, how can you say that?' Louisa said.

'What? Hell is for bad people,' Dot said, indignant. 'I mean really bad people, Oliver. Like murderers, like Hitler–'

'Not Mum?'

'Of course not.'

'Ollie,' Louisa said, 'I don't think there is such a place as Hell.'

'Neither do I,' Grandma Milly chimed in. 'The afterlife is like one big holiday with lots of happy, smiling friends, lots of singing and everyone eating lollies and cake.'

'Mother, really!' Dot said.

'What do you think, Auntie Louisa?'

Before she could answer, they reached Jesse's room and everyone fell quiet. The afternoon sun made the room brighter and warmer than it had been that morning.

Ollie was the first to approach Jesse. He took her hand and put his head down on the bed beside her. After a few moments, he turned around to Louisa. 'Are you thinking about Heaven?'

'Oh,' she said, choking back tears. 'Yes ... I think Heaven must be a happy place where people who've died watch over and guide us.'

'Like angels?'

'Yes, like angels.'

'Do you think Mummy will be an angel soon?'

'Goodness, I hope not. Maybe far, far in the future.'

'What if you have a really bad person guiding you?' Ollie continued.

'There aren't any bad people when you die,' Louisa said.

'Then where do all the bad people go?' Emily asked.

'Yeah,' Ollie said. 'We don't want them hurting Mum.'

'No one's going to hurt your mum, Ollie. Besides, she's not going to die.'

'Do you know that for sure?'

Before Louisa could answer, Dot rushed in with, 'Of course we do. Now, come on. Why don't you tell your mum about your day at school? She'd love to hear all about that. Emily, you start.'

'My class said prayers for Mummy ... and I read a book. My teacher said I didn't have to do any work today, but I wanted to.'

'I drew Mummy some pictures,' Ollie said. 'But I left them in the car.' He stroked Jesse's hand and whispered, 'Don't be lonely, Mummy. I love you always. I do.'

Dot sniffed back tears while Bernard blinked furiously to stem his.

'Who wants to come with me down to the chapel?' Dot said suddenly.

No one responded.

'Emily? Ollie?' Dot asked.

'I want to stay with Mummy,' Ollie said.

'You come then, Emily,' Dot said. 'Grandma will come too, won't you?'

'If I must,' Milly replied.

'Then we'll put some fresh water in those vases, okay?' Dot said to Emily as they walked out of the room together.

'How about you put on some music, Louisa,' Bernard said moments later.

'I was just thinking the same thing. Oliver, do you want to help me set up the iPad? Then you can choose some music you think Mum would like to listen to.'

Ollie's eyes stayed firmly on Jesse.

'She's got a lot of music on here,' Louisa said, scrolling through the list. 'Your mum sure likes Robbie Williams. She's got a zillion of his albums downloaded.'

'Yeah, she loves him,' he agreed distractedly.

'Any one in particular?'

'She likes them all. Maybe this one,' he said, pointing to one. 'I gave her the poster for her birthday. She says it's her favourite.'

'Great choice.'

'Your mum'll love this,' she said as Robbie Williams's voice kicked in with 'Better Man'.

Louisa and Bernard listened to the music while Ollie rubbed his mother's hand.

'Mum wouldn't leave me, not if she didn't have to,' Ollie said. 'She loves me.'

'She adores you,' Louisa said. 'She loves you and Emily more than anything in the world.'

'And you don't leave somebody if you love them, right? You just don't.' Ollie stamped his right foot three times on the carpet.

Louisa glanced at her dad.

'You just ... hey, did you see that? Mum just squeezed my hand. She squeezed my hand! She's waking up!' Ollie shouted, tears streaming down his red cheeks.

'Quick. Call the doctor,' Louisa said to Bernard, but he was already out the door.

Within moments, Doctor Thompson and several other doctors and nurses appeared in the room, examining the monitors around Jesse. Steve followed close behind. Louisa assumed he must have just arrived.

'We'll run some tests,' Doctor Thompson said, 'before you get too excited, you need to know that sometimes a patient in a coma exhibits behaviour that mimics conscious behaviour. For instance, they may turn their head towards a sound or squeeze someone's hand. It doesn't necessarily mean it's a purposeful movement.'

Louisa could see that Ollie was looking more and more

distressed as the reality dawned on him that Jesse wasn't going to leap out of bed any time soon.

Steve saw it too. 'Ollie, let's go to the café and have a milkshake.'

The little boy's eyes remained fixed on Jesse. 'I want to stay here with Mum.'

'Come on, let's leave the doctors to check on Mummy. You can tell me about your day. We'll come back soon.'

Steve looked tired and, Louisa hated to admit it, miserable.

'Okay,' Ollie said. He turned to Louisa. 'You'll look after her, Auntie Louisa?'

Louisa nodded. 'Yes, Pop and I will.'

Ollie took Steve's hand and they left together.

Bernard waited until they were out of earshot before speaking. 'What exactly are you saying?' he asked the doctor.

'It's certainly encouraging,' Doctor Thompson said, 'but I don't want to give you false hope. Maybe her hand squeeze was purposeful, but it could also have been an involuntary movement.'

Louisa's heart sank.

'Now, if you'll excuse me.' Doctor Thompson left the room, the other doctors and nurses trailing behind him.

Bernard shook his head and banged his fist on the table next to the iPad. 'There must be something more we can do.'

Louisa reached out to hug him, and he collapsed, sobbing, into her arms. She felt useless. This was so unfair.

'Dad, I'm really sorry about everything. What I mean is–'

'I know what you mean, Lou. I'm sorry too. I could have handled the situation better.'

'No–'

'Yes, I could have. I'm your father. I treated you unfairly. I'm sorry.'

This was the longest conversation she'd had alone with her

father in years. So much time lost, so many words unspoken. Time couldn't be reclaimed. But at least they could talk now, she hoped.

'Am I the reason you haven't been back?' he asked.

Louisa shook her head. She could see how hurt he was, the tragedy of Jesse's accident compounding his grief and sadness. She didn't want to add to that.

'Why, Louisa? Why did you stay away so long?'

'I'm sorry,' she said, her voice breaking. 'I thought you wouldn't want to see me. I was ashamed ... I'm still ashamed. My own father knowing...'

Bernard hugged her. 'What you do and how you live your life is nothing to be ashamed of. If anyone should be ashamed, it's me.'

'Dad...'

'Louisa, I was shocked. Worried about your safety. I didn't want to think–' Bernard stopped.

'I never did anything I didn't want to do.'

'You left Australia.'

'Dad, can we leave the past behind?'

He nodded. 'I'm so proud of you, Looey-boo. You're my daughter and I love you. Have always loved you, no matter what.'

Hot tears fell down Louisa's cheeks.

'I'm glad you finally made it back to us.' He shuddered. 'But I'm so heartbroken it's under these circumstances.'

They both turned to look at Jesse again, and Louisa thought she saw a brief movement.

'Dad, her eyes fluttered!'

CHAPTER FIFTY-FIVE

STELLA

After dropping Louisa home, I spent the afternoon dithering, picking up groceries, running errands, doing anything I could to distract myself from thinking about Jesse. I drove halfway to the mountains with the radio blasting just so I wouldn't have to think. But none of it worked. Jesse was always on my mind. My head throbbed. I felt so bloody guilty. Jesse was lying in hospital, in a coma, and it was my fault. If only I'd left with Jesse after Liz had sacked her, insisted we go to a café and talk.

June was out the front, raking leaves when I arrived home late in the day.

'June!' I walked over and took the rake from her. 'Give me that! It's blazing hot out here. You should be resting.'

'All I do is rest. I like to keep busy.'

'At least come inside and have a cold drink or a cup of tea.'

'Good idea. How's Jesse?'

'No change, I'm afraid. The doctors were running more tests as I was leaving. The good news is that her sister, Louisa, has arrived from the States.'

June nodded and took a seat at the kitchen bench.

I busied myself filling the kettle with water. 'It's so tragic. I keep thinking about Oliver and Emily.'

'You never know what's around the corner.'

I shook my head. 'No, you don't. How are you feeling? You're looking bright.'

'Stella, I'm not an invalid. I'm feeling fine. And I'm not going crazy either.'

'I never said you were crazy.'

'Really? Then why all the memory tests with your doctor friend?'

'I don't know what you're talking about.'

'Don't give me that. Those tests weren't run-of-the-mill. They were specific tests for Alzheimer's. I know. I've done them before. It's not as if I haven't been worried about it myself.'

'June, I'm sorry. I thought you might fly off the handle or get embarrassed. Or worse, not know what I was talking about. It was wrong of me.'

June raised her eyebrows.

I poured boiling water into the teapot and took a couple of cups from the cupboard. 'Come and sit out on the deck.'

'I know I can be absent-minded and forgetful,' she said once we were settled, 'but I'm old. I can't be bothered remembering every specific detail of all the thousands of things I've done or am doing. Not to mention keeping up with everyone else's dramas. And I still think Garth was a fool to leave you.'

'It was mutual.'

'I know, but I don't think it's ideal.'

We sat in companionable silence for a while.

'I can't bear the thought of Jesse lying in hospital, lifeless,' I told her.

'Then don't,' she replied. 'Imagine her doing something she loves, like being with her children or working at the library. Thinking about her lying in some awful hospital room isn't going to help anyone, least of all Jesse. You need to stay positive. It's your only hope of getting through this.'

'You're right.' My mobile rang. 'Garth,' I mouthed to June as I pressed the answer button. 'Hey, what's up?'

'Just checking in.'

'That's nice.'

'How's Jesse?'

'No change. How's everything with you?'

'Not so good, I'm afraid.'

June started clearing the cups away. 'Leave those,' I whispered. 'Relax and read your book.'

'Is that Mum? How is she?'

'Very good.' I smiled. 'Excellent. Now, about you not being so good: why?'

'Things aren't working out with Amanda.'

'But you've only been living with her a month.'

June rolled her eyes and walked into the kitchen taking empty teacups with her.

'And she wants to marry you,' I whispered so that June wouldn't hear.

'Exactly. Too much pressure. Can I come home?'

'Which home? This home? My home?'

'Yes.'

'The short answer is no. I'm sorry, Garth.'

'But why? I don't want to live with Amanda.'

'Then don't. Live by yourself.'

'I can't do that,' he said, sounding bemused by the notion. 'I'd be alone. I don't want to be alone, Stella.'

'What's the alternative? Find a replacement and move in with her?'

'Funny. No. After everything that's happened, I thought that maybe you and I could try again?'

Oh, Garth. I loved him. I truly did. He was the father of my children and a damn fine father at that. As much as the kids went on about him, they loved him too. But as for us resuming our marriage? Not a chance. Garth was one of my closest, dearest, friends and I hoped he'd always remain so, but the idea of having sex with him again? Well, that wasn't going to happen, no matter how many tequilas I slammed down.

'Tempting as that is, I'm afraid my answer is still no. Regardless of any problems you're having with Amanda, running back to me isn't going to solve anything.'

'Really, Stella, you can be so hard. Can I speak to Mum, please?'

'Sure ... and Garth, everything will work out. Okay?'

'Thanks.'

I found June hovering by the kitchen sink, handed her the phone, and left them to talk in private.

Garth was a good bloke. He'd always be in my life, but I didn't tingle anymore when I thought about him. Not the way I tingled when I thought about Mike. Maybe, just maybe, I could give it a go with him. The timing was rotten, the kids would object, but if we kept it quiet for a while until we were both sure, then maybe. All I knew was that I wanted to keep an open mind, and if Mike wanted to take me out to dinner again, that wouldn't be such a bad thing.

CHAPTER FIFTY-SIX

I was in bed reading that night when Mike called. Date call, I thought, then checked the bedside clock. Ten thirty. A bit late for chit-chat. The thought vanished instantly at his first words after 'hello'.

'I might have good news for you.'

'What? Really?'

'Yes, really. Jesse's eyes fluttered open three times this evening. She's definitely showing signs of emerging from the coma.'

'I'm coming straight in.'

'Hang on. I'm not saying she'll wake up in the next hour or two. She's still not responding to requests to squeeze her hand or blink. But the signs are encouraging.'

'That's good enough for me. Thank you, Mike.'

I hung up, threw on a pair of jeans and a T-shirt and raced over to Carly's. I had to knock several times before Brett finally answered.

'What's up?' he said, looking dazed.

'It's Jesse,' I said breathlessly. 'She might be waking up.'

'Waking up?' Carly said, emerging from the guest room. 'What are we waiting for?'

She and Brett were obviously having problems, but now wasn't the time to ask. We needed to focus on Jesse, and hopefully, some good news.

Within twenty minutes, Carly and I had arrived at the hospital and were treading the familiar path up to the third floor. Louisa and Dot were sitting by Jesse's bed. They waved us in, and we hugged before turning to Jesse.

'It's going to be okay,' Dot said, sighing with relief.

The four of us crowded around the bed, willing Jesse to make some further sign, but she looked just as she had the past few days – all bandages, bruises and tubes. My heart felt like it was breaking all over again. It wasn't as if I was expecting her to jump up and dance the Macarena, but I'd hoped for some confirmation, no matter how small, that she was on the mend.

'Where are Ollie and Emily?' I asked.

'At home with Bern,' Dot said. 'After what Ollie went through earlier today, we don't want the children seeing Jesse again until we've got firm news about her recovery.'

'And Steve?' Surely he should have been rearing his ugly head by now.

'No one's been able to contact him,' Louisa said. 'He came in briefly this afternoon but left just before Jesse started responding. He asked Mum and Dad to take Em and Ollie for the night. We've called his mobile and left messages, but he seems to have disappeared.'

Good.

My expression must have revealed what I was thinking because Dot said, 'Perhaps it's for the best at this stage. It certainly feels calmer when Steve's not here.'

'If my partner was lying here, I'd never leave, not if I could help it,' Louisa said.

Dot looked at Jesse and then at Louisa. 'He has to give the kids some sense of normality and continuity. And who knows why people behave the way they do. Perhaps seeing Jesse lying here is too much for him to handle.'

'Too bad. She's his wife.'

'I agree, but when the going gets tough, sometimes people run away rather than face their responsibilities,' Dot said.

I tried to catch Carly's eye, thinking that we should leave Dot and Louisa to their private conversation, but she was in a daze, staring at Jesse.

'Steve has the twins to consider,' Louisa said. 'He should be thinking of them instead of himself.'

'Some people never learn, never grow up,' Dot said. 'Maybe Steve...' She trailed off, then added, 'How many of us do silly things when we're young, never thinking about the consequences?'

'And when we're not so young,' Carly said. 'Never thinking about how our stupid actions and their repercussions will haunt us later in life.'

'I'd do some things differently if I had my time over again,' Louisa said thoughtfully.

Mike arrived at the door. He looked shocking – pale and exhausted. He motioned for me to come outside.

'What's up?' I asked. 'Please don't tell me it's Jesse. We're all so hopeful. She's–'

'Stella, Jesse's going to be fine. Her physical recovery will take time, but the signs are positive. I believe we're through the worst. There's something else, though...'

'What?' I could barely contain myself. 'Mike, what is it?'

'It's Steve.'

I raised my eyebrows. Steve was the least of my concerns. If he wanted me to leave Jesse's room, he'd have to come in and personally frogmarch me out. I was staying where I was until she regained consciousness. Carly, me, Dot, Bernard, even Louisa – we'd all been a hell of a lot more attentive than Steve had been the past few days.

'Okay,' I said. 'What about him?'

'He's in emergency ... an overdose.'

'Pardon?'

'Cardiac arrest. Looks like he's been on a bender. Most probably cocaine and–'

'Faark! Will he be okay?'

'Yeah, but it was touch and go.'

'Shit, shit, shit.' I shook my head. 'Does he have a dodgy heart?'

'Maybe. We'll run some tests over the next couple of days. Then again, maybe he just overdid it tonight.'

'You're kidding me.' Louisa had appeared beside me. 'Talk about karma.'

Dot and Carly joined us, and, dumbstruck, the four of us listened to Mike's summary of the situation. Then Carly laughed. We all stared at her, horrified.

'I don't mean anything by it,' she said, but she'd set Louisa off too.

'But Steve,' Dot said. 'He's had a heart attack?'

I rubbed her back. 'It seems so.'

Louisa was shaking her head. 'What an idiot. I mean ... why?'

'Maybe the pressure,' I said. 'And tonight, he finally flipped.'

'We've all certainly been under a lot of strain in the last few days, that's for sure,' Dot agreed.

Carly nodded. 'It's been a difficult week,' and within seconds her and Louisa's laughter had turned to sobs.

Dot shook her head sadly and sniffed back her own tears. 'Those poor children,' she kept saying.

I was too stunned to make a sound.

Mike did his best to calm us down, while a nurse organised cups of tea. By the time we'd composed ourselves enough to walk back into Jesse's room, it was well after two in the morning. We gathered around her bed, Louisa holding her hand. Fittingly, Robbie Williams's 'Angels' was playing as we sat there quietly, not knowing what to say or where to look.

Dot broke the silence, reminiscing about the birth of Jesse's twins. 'They were big babies. Huge.'

'That would have been the last time Jesse was in a hospital,' Louisa said.

'Cracked rib,' Jesse croaked, barely audible. 'Two years ago.'

I felt as if I'd stopped breathing.

'Jesse?' Louisa said.

Jesse's mouth moved. 'I'm here,' she whispered. 'Always have been.'

I wanted to jump on the bed and hug her, but instead I ran out into the hallway. 'Jesse's awake,' I shouted towards the nurses' station.

CHAPTER FIFTY-SEVEN

JESSE

Jesse was alone in her room, resting after yet another team of doctors had done numerous checks and tests, when Mike walked in.

'Remember me?'

She smiled weakly. 'Mike?'

He nodded. 'Yeah, Mike. How are you feeling?'

'Groggy, tired, sore.'

'That's to be expected.' Mike pulled up a chair and sat down beside her. 'Do you feel up to talking?'

Jesse nodded, tears in her eyes. 'I lost the baby?'

'Yes. I'm sorry.'

'It's...' Jesse's words caught in her throat.

'I know this is hard for you, but there's something else. It's about your husband.'

Jesse took a sharp breath. What had Steve done now? Caused a scene in the hospital? Abused the doctors?

'Steve's fine. That is, he's going to be okay, but he's also in hospital.'

'Did he have a car accident too?' Jesse asked, panic rising, her stomach churning. 'My children?'

'They're fine. With your parents. I'm afraid your husband overdosed.'

'As in drugs?'

Mike nodded.

Jesse's eyes filled with tears. How much more could she take? 'But he's going to live?'

'This time.'

She sighed deeply. Whatever she thought about Steve, she certainly didn't want him to die. He was the father of her children. They didn't deserve to grow up without their dad.

'Are you all right?' Mike said. 'I know it's a lot to absorb.'

'What drugs?'

'Cocaine. We're running tests for other narcotics as well.'

Jesse turned away. She was embarrassed, humiliated and so, so unhappy. Life wasn't meant to be like this. Her poor children. How would they ever cope?

It seemed like hours before Mike spoke again. 'Jesse?'

What now, she thought, nodding ever so slightly.

'The afternoon of the accident ... can you remember what happened?'

'I was angry and upset.'

Mike said nothing.

'Everyone had let me down. My husband, friends. My sister. My job at the library ... I was shaking so much it was almost impossible to drive. I could barely see the road through the rain and my tears.'

'And?' Mike prompted gently.

'I knew I had to pull over.'

After Mike left, Jesse thought more about that afternoon. The shaking had become so bad she'd had to stop the car. With minimal visibility because of the rain, she'd chosen a spot on the long, straight stretch of road, a grassy area where she could pull over safely and take a few minutes to calm down, collect her thoughts and focus on deep breathing.

As she sat there, the rain eased. Across the road, she noticed a man in a lightweight raincoat with another person, male, walking a Labrador. He looked content, at peace. That's what she wanted, to be at peace. She focused on the man, the easy way he laughed with the boy and the way the boy held the dog's lead, then on the animal itself, its even gait. Watching the Lab, Jesse's breathing slowed. Ollie and Em would love a puppy. She forced a smile, slightly less anxious.

She wiped her eyes, then started the car again. Before heading off, she pulled a lipstick from her bag and turned the rear-view mirror slightly so she could see her face. It was red and blotchy. Despite appearances, she had to believe she could get through this. She certainly wasn't going anywhere without her children.

As Jesse went to apply the lipstick, she dropped it on the floor. Her leg jerked and her foot tapped the accelerator. She slammed her foot on the brake and bent to retrieve the lipstick. As she did, her foot jerked again, hitting the accelerator. Hard.

Now look where she was ... in hospital. Melancholia had set in – about losing the baby, about Steve – but at least she was alive. Imagine if she never got to see Ollie and Emmy again? They'd be in to visit her soon and the three of them would get through this together. Jesse was going to come out of this a much stronger woman: secure in her beliefs and the direction she wanted her life to take.

As for Steve? It was a fait accompli. She was leaving him, no doubt about it.

When Jesse was finally allowed to see Oliver and Emily, she couldn't hide her delight. 'My darlings,' she cried when they tentatively entered her room. 'Mummy's missed you so much. Come and give me a big hug.'

They barged at her with every bit of their nine-year-old energy. The impact almost wiped Jesse out, but she'd never admit it.

'So, what have you been up to?' she asked once she'd caught her breath.

'Mummy,' Oliver said in an exasperated tone, 'we've only been thinking about you since the accident.'

'And that's been like forever!' Emily said.

Jesse attempted a smile. 'Thank you. I knew you were thinking of me. I could hear you. I missed you both so much.'

'Did you really hear us talking to you?' Oliver asked.

'Of course,' she replied. 'Especially when you squeezed my hand, Ollie.'

He beamed. 'I knew you could feel it. I just knew. But, Mummy,' he was suddenly serious, 'I was very worried that you wouldn't wake up.'

'Thank you, darling. I know you were but...'

'But in my head I kept saying *Silenzio, Bruno!*'

'That's right,' Jesse whispered, '*Silenzio, Bruno!*' She faltered and started tearing up. 'You know Mummy loves you and would never leave you ... will never leave you?' She kissed her son's cheek. 'I love you, Ollie.'

Jesse pulled Emily in closer. 'Love you, sweet girl.'

Dot appeared in the doorway. 'Come on, Ollie, Em! It's time Mum rested. And Grandpa needs an ice cream.' Dot winked at Jesse before leading her grandchildren out into the hall. Moments later, she was back. 'Love, how are you doing?'

'Fine, Mum.'

'About Steve...' Dot hesitated for a moment. 'I'm so sorry. I had no idea.'

'Neither did I, but the good news is, he's going to be okay. He and I aren't going to be together, but we'll both get through this. I'm sad, but...'

Jesse couldn't help herself. As the tears came, Dot rushed to her side.

'You have a family that loves you,' Dot said. 'We'll be here for you. Speaking of which, Louisa's here. Are you up for another visitor?'

'Am I!' Jesse said, wiping her eyes as Louisa walked in. 'Sis!'

'Darling,' Louisa said, tears streaming down her face. 'You had us all so worried.'

Jesse smiled. 'Thank you so much for keeping me company while I was asleep.'

'Jesse, I've missed you so much. Can you ever forgive me?'

'Probably not.'

'Oh.' Louisa looked stricken.

'I'm joking. But you should have told me, Louisa. After all, blood is thicker than water and all that.'

'I'll never forgive myself.'

Jesse sighed. 'You have to, and you will, because if I hadn't been with Steve, I'd never have had Ollie and Emily.'

'Oh,' Louisa said again, remembering. 'Do you know about...'

'Yeah.' Tears welled in her eyes. 'Obviously it wasn't the right time. Maybe in the future...'

'Yep,' Louisa said, fighting back tears as she kissed Jesse on her cheek.

'Anyway, I'm sick of talking about me,' Jesse said. 'Tell me about Philippe.'

Louisa grinned. 'You're unbelievable, you know that?'

'Enough with the stalling. Tell me about this Adonis of

yours, and you'd better have pictures on your phone or there'll be trouble.'

After Louisa had shown Jesse several photos of Philippe and Ziggy, she said, 'Can you ever forgive me for running away six years ago? I'm so sorry. I was scared and ashamed and I didn't want to ruin your perfect life.'

Jesse looked at her. 'My perfect life? Really?'

'Okay, it doesn't seem so ideal now, but back then...'

'Back then, I was living a lie.'

'I'm sorry,' Louisa said. 'I didn't realise the extent of it – Steve's drug taking and everything else.'

'Hello?' came a voice from the doorway. It was Stella, and Carly was with her. 'Do you have room for a couple more visitors?'

Jesse smiled. 'I sure do.'

CHAPTER FIFTY-EIGHT

LOUISA

Louisa left Stella and Carly to catch up with Jesse while she walked outside and made a phone call.

After her text the previous afternoon, she'd received one back from Philippe saying simply: *I love you. If you need me, I'll be on the next flight.* She'd read the words and wept. She hadn't known it before, but those were the exact words she'd wanted to hear. She loved Philippe. She just needed to tell him.

'Hey,' she said when she heard his familiar voice.

'Lou, I've been so worried. How's your sister?'

'She's going to be okay.'

'Babe, I'm so glad. I haven't been able to concentrate on my studies since you left. Might need you to write me a note–'

'Philippe,' Louisa said, interrupting him.

'Yeah?'

'I love you.'

Silence.

'Philippe?'

'I'm still here. Could you repeat that, please?'

Louisa smiled. 'I love you. Can't live without you. Want to be with you forever.'

Philippe sighed. 'Well, it's about fucking time.'

Louisa got off the phone feeling happier and more content than she had in years.

Was it possible that, after all this time, she could truly be in love?

CHAPTER FIFTY-NINE

STELLA

As happy as Carly and I were to sit with Jesse, we knew she was tiring. It would be weeks, maybe months, before she was back to her old self. Mike had told me that Jesse's accident had been exactly that. Thank goodness. The hospital didn't believe she was a suicide risk, but she was still fragile, so we needed to take a softly-softly approach.

'You sure you're okay?' I asked.

'I think so,' Jesse said quietly. 'Stella, I'm so sad for Ollie and Em. And I'm sad for Steve too. But I'm relieved he's going to be all right. He'll probably only need to be in hospital one more day.'

'Good.' I glanced at my watch. Carly and I had been at the hospital over twelve hours. Tired, smelly, hungry and wrung out, I needed a long bath and a deep sleep. It was time to leave. Besides, Jesse was starting to nod off.

Just as I was about to kiss Jesse goodbye, Louisa reappeared.

'How about I get us more coffees?'

Carly and I glanced at each other. Jesse was asleep.

'Sure,' I said, yawning. 'And then I've got to go home. I reek.'

Carly laughed. 'We're way beyond that.'

Louisa left to fetch the coffees, and I took the opportunity to ask Carly about the situation between her and Brett. 'What's going on?'

Carly shrugged. 'I don't know. But I do know I'm going to talk to him when I get home, try to make sense of everything ... I've really lost my way the last couple of years, and then with Nicky moving overseas, I fell apart. I might fantasise about fuck buddies and leaving my husband, but it's not what I want. I say and do things without thinking them through.'

I hugged her. 'You've always been impulsive. It's one of the things I love about you.'

She sniffed back tears. 'Thanks.'

I reached for her hand. 'I like Brett.'

Carly smiled. 'Yeah, so do I. When I think back to how it was in the beginning for us – we were so in love. Maybe we could get back to that place.'

'Absolutely.'

'I've been scared for a long time, thinking that love has gone. But maybe we can get back on track. It won't be the same, of course, but hopefully it can be just as strong. You?'

'I'm doing fine,' I said, and I meant it. 'Though did I tell you Garth's having issues with Amanda?'

'No!'

'She's pushing for more commitment. He's terrified.'

'I bet. And?'

'His solution is to run back to me.'

'You're not serious?'

'I'm not, but Garth seems to be. I told him no, and that's about as far as I'm going to get involved. He needs to decide what's right for him on his own.'

'True.' Carly threw me a sly grin. 'And Mike?'

I smiled. 'Nothing. I mean, he's nice.'

'And?'

'And that's it.'

'You know meeting those guys the other week doesn't have to be all bad. Love–'

'Carly, enough. I am not about to fall in love.'

'Just saying. Besides, you have no control over who you fall in love with ... it's destiny.'

'Thank you. Let's change the topic.' Thinking about Mike was making me feel a tad too excited.

'Talking of destiny,' Louisa said, walking back into the room with three coffees, 'I've just told Philippe I'm moving back to Australia.'

'Jesse will be ecstatic,' Carly said.

Louisa glanced at Jesse, who was still asleep. 'I know. San Francisco is wild and crazy, and I love the place, but I think I could love Sydney too. Anyway, I'm giving it a shot. It means bringing my beloved Ziggy out here and putting him through quarantine, so I wouldn't be doing that if I didn't have serious long-term goals. I want Jesse to know it's not because I feel obliged. I want to be here. And...' She trailed off.

'Come on,' I said. 'And what?'

'Philippe's coming out too. We'll see how it goes.'

'Wow.' I almost spilled my coffee. 'That's great. I'm so happy for you.'

Louisa smiled. 'Yeah. Perhaps I haven't been entirely honest with myself about my feelings for him. It might end in tears, but if I'm ever going to take the next step with him, now's the time. We'll see out the academic year at USF, then come over. I should be able to pick up work here. Anyway, it's an adventure.'

'Absolutely,' I said, raising my coffee cup. 'Here's to life. It's definitely one hell of a rollercoaster.'

CHAPTER SIXTY

CARLY

Carly was finally home ... and she was wrecked. All she wanted to do was shower and fall into bed. When her phone rang, she assumed it would be Brett. She hadn't spoken to him except a very brief and tearful conversation letting him know Jesse was awake. But when she glanced at her screen, she saw it was Nicholas. She hesitated, given her tired and emotional state, but he rang so rarely.

'Hello.' Her voice was croaky and uneven.

'Mum? Are you okay?'

Tearful, she said, 'Yes, darling. It's good to hear from you.' She told him about Jesse, then said, 'I'm worried about you too.'

'Yeah, I know. That's why I'm ringing. Mr Sinclair said he's going to email you and explain everything, but basically this kid, Jeremy Middleton, doesn't like being away from home. He makes up stories about other students, the assistants, ground staff, everybody.'

'He made up the story about the towel flicking?'

Nicholas laughed. 'No, we were flicking towels, but there were loads of us involved. He made a big deal because he wants his parents to pull him out of school. Fair enough – he hates being a boarder, and his parents only live two miles away. Seems a bit weird, but I'm learning some parents prefer to parent remotely.'

'You're not about to be kicked off campus?'

'Of course not. The guys think I'm great.'

'I'm so relieved.' Carly hesitated a moment. 'Nick, there's something else. Dad told me about Mr Busby–'

'What? I told him not to.'

'I'm upset that you couldn't confide in me.'

'Why would I? It's embarrassing. He sent me crazy letters.'

Carly took a deep breath. 'I know. I found them.'

'Mum! I knew you'd freak, that's why I told Dad. He dealt with it. He had a word with Busby and the principal, and next thing I knew Busby was gone.' Nick sighed. 'I thought I threw the letters away.'

All these revelations were doing Carly's head in. 'Are you gay? Because as long as you're happy...'

Silence.

'Nicky?'

'Honestly, I'm not sure if I'm gay or not.'

'So you're a work-in-progress?'

Nick laughed. 'You could say that. Are you disappointed?'

'How could you even think I'd be disappointed? No. I love you unconditionally. Your dad does too. As long as you're safe.' Carly took a moment. 'You are having safe sex aren't you, regardless of gender.'

'Mum!'

'I've been so worried. I miss you so much. I hope in the future you can confide in me.' Carly smiled to herself. 'Within reason. I don't need to share the minutiae of your everyday life.'

'I'll say. You're not supposed to know everything about me. I do have some secrets.'

'I can't help worrying. I'm your mother – it's what I do best. So you're okay? I didn't fail you?'

'How?'

'By not picking up on the Mr Busby signs.'

'Mum! There weren't any Mr Busby signs. Nothing happened. Sure, he was annoying and sent me letters, but he was harmless and unhappy. There was never a time when the two of us were alone.'

'You're sure?'

'I'm sure. Look, if I need therapy later on, you can pay for it.'

'Deal.'

'Mum.' Nick took a breath. 'I've been talking to Will. You need to step up.'

'What do you mean?'

'He needs you ... and you need to step up.'

Carly breathed deeply. 'Yes, I do. Things have been a bit crazy.'

'No kidding.'

'Okay.' Carly stopped. 'Nicky, you haven't answered my question. Please tell me you're practising safe sex–'

'Yes! Hanging up now, Mother.'

'One more thing, I don't like remote parenting.'

'Yeah. I know. I'll be home at the end of the year.'

'Promise?'

'Promise? I'd love to promise but what if I break that promise? There are no guarantees in life. Love you.'

'Love you too, Nicky.'

On autopilot, Carly walked into the kitchen and opened the fridge. She pulled out a bottle of wine. It was so strange how a single action like meeting Toby and going to that party could have caused so many lives to veer off in directions no one could have imagined. Carly's behaviour that night had set in motion a chain of events that had led to her friend lying in a hospital bed in a coma.

She stared at the bottle's label for a minute, Steve's words from a week earlier playing in her mind: *I can recommend the Oyster Bay Riesling this week. It's on special for a hundred and thirty bucks a dozen, and since you buy your liquor by the crate, you'll save a bundle. Or rather, Brett will.*

Wine had been a crutch she'd relied on for too long. Now, Carly had a picture in her mind of what her future looked like, and it didn't include her passed out every night from too much alcohol. She put the bottle back in the fridge and closed the door.

What she needed was sleep, not wine. She walked into her bedroom, took off her shoes and fell into bed.

She woke when Brett sat down on the bed beside her.

'Carly,' he said softly, 'are you okay? I'm so happy about Jesse.'

She opened her eyes slightly, adjusting to the dim light. 'Jesse? Yes ... so happy.' She closed her eyes again.

'Hon, are you okay?'

She nodded. 'Tired. Spoke to Nicky.'

Brett sighed. 'I'm sorry for not telling you. I was trying to support Nick the best way I knew how, but I stuffed up.'

Carly forced herself to wake up fully. 'I'm sorry too. I know you were trying to do the right thing.'

She sat up, and Brett stroked her hair, then put his hand around the back of her neck. 'Are we okay?'

She shook her head. 'I don't know. After everything that's happened with Jesse, I'm an emotional wreck.'

'I'm here for you, you know, and I always will be.' When he

pulled her into him and kissed her on the lips, she felt instantly comforted.

'What did Nick say?'

'You were right. Everything's been sorted with the sports master. Oh, and he's probably gay.'

'As a percentage?'

'I'm leaning towards ninety per cent, but I think you might already know that.'

Brett lay down on the bed and wrapped his arms around her, drawing her close. 'Maybe.'

'I want to fly over to Cornwall and hug him.'

'We can. Let's plan a holiday in the middle of the year so Will can come too.'

Carly nodded. 'I'm not going to cry.'

'No,' Brett said. 'There's been too much of that lately.'

When he kissed her, she felt herself responding to him in a way she hadn't for months. The kissing was slow and intimate and felt divine. Carly pulled back and glanced at the door. 'What about Will? What if he comes home?'

'He's at basketball practice till eight. Let's live dangerously, hey?' Brett whispered, massaging her breasts through her dress.

'But I've been so stupid.'

'We both have. I know you've been unhappy. I was trying to wish it away.'

'With all that's happened to Jesse, I realise how selfish I've been. I do love you, Brett.'

'I know. I love you too.'

They shrugged off their clothes.

Brett pulled her down on his chest and kissed her neck. Carly knew every inch of his body. He was so familiar; his scent, the freckles on his stomach, the perfect way their bodies fitted together.

'Feels good,' she said, positioning herself above him so Brett could enter her. A couple of thrusts, and he was inside.

He smiled. 'Just good?'

Carly stared into his deep brown eyes, her pleasure obvious.

'Fucking fantastic,' she said finally as they found their intimate rhythm and rocked together, revelling in the moment.

CHAPTER SIXTY-ONE

STELLA

I was home, tired and exhausted, but happy to be with Hannah, Harry and June. I was so grateful for the love and joy my children brought me, for the loving marriage I'd enjoyed with Garth, and for the continuing presence of June in my life. That's what got you through in the end: the love of family and friends, and a belief that you were doing the right thing, or at least the very best you could.

I thought back to my conversation with Jesse that evening, just as I was preparing to leave. She'd woken up briefly and motioned me to move closer to her.

'Steve and I ... finished,' she'd whispered. 'Feeling sad but strong too ... How do you do it?'

I'd taken her hand. 'One step at a time, one day at a time, angel. When Garth and I got together, he told me he'd love me forever, and I know he meant it. But forever is a long time and maybe it's just too much to ask.'

Jesse had nodded slightly.

'We're all here for you, Jess,' Louisa had added.

'Yes,' I said softly. 'We're all here. I'm leaving now, but I'll be back, darling.'

'Tomorrow?'

'You bet.' I'd kissed her lightly on her forehead through the bandages before heading out the door.

Now, I sat at the kitchen table, staring at my beautiful pink hydrangeas in a blue ginger jar, drinking tea and enjoying June's company as she filled me in on the last few days of family life. She'd been marvellous while I was spending so much time at the hospital. She'd organised the kids, supervised the making of their school lunches and had even made sure they stacked their dirty plates in the dishwasher. Not only that, but the past few nights she'd persuaded Hannah to log off Farmville and do her maths homework.

'Only after I agreed to sign on to Facebook,' she told me with a chuckle.

'Facebook?'

'Don't look so surprised. I'm not that ancient. Besides, it will open up a whole new world to me. I've already got two friends,' she said proudly. 'Hannah and Harry.'

'Really? Well done. They keep rejecting me, but I'm trying not to take it personally.'

'Sweetie,' she said wisely, 'they're never going to accept you. You're their mother. I'm a harmless old lady. I pose no threat.'

'So you'll spy on them for me?'

'Of course, dear. Why else would I join?'

We were laughing together when the doorbell rang.

'Expecting anyone?' I asked her.

She shook her head and Barney bounded down the corridor, barking madly, tail wagging. I followed.

I opened the door to see Mike standing there. He was looking tired but still gorgeous, wearing denim jeans, a collared blue shirt and a big wide smile. Barney jumped up at him, always needy for pats. Some guard dog!

'Mike?' My heart was dancing. Until a split second later when I remembered. I gulped for air. 'Is it Jesse? She was fine–'

He bent to stroke Barney. 'Shush,' he said, putting his forefinger against my lips. 'In my expert opinion, I'd say she's doing very well. Better than expected given everything that's happened.'

My heart skipped a couple of beats – relief or desire, I wasn't sure. But I was enjoying the erotic sensation of his finger on my lips.

'How are you doing?' he asked.

'Okay, though I'm a bit puzzled as to why you're standing on my front doorstep.'

'Yeah.' He kissed me lightly on the lips. 'Must be confusing for you because I know you're definitely not looking for romance.'

He put his hands around my waist, and I couldn't help melting into his arms. Still, I stuck to my guns. 'That's right.'

He moved towards me, his body close against mine, and I could smell his fresh woodsy scent. 'We need to work on that.' He kissed me again, this time with greater ardour.

He tasted like peppermint. I wanted more. A lot more. In fact, my legs went wobbly. If I could have whisked him up to my bedroom right then, I would have.

'Mum!'

I heard Hannah's voice in the background and pulled away. 'I guess we should stop,' I said half-heartedly. Barney yawned.

Mike grinned, still holding me in his arms. 'I guess. After all, we've got time on our side.'

I liked that.

'So,' he said, stealing another kiss, 'dinner tomorrow night?'

I smiled and nodded. Yes, I was going to dive into whatever lay ahead for me. Rather than hover around the periphery, worrying about whether I was making the right decision, I was going with my heart – and my heart was screaming at me to seize the moment, to accept what the universe was offering.

I took Mike's hand and led him inside.

THE END

ACKNOWLEDGEMENTS

I am thrilled that *Should You Keep A Secret?* previously published as Stella Makes Good, has been offered a new lease of life. It was great revisiting revisiting Stella, Carly and Jesse's lives and editing their stories for a 2022 audience.

Many thanks to Betsy Reavley at Bloodhound for loving *Should You Keep A Secret?* as much as I do and for publishing this updated version. To Fred Freeman, my editor Morgen Bailey, editorial manager Tara Lyons, and proofreader, Abbie, thank you. You are all a joy to work with.

Thank you to my amazing agent Michael Cybulski, and all at New Authors Collective Literary Agency, especially Ros Harvey and Dennis Fisher who continue to make my feel like my writing is worthwhile and occasionally amusing.

Thank you Andrea Barton, my editor at NAC. You are wonderful. Always insightful, I love/hate that you always push me to go that little bit further with my manuscripts.

Thanks also to my NAC stablemates, Susannah Hardy, Sarah Bourne and Sarah Hawthorn, I'm glad we're on this journey together.

To friends, old and new who have supported me along the way with encouragement, honesty and camaraderie, cheers!

Josh, Noah and Mia, I love you... and like I say with all my books, maybe one day you'll read one of them – or at least the acknowledgements.

Thanks Chris for your unwavering support, love, and for making me laugh on hard days when I feel like my writing sucks.

Finally to readers who email, Facebook, tweet @me, and write lovely reviews on Amazon, Goodreads, and beyond, thank you, thank you, thank you. When I'm consumed by self-doubt, then read the reviews, you give me the enthusiasm and courage to open my laptop again!

A NOTE FROM THE PUBLISHER

Thank you for reading this book. If you enjoyed it please do consider leaving a review on Amazon to help others find it too.

We hate typos. All of our books have been rigorously edited and proofread, but sometimes mistakes do slip through. If you have spotted a typo, please do let us know and we can get it amended within hours.

info@bloodhoundbooks.com